The Poppy Killer

A Psychological Thriller

George Peters

Only the living understand the pain of death.
Only the dead are relieved from the pain of living.

He stood motionless in front of the gravestone.

He thought of his mother…of her funeral. It seemed such a long time ago and yet it felt so raw.

A lady who was visiting the grave opposite looked at him…she felt uneasy. She had never seen such disturbing looking eyes before.

His mind was pitch black.

Then…

Clarity.

That feeling inside.

There was no other way. Life had signed him a blank cheque. Life had given him permission to do whatever he wanted. And what he wanted was retribution.

The following year on 7th June 1986, he started to pay life back.

PART 1

1

The Poppy Killer
First Victim. Saturday, 7 June. 1986

A figure appeared.

Man, woman? It was too dark to see.

A man – surely?

Where had he come from?

He was dressed in all black. Slightly bent over. Head down. The gait of an old man. But there was something disturbing about the way he was approaching.

Don could feel his heart rate rising rapidly.

He held his breath.

The man walked slowly by, not looking up. Not uttering a word.

Don let out a sigh, relaxed a little. Let down his guard a fraction. It would cost him his life. Suddenly the man turned around and in one terrifying continuous move he straightened up and bore down on Don like a huge black cloud.

6 Years Later

The Poppy Killer
Fifth Victim. Sunday, 5 July 1992

It was approaching one o'clock in the morning.

The killer waited. Still. At one with the darkness.

His van was lost in the night sky by the dark blanket that covered it. Camouflaged. Out of sight, out of mind.

The killer looked through his night vision binoculars.

A target was approaching.

Total silence. The conditions were right.

He made his move.

All Marie's senses were consumed by the inescapable shape that fanned out in front of her; tall, twisted, grim, malevolent. She tried to wake herself up – escape the nightmare. But instead she descended into darkness.

A Few Hours Later

Marie Hurst woke up feeling nauseous.

Alone.

Afraid.

There was a dim light.

A cage.

Days passed.

And then…nothing.

Nothing.

Marie Hurst's emaciated body was discovered in secluded woods on the outskirts of Warwick in the early hours of August 4th 1992.

A red poppy was found under her feet.

The police informed the media that they were treating the murder as the work of the *Poppy Killer* (they continued to withhold information relating to where the poppy had been placed).

This was the first time the police had used the sobriquet that the press had been using since the third murder. The sobriquet of the *Poppy Killer*.

2

August 3rd 1992

William Marshall worked as a delivery driver for Children's First Class Catering, a business dedicated to delivering food to schools.

He was on his way to work.

He'd worked for the company since he was sixteen, but now he only worked part-time, covering the busy Monday slot. He had his own gardening business, so he was financially secure.

As he was driving the one and a half hour drive from his Ludlow cottage - called Tawelfan - to the headquarters of Children's First Class Catering in Birmingham he thought about his father.

His father.

That day.

That day in 1950. Standing on the roof of a soulless Birmingham factory. A full moon lighting up the night sky. His father on the roof ledge. Talking. Telling William things he didn't understand. He recalled watching him take out a red poppy from his pocket and laying it by his feet. His eyes were reaching, yet distant. Then, without any hint of context, he said

Blinded. And then he jumped. William remembered the eerie silence, giving way to the sound of screams, then that strange feeling inside of him as the old Erdington factory creaked in the cold Birmingham wind. He could see himself - a twelve-year old boy, walking over to the ledge and calmly picking up the poppy.

The red poppy.

3

The Poppy Killer
Tenth Victim. Friday, 14 September 2001

Kevin Kenny had reached the industrial link road between the city centre and his neighbourhood. His mind was feeling pleasantly absent - unconcerned about the darkness...about the lack of street lights...he could look after himself, or so he thought.

Suddenly a sweet smelling rag was smothering his face. A thunderbolt of adrenaline went through his body. KK instinctively swung out. His assailant was knocked off balance. He noticed, just for a split second, that his attacker looked old. It gave him a glimmer of hope. But he felt disorientated. He randomly threw out punches - air punches. He could feel his senses failing him and he couldn't make out where his attacker had gone. He was now rooted to the spot swinging wildly. Suddenly the old man reappeared rising up from his crouched position to within inches of KK's face. KK could feel his limbs go weak before the full force of the chloroform reduced him to a helpless slab of meat.

Driving away from the industrial area, the *Poppy Killer* felt mixed emotions. He'd been careless. His speed reaction time had been too slow. Everything had felt like it was taking more effort. Yes, he'd executed a clean and detection-free operation, but his mind had been slightly out of sync. As if it was following a time-lapse version of reality.

He wasn't getting any younger, he knew that, but this felt different. Like there was a fault in the electrical activity of his brain. He'd still had enough guile to overcome tonight's victim, but if the person had been quicker on his feet, less predictable; if he'd dropped the chloroform-soaked rag…if…if…too many ifs were entering his head. He let them fade into nothing and then his thoughts, as they often did, turned to Julie.

Julie.

Their first meeting in December 1983 at the Grange Comprehensive School in Lye, near Stourbridge. He was delivering food for the school meals. Polite exchanges at first, then friendly gestures, then more meaningful exchanges. Until one day he asked her out and gradually, over the months that followed, they grew closer and closer. Everything was perfect.

Perfect.

Until.

Until that terrible day: Saturday, 17 August 1985. When events would cause that thing that had been nesting inside of him to rumble with such force that it awoke the *Poppy Killer.*

When he got back to Tawelfan cottage it was almost 1.30 in the morning. It took him longer than normal to get the victim from his vehicle down into the cellar. William Marshall was still strong, very strong for his age, but the victim was heavy. Clichés flooded his mind.

With his tenth victim locked in the cage he returned outside to close the van door.

At that moment, he felt something. He wasn't sure what. Just a feeling. He looked around. The trees, the darkness. Everything, and nothing.

Everything, and nothing.

He walked back to the cottage, took one last look out into the night sky, then closed the door...oblivious to the fact that someone had been tracking his movements. Oblivious to the fact that his next victim – his eleventh – would be his last.

His last.

PART 2

4

Harry
February 2018

It had been 17 years since the *Poppy Killer* last struck and even though the case had to all extent and purposes gone cold, every now and then - usually when there was little other news to cover - the press would exhume the case and run a feature on the failure of the West Mercia Police to identify a suspect, let alone apprehend the killer. The press were very good at mobilising public opinion. And public opinion was very good at mobilising police action. And the police were very good at denying the investigation had gone cold while simultaneously reigniting it. It was all highly reactive and had little longevity because the police knew that it wouldn't be long before a politician transgressed or a celebrity self-imploded and the tabloids and the public would move on to current, fresher topics...and the police investigation into the *Poppy Killer* murders would once again be wound down.

But for now, they needed to be seen to be doing something, and so the job, in recent times had been given to either a detective nearing retirement or one who had fallen out of favour.

DS Harry Black got the case.

5

May 2018

Harry wasn't sure what he was doing. Well, he knew what he was doing, he just wasn't quite sure *why* he was doing it. All his *friend* Mickey Maguire, the private detective had told him was that the property he was heading for was his birth father's last known address – that he'd moved there in 1963.

Harry was born in 1985. He grew up in Malvern, a spa town in Worcestershire. He was an adopted baby. He was told this when he was young. On the surface he absorbed the information in the same way as if his adoptive parents had told him they were going out shopping. But deep down it created an imperceptible sense of detachment from his parents and from his sisters. As if he was a member of the club, but not part of the inner circle. After that, the feeling of not belonging, the feeling of his birth mother deserting him, grew slowly and coarsely inside of him. And increasingly he felt more comfortable when he was in his own company.

Harry very rarely heard his dad talk about the adoption. All he knew is they'd been left with no choice but to go down the adoption route. The birth of their second child, the youngest of Harry's sisters, had been a difficult delivery and his mother was told some months later that she would no longer be able to conceive. That just made her yearn for a son as much as Harry's father yearned for a son. So they adopted.

Harry and Mickey Maguire, the private detective, called each other *friends* but in truth they hardly knew one another beyond their professional relationship. A relationship that was founded on the two-way exchange of information. A constant merry-go-round of favours given and favours owed. This time the private eye owed Harry. So Harry had asked Mickey to investigate his birth father and mother. He didn't say why and Mickey didn't ask. That was all part of their unwritten code of conduct...not to ask questions. And a fortnight ago he'd received a call from his *friend* – telling him his father's last known address. Now, two weeks later Harry was on his way to a cottage in Ludlow, Shropshire. He was fully aware that his birth father may not have lived there for years. That the whole journey might turn out to be a waste of time. But the urge to make the trip had overridden all of his rational thoughts - he just knew that he had to do it.

As he drove to Ludlow he thought about who he might find at the cottage. Then, as if somewhere in his mind they were competing to be remembered, images of his adoptive mother and father flooded into his consciousness.

His dad had been a magician. Not a celebrity magician, but a grafter who, in the early years of Harry's life had worked the clubs and cruise ships, providing a financially secure environment for Harry and his two sisters to grow up in. But his time away at sea and his weekend late night slots meant things on an emotional level had been less secure.

This was exacerbated when his mother killed herself.

One afternoon Harry found her asleep in her bedroom and she never woke up. He was eight. The memory still haunted him. Not just the memory of his mother but the look on his father's face as he ran into the room. Harry standing there – unmoving, expressionless.

Soon after, grandma became his surrogate mother, until his father re-discovered his mojo and married his assistant. One minute he was sawing her in half and the next minute they were married. Harry always thought there was a metaphor there somewhere, but he never came up with one.

****

It took him a while to find the property. Driving out of Ludlow on the Whitcliffe Road, which turned into Killhorse Lane, the cottage was nestled in the hills at the end of a quiet country lane. Harry figured the only people using the lane would be the occupants of the house and the postman.

He parked in front of the cottage. There was a sign: Tawelfan. It was the right cottage. He looked around. No other car on the drive. There was a garage. There was still hope.

He looked at the building; it was old. He tried to take in more detail but his mind was elsewhere. He walked to the door and rang the bell. He waited. He felt calm. No sign of any life so he rang the bell again. And waited. Hope was fading. And then…

…he heard footsteps…

…and then…

…the door gradually opened.

And Harry wondered to himself if he would be greeted by his birth father…William Marshall.

6

Jackson
Tawelfan Cottage - May 2018

Jackson Brown had been sitting on the toilet when he'd heard the car pull up. It was mid-morning. Dead-cert it was the postman. But it didn't stop his heart missing a beat when the doorbell rang. When you have something to hide it's a natural reaction – he knew that.

When he finally got to the door he was expecting he would have to sign for something, but instead, he was surprised to see a stranger standing there. He thought he noticed a look of disappointment on his face.

The stranger introduced himself as Harry Black. His name sounded familiar but Jackson couldn't place it. He was dressed casually but smart. Jackson thought he had a slightly old-fashioned look about him. Probably in his early forties. Perhaps his appearance made him seem older than he actually was? Maybe he was mid-thirties? His hair was black, swept back – stylish but without a specific style. Every feature seemed prominent, yet contradictory: smiling, yet dark eyes; faint laughter lines, yet stern-set cheekbones; approachable yet distant.

The stranger apologised for the intrusion and informed Jackson that he was researching his biological parents and that his birth father had previously lived at the property.

7

Jackson

Jackson Brown was born on Saturday, 17 August 1985 and christened two months later. He grew up in Stourbridge, west of Birmingham. And lived half a mile from the town centre. It was a modern detached house – a designer house.

Both his parents had come from poor backgrounds and had worked their way through society to be rewarded with the appellation *upwardly mobile*.

To Jackson, they were like occasional parents. There, but not there.

By the time he reached his teenage years, he had begun to develop a confused sense of insecurity. And, as he observed his mother and father going about their daily lives, quite often indifferent to his presence, he felt a sense of remoteness from his surroundings, from himself. Like they'd purchased him from a superstore, unpacked him and then hadn't even bothered to look at the instructions as to how to put him together.

On one occasion, when his parents had been entertaining friends, and he'd been confined to his bedroom, he'd imagined them, at the end of the evening when all the guests had gone, sitting together at the dining table, smiling, ticking off the boxes: successful careers – tick; married – tick;

home owners – tick; good social circle – tick; child – tick.

Jackson had no brothers or sisters. Maybe he'd been adopted? Maybe adoption was just that, a shopping trip? It had crossed his mind, but he'd never broached the subject with his parents. And in truth, because he didn't fully understand his own feelings, it didn't seem to matter that much.

He possessed a personality that was easily misunderstood. What his parents saw was a reticent, mysterious, slightly diffident boy. What he was however, was a follower. His fragile self-belief meant he didn't create things, he latched on to them.

He had a small circle of school friends, but he wasn't close to any of them; he was never an integral part of any one group or set of friends. He was happy with that - to a degree. He felt that friends were a necessary hassle. And besides, he had Mel. At least that's what he thought.

He was fourteen when he first started dating her. Mel. They were in the same year at school. They became inseparable. People…his parents, told him fourteen was too young to be in love. But Jackson had been overpowered by the force of his desire. Mel had opened up and exposed everything that Jackson had, subconsciously, tried to hide. His love became all-consuming. And any lingering sense of self was forgotten…his world had become Mel. And for a while his personality changed; some people even used the word *happy* - but it was not to last.

When Jackson turned sixteen he asked Mel to marry him. It seemed like the natural next step. For two to become one. For him to become a part of her. Of course he didn't see the obvious…he was blinded by love. It was too much for her. Too much too soon. She did not want to become a part of him. She cried when he asked her – but they were not tears of joy. That was the last time she ever spoke to him.

After that, he really went into his shell…back into his own world. He was confused. That was not how it was meant to be. He couldn't see forward and he didn't want to look back. And for a while he even forgot the things he couldn't remember. His confidence was at an all time low. He felt alone, drifting aimlessly to nowhere that mattered. Until, in 2003, an unexpected encounter would prompt him to move to Ludlow and his life would change forever.

8

Harry
Tawelfan Cottage - May 2018

After Harry had introduced himself and explained his reasons for visiting, he was invited in.

Harry asked the question and found out the name of his host was Jackson Brown.

Harry noticed he was a similar height to himself: 6 feet 1 inch tall and he looked in reasonably good shape. Youthful in an early thirties kind of way. His smooth complexion was of a man who found little pleasure in sunbathing. And he wore the clothes of a man who found little pleasure in fashion. A simple but functional style.

He had something about him, something Harry couldn't put his finger on.

Harry accepted the invitation to sit down and he made himself comfortable on a modern functional plain brown sofa while Jackson sat opposite him on an older shabbier-looking armchair.

Jackson asked Mr Black *how he could help him.*

'Please, call me Harry.' He looked around the room. It was something he did without thinking. Then his eyes settled back on Jackson.

'As I said, I'm looking into my immediate birth family.' He let out a deep breath. 'I was adopted.' Gave a faint shrug. 'I've known this since I was young but, until recently I've never felt the inclination to delve into the past. But since my adoptive father died...' He paused. His eyes hid a private memory.

'...well, now just seemed the right time to do it.' He straightened up. 'It's a long shot; my father's name was William Marshall; I was wondering if you knew anything about him? Maybe you bought the cottage off him?'

9

Harry

Harry's curiosity as to where he came from started in November 2017, nine months after his adoptive dad died. It was like his father's worst magic trick; one day he was there and the next day he was gone. Heart attack: 18th February 2017.

Soon after, Harry left the family home and lost the quasi-closeness he'd had with his sisters. Quasi, because in truth Harry had never felt comfortable or confident in the company of the opposite sex. He felt they possessed an unknown power. It made him feel uneasy. So he preferred to remain emotionally silent. To look away. Stare out of the window...detach himself. But for how long could he stop himself from yearning...yearning for love...yearning to *be* loved? That was a question he was unable to answer.

His parentage though, for reasons he couldn't even articulate to himself had suddenly become important. Maybe it was a distraction, maybe it would help him in some way? Maybe?

So in November 2017 he'd filled in an application called Birth Certificate Information Before Adoptions Service. It was a form that allowed for the fact that people who had been adopted may not know their original birth details. Four months later in February 2018 Harry received his full birth certificate.

He made himself a cup of tea.

He sat down on the faux leather arm chair that straddled the window and looked at the envelope. He felt odd; a strange sense of guilt. As if delving into his ancestry was wrong – a betrayal of his adoptive parents. He thought for a moment. Then he opened the letter.

He gently eased out his full birth certificate and placed it on the table. He looked straight ahead. He tried to get a sense of the moment but his mind went blank. He looked down. The first name he saw on the certificate was William Marshall.

****

William Marshall. Harry's birth father. It was not a name he recognised. *Why should it be* he asked himself as if he was expecting the disclosure to answer all the questions that had been knotting up his brain. He felt a sense of anti-climax; bordering on embarrassment for having let himself get carried away. He looked at the cup of tea that was sitting untouched on the glass table. He gazed around the room and breathed a deep sigh as if communicating his own stupidity to the four walls. He leant forward, picked up his birth certificate and stared at it. The name of his biological mother was Julie Kendrick. He pondered over the name...how one-dimensional it seemed. There was no face, no smile, no motherly warmth...just a name. Then suddenly he felt a thud in his heart. The walls started to close in. His birth certificate was enlarging and shrinking in front of his eyes. He dropped it and put his head in his hands.

He squeezed his eyes shut as if to rid his mind of what he'd just seen. Then he slowly re-focused his gaze. He had not been mistaken. There was a word on it. One word that would change everything. Triplet.

10

Jackson
Tawelfan Cottage - May 2018

Jackson could feel the blood draining from his skin – as if his blood was abandoning him. Leaving him cold and alone with his guilty secret.

How could this be? He was totally confused - struggling to weigh up everything. The threat, the reality, the implications…his mind was turning over too quickly for him to hold onto any meaningful thoughts. He could just about remember the question… *my father's name was William Marshall; I was wondering if you knew anything about him? Maybe you bought this cottage off him?'*

'I'm afraid not.' There was a long pause. Jackson knew that Harry was using the silence to prompt him to add more flesh to the brittle bones of his reply. *Give nothing away*. That's all Jackson could think of.

'You're welcome to have a look around.' There was nothing for him to see so Jackson was happy to make the offer. But more than that, he needed time to process what Harry Black had just told him...that William Marshall was his birth father. He repeated the same question in his mind over and over again…*how could that be*?

Of course, Jackson knew the immediate implications of what Harry Black had said. But he couldn't see beyond the first link. He couldn't see whether this new dynamic would pose a potential threat to his own situation.

Now he felt an overwhelming desire to get rid of Harry Black and give himself time to think. So he continued to be evasive. 'Sorry I can't be of more help, but next time I'm in town I'll ask around; see if I can find anything out about William...Marshall?' He saw Harry nod and get up out of his chair. Jackson mirrored his action.

11

Harry

When he'd first found out, back in February 2018, it had taken Harry a few weeks to digest the information that he was a triplet. When he'd seen the word on his birth certificate he'd felt like the fuse box in his brain had tripped. But the passage of time had allowed him to reset his mind and focus – to ask himself the question...what had actually changed? He still wasn't sure. On the one hand he felt, in a strange way, part of a club that he'd always been excluded from, but on the other hand it didn't seem to matter. The moment had gone. The Harry that could have been – Harry the triplet – had long since faded from the Harry of today. But, having viewed his full birth certificate it had made him sufficiently curious to want to know more about his parentage, about his siblings. That's why in March he'd contacted his *friend*, Mickey Maguire, who had found out his father's last known address: Tawelfan cottage in Ludlow. And now Mickey was looking into the whereabouts of Harry's birth mother - Julie Kendrick - and the names of Harry's two triplet siblings.

12

Harry
Tawelfan Cottage - May 2018

Jackson was definitely spooked. Harry couldn't remember the last time he'd seen such a rapid paling of the skin. Even when he'd arrested people for murder he'd seen less of a dramatic response.

It was obvious to Harry that Jackson was hiding something. But he was aware that it wasn't the time to start probing. Harry was a good detective...he knew when to push and he knew when to hold back. This was a time to hold back. A brick had been removed; he knew it wouldn't be long before the wall would start crumbling. He just needed to be patient. He could see that Jackson was anxious for him to leave so he made it easy for him.

'Thank you for your offer to have a look around but it was just a curiosity trip more than anything. It was very kind of you to invite me in. Just by stepping into his old cottage I feel the experience has allowed me to connect with his spirit in some way.' Harry walked towards the door. 'And thank you for offering to ask around. Here's my card. Please let me know if you find anything out about him...William Marshall.' Harry watched Jackson put the card in his pocket, while he continued to hold his stare. He then shook hands with Jackson, turned around and made his way back to his car.

Jackson

Jackson was about to close the door when he found himself calling out to Harry. He knew it would sound odd, but he had to know. He had to ask him.

'I hope you don't mind me asking, but when were you born?'

Harry was a few paces from his car. He turned around.

Jackson watched as Harry stood there in silence. He wondered if he'd gone too far. Then suddenly Harry replied...*17th August 1985, why do you ask?*

Jackson felt his legs go weak. He tightened his grip on the door handle to stop himself from collapsing. He was struggling for breath. His mind was a whirlwind of frantic thoughts. And then, just as quickly, his mind froze. He couldn't think. He had no reply. But he had to do something. He looked up to the sky. It planted an answer in his mind. 'Nothing really, I'm just interested in astrology.' Harry nodded and got into his car.

Harry

It was an odd question...wanting to know when he was born. Harry had given himself time to think before answering. Could there have been anything hidden, anything underlying the question? Nothing had come to mind so he'd answered. And for a moment Jackson had looked like he was going to faint. But why? Whatever his reasons for asking,

Harry was sure of one thing, it had nothing to do with astrology.

His visit to his birth father's last known address had started something. He was sure of that. He didn't know what, but he knew for certain it was just the beginning.

Jackson

Jackson closed the door and sat back down. The room suddenly seemed claustrophobic. He sat for 30 minutes staring at the wall. His mind was so full of questions, so full of conundrums. He didn't know whether to feel happy or sad. Eventually he reached into his pocket and took out the card Harry had given him. He read the name: Detective Sergeant Harry Black. He looked at it in disbelief.

As if zombified he got up out of his seat and walked towards the stairs. He paused. The doors under the stairs triggered a memory. Suddenly a whole cascade of memories flooded into his mind. He quickly opened the cupboard doors and removed the boxes stored there. He took up the dark oak laminate flooring that revealed the hidden trap door. Jackson took a deep breath and lifted the door open. He turned on the light, made his way down the rickety old stairs and walked dreamlike over to the far wall of the cellar where an old wooden chair waited in isolation. He sat down, closed his eyes and let the tsunami in his mind take him back to late June 2003…to the day *it* all started.

The day he met William Marshall.

13

West Mercia Police Headquarters
February 2018

The directive from his DI had been simple and brief. *Sorry Harry, you've drawn the short straw…the Poppy Killer case needs reviewing. Be thorough.*

DI Trish Bond stood in front of Harry's desk, the expression on her face indicating that she wanted Harry to acknowledge he had understood what she had meant. Harry nodded. He unscrambled her words in his mind. *Be visible. Show you're giving the case a thorough re-examination. But don't forget it's a cold case and it's a cold case for a reason…there is no new evidence. Don't waste your time re-investigating what has already been investigated. And most of all don't let it get in the way of any of your existing workload.*

DI Bond looked at Harry. She felt bad for having to give him the case but she knew he was his own worst enemy – that he'd brought it on himself. That thing inside of him, that switch he pressed every time anyone tried to get near him. It was a defence mechanism, she knew that. And doing things his own way was just a manifestation of that defence mechanism. But the deeper meaning, the root cause of his behaviour - she'd never got close enough to find out what really lay beneath the surface.

Harry went to the store room at the back of the building and retrieved the files relating to the *Poppy Killer* investigation. He was old school…he always liked to *feel* the case notes. As if touching them could reveal secrets that the computer files could not.

He opened the file.

His mind went AWOL.

He stood up and tried to compose himself. Everybody knew about the *Poppy Killer* case. The press, the public, his fellow officers. *The poisoned chalice,* that's what his colleagues called it. *Don't over think it or it will drive you mad* was one of the comments he'd received from an older, supposedly wiser detective.

He sat back down. He let the minutes drift away. Then, as if some undefined moment had been reached he re-focused on the file. An hour passed, then another, then another, page after page, then suddenly without warning he felt something. Something he had not felt since his father died. A longing. For reasons he didn't fully understand the *Poppy Killer* was creating a yearning deep inside of him. He knew it wasn't unusual for cops and criminals to admire and respect each other. Adversaries on the opposite sides of the law, drawn together by their dedication to their respective *professions.* But this felt different. This had touched a nerve with his profound loneliness. He tried to make sense of things. He stood up. He was afraid to look out of the window but he couldn't resist the urge. He saw him, in his mind's eye, the *Poppy Killer,* smiling, contented, as if at one with himself. Harry longed for that moment. He longed for someone, something...anything but the horrible emptiness he felt inside. He sat back down and put his head in his hands. He felt an overwhelming urge to cry, but somehow he resisted it.

PART 3

14

Mary Stevens Park, Stourbridge
Saturday, 28 June 2003

After the *episode* with Mel, Jackson retreated. Physically and emotionally. And even though he was now taking his A-Levels, his stunted social circle had contracted even more. The only time his mind felt a surge of positivity was when he was out walking. And every Saturday morning he would spend time in Mary Stevens Park, Stourbridge – a local community park situated about a mile from where he lived. Jackson felt a fondness for the park, especially its features: the lake, the trees, the cast iron bandstand, the café. He felt at peace there. In a bubble. As if, when he entered the park, it somehow shielded him from all his troubles.

He was sat on *his* usual bench - on the east slope, away from the hustle and bustle of the park. From his vantage point he liked to observe the Saturday morning rituals: the dog walkers, the joggers, the strollers; the same people doing the same thing every week. Today there was a new member of the cast. An old man - perhaps in his sixties? Certainly an age that felt old to Jackson. He watched the stranger complete a circuit of the park. Then, on his second time around, totally out of the blue he stopped - right in front of Jackson. At first the old man remained in profile, slightly bent over, but strangely still. Then, he slowly turned his head and looked directly into Jackson's eyes. There was no smile. For a moment Jackson thought he was unwell. But then he walked towards him.

'Do you mind if I join you? Take the weight off my feet,' said the old man.

Without waiting for a reply he sat down.

Normally such an act would have annoyed Jackson, but on this occasion he remained unflustered. Ambivalent.

They sat in silence for a while, both staring outwards - watching the morning unfold. A gaggle of geese flew overhead making a loud honking sound to announce their impending landing on the lake. Then, the old man turned his head to look at Jackson, and in an assured, slightly mesmeric way he asked him his name. Jackson surprised himself by answering immediately and reciprocating the question. *William Marshall* was the reply. For no reason, it sent a shiver down Jackson's spine.

'It's a nice spot you've got here, looking out at the…' The old man paused, as if he'd forgotten what he was going to say.

Jackson followed William's line of sight to try and add some meaning to what he hadn't said, but nothing stood out.

Silence re-filled the space between them. It felt slightly strange to Jackson, but, as he was not a great conversationalist, he soon felt comfortable with it.

He heard William sigh.

'I come here a lot. Have you ever noticed me?'

Jackson was surprised by the directness of the question and was unsure how to answer it. He'd never noticed him, but there again his mind was often elsewhere. 'I…I don't think so,' he said.

William continued talking as if he'd not heard Jackson's reply. 'In the old days I used to come here after delivering the food to the local school. After I'd made the drop I would visit…' William cut himself off mid-flow, as if whatever it was he was going to say was too personal to be put into words. Instead he pointed to his right, out to a place hidden in the distance. Jackson instinctively looked in that direction. 'Then I would drive here and walk around. Reflect. I've seen you here many times.'

Jackson suddenly started to feel uneasy, but at the same time he felt an odd sense of exhilaration. As if something exciting was happening in his life.

Another prolonged silence engulfed their bench.

William suddenly began rubbing his hands together as if he was cold. 'Solitude can be a good friend, can't it?' he said. 'It's non-judgemental. It's always happy to agree with your thoughts.'

Jackson gave a faint nod. He'd spent enough time in his own head to know the old man was right.

William sat back and tilted his head upwards as if he was making a special effort to breath in the air.

For the next few minutes their fragile rapport switched between silence and idle chatter.

Then suddenly the tone of William's voice changed.

'You see all those people.' Jackson followed Williams gaze out to the epicentre of the park. 'What do you see?'

Jackson shrugged, as if the question was either too obvious to answer, or he didn't really understand it.

'You see what you want to see. You perceive what you want to perceive. But are you doing what you want to do?'

Jackson looked blankly at him.

'Think about it Jackson. You see, you perceive, but do you do?'

It flashed through Jackson's mind that perhaps the old man was suffering from some form of mental illness.

William looked back out towards the park.

'Soon your life will change, and when it does, don't forget to look beyond what you see. Because that's where you will find the courage to take action.'

Jackson's emotions were changing rapidly. Now he wondered if this is what old men do? Talk in riddles. Blather philosophical nonsense.

William looked up to the cloudless sky and then lowered his head as if he was staring vacantly into his own thoughts.

Then he looked at Jackson. 'Look at me son.'

Jackson suddenly felt small. Like a child. Inadequate. Ill-equipped to offer the stranger whatever it was he wanted. He tried to make sense of what was going on but in that moment as he looked into William's eyes he felt completely lost.

'Jackson.'

'Jackson.'

Jackson snapped out of his haze.

'Our meeting today. Don't always take things on first impressions. Do you understand?' He paused. 'Do you Jackson?'

'I...I...I don't know.'

William stood up and extended his hand and Jackson rose to his feet accepting the offer as if compelled to do so.

William's eyes seemed opaque.

'I need to tell you something.' William paused for what seemed like an eternity. 'No, no...this is not the right time. *He* will tell you.'

Jackson felt stunned. So stunned that he failed to ask the questions that would reverberate in his head for years to come.

William walked two paces away, then stopped. Jackson watched him intently, oblivious to his surroundings. The seconds ticked by slowly before William turned back around.

'Sometimes in life things happen for a reason,' William told Jackson. 'And you must learn to grasp the nettles with the same consideration and care as you would hand pick a rose.'

And with that he was gone.

Jackson stood there dumbfounded. Had he been dreaming? He shut his eyes sharply, then opened them. He looked around. There was no sign of the old man. His heart was pounding. His head movement became more animated. He strained his eyes but still there was no sign of him.

He sat back down. He couldn't quite believe what had just happened. And yet, the strangest thing of all was that despite the surrealness of the whole scenario, it had felt so real.

15

Tawelfan Cottage
2018

Jackson came out of his trance. He looked around unsure of where he was. He thought he heard a noise. He sat up straight. Then he remembered. He was in the cellar. A chill ran down his spine...the cellar trap door was still open. He listened. Silence. When he was sure of the reliability of his senses he relaxed. Looked around. It was the first time he'd been in the cellar since 2003. He wasn't sure how he felt. He thought back to the time after *it* had all happened. When he'd dismantled and then disposed of the contents of the cellar. And then, shortly after that, in early 2004 the doors had been fitted under the stair case and the hatch leading to the cellar had been covered with laminate flooring. A room hidden. But never forgotten. And now Jackson was sat on the one piece of furniture that had been left – the old wooden chair. He stared at the floor, he noticed the marks: four small circles. He'd hoped they would have vanished when he'd filled the bolt holes in, back in 2004, but the new concrete had dried a slightly different colour to the old stone floor.

He put the holes and their significance to the back of his mind. Instead he thought back to the Saturday after he'd met William, how hyped up he'd been, waiting to see him again. Anticipation that had gradually turned to disappointment when William Marshall had failed to appear. He'd only met him once but it had already begun to feel like an established part of his Saturday morning routine. So when William didn't show up, Jackson had been overcome by a foreboding sense that something terrible had happened.

He stood up and paced around the cellar like a prisoner in solitary confinement. He was struggling to concentrate - to project the next image in his mind. He sat back down. His eyes went vacant...waiting for the memories to flow back into his consciousness. Then as if the lights had gone down and the movie had re-started he was transported back to Saturday, 12 July 2003.

16

Mary Stevens Park, Stourbridge
Saturday, 12 July 2003

Jackson was sat on his usual bench in Mary Stevens Park, waiting out of hope more than expectation for William Marshall to appear, but instead he noticed a smartly dressed middle-aged man approaching him. He looked like an accountant. A flustered accountant. He was certainly not part of the usual Saturday morning crowd.

Jackson felt his heart sink. He knew the man was there to see him – he just knew it. Not long ago he would have thought it odd – sinister even, but now it just seemed like it was meant to be.

He saw the man take out what looked like a photo from his jacket pocket, glance at it, then at Jackson, then back at the photo. He then came over to where Jackson was sitting.

'Jackson. Jackson Brown?' The man said, seemingly confident that he already knew the answer.

Jackson said nothing. He just stared into space.

The *accountant* seemed slightly irritated by his offishness.

'You mind if I sit down?'

Jackson shrugged.

'I'm Huw, Huw Morris. He said I'd find you here.' He refrained from offering Jackson a greeting hand.

Jackson continued to say nothing. The reels in his mind were spinning.

'I'm from Morris and Price solicitors in Ludlow. I'm here about a deed of gift.'

Jackson's mind gradually stopped spinning and came to rest on the word *gift.*

'You knew William Marshall.'

Jackson wasn't entirely sure if it was a question or a statement. His mind went blank.

Huw Morris opened his briefcase and took out a photo.

'Here, he gave me this.' He handed it to Jackson reiterating 'William Marshall.'

Jackson looked at the photo. He nodded.

Huw Morris continued as if his mind was mechanically driven - totally automated.

'A week last Tuesday, William Marshall came into my office, requesting me to act on his behalf.'

'You said gift, what gift?'

'Deed of Gift to be precise. A deed of gift is a signed legal document that voluntarily and without recompense transfers ownership of a property from one person to another.'

'What has that got to do with me?'

'To put it simply, he has given you his house.'

Jackson was speechless. In shock. Huw Morris asked him if he was okay, but in a way that implied he wasn't interested in his reply.

Jackson continued to stare into space.

'You are his son. I cannot word it any differently or add anything to make that statement easier for you to hear.'

'What...'

Words, thoughts, drifted in and out of Jackson's mind.

'I…I don't understand.'

'What don't you understand Jackson?'

'I mean, how can that be? How do you know? How can you be sure?'

Huw Morris said nothing. He had a look of impatience.

'But I hardly knew him. Why would he do such a thing?'

'I am not the person to ask. And besides, mine is not to question the logic or motives of my clients. Do you think Mr Jaggers questioned the motives of Abel Magwitch?

'*What*?'

'Sometimes people do strange things. I've known people leave their entire estates to their pet dog or cat…don't worry about it.'

Huw Morris stared impassively at Jackson.

'This can't be…this can't be happening.'

Huw Morris nodded his head, raised his eyebrows and gave a slight smile to indicate it *was* happening.

'But how did you know? To be here, today…now?'

'He gave me very specific instructions.'

'Tell me what happened. What did he say?'

Huw Morris huffed and then glanced at his watch.

'Please.'

He looked around, then shrugged his shoulders. 'Okay, but it may not be easy listening.'

Jackson sat up straight.

'Like I said, it was a Tuesday. He told me he wanted to set up a deed of gift…his own home.

'But why?'

'He told me he had Alzheimer's. He seemed lucid enough, but he said he didn't want to wait for it to get any worse. He said he was going to travel to Europe that coming weekend - to find a country offering euthanasia.' He paused. 'In a nutshell, he wanted to die.'

Jackson shook his head. 'And you didn't try to stop him.'

'I'm not a counsellor. He said he didn't want to become a vegetable. That seemed a perfectly acceptable reason to me. He came back on the Friday, signed the necessary papers and that was that. Yes, the time frame was a bit tight. And yes, I've had to cut a few corners to make this happen so quickly. But he was very adamant. Very persuasive. So I've set up an arrangement in the short term to allow you to take up residence at the property and then I'll sort out the raft of official forms that will need to be dealt with at a later date.'

'So he's gone. He's...*dead*.' Jackson could hardly bring himself to say the last word.

'I just don't get it. He came to you...needing help. And all you did was take his money?'

Huw Morris looked surprised. Slightly vexed. 'Like I said, I'm a solicitor not a counsellor. It *is* what it *is*.'

It was Jackson's turn to look surprised.

Huw Morris ignored the expression on Jackson's face and proceeded to talk to him as if he was speaking into his Dictaphone.

'There was one key clause. I was to deliver the keys to you today. He was very specific on that point, on the need for urgency.' He delved into his briefcase and took out the keys, together with an envelope and handed them to Jackson. 'You asked me how I knew…how I knew you were his son. He didn't tell me directly, it was written on the form he'd completed, against the question that asked the relationship of the Donee to the Donor. He'd put *Son. Adopted.* And in brackets he'd put *He doesn't know.* Nothing more.' Huw Morris shook his head. 'I guess it was hard for him. Strange though, how clinical it looked when I read it.'

For a moment Jackson started to think he'd got Huw Morris all wrong, that he did have feelings after all.

'Still, he paid well. And who am I to pass judgement.'

Jackson stared at him with disbelieving eyes. His brief moment of sympathy for Huw Morris a forgotten thought.

Huw Morris gripped his briefcase.

'Like I said, I'll sort out the paper work, the legal transfer and other matters in due course. For the moment just make sure you get the appropriate insurance and sort out the utilities. There's a list in the envelope. You'll also find the property details in there.' He flipped back the latches to his briefcase, got up and stood in front of Jackson.

'Cheer up, you've just been gifted a valuable asset.'

Jackson gazed vacantly at Huw Morris's briefcase. It was black leather. Pristine. No marks.

No stamp of individuality. A brief case without personality. Unloved.

Huw Morris looked at Jackson as if he was waiting for him to say thank-you. When Jackson continued to stare into space he shook his head. He didn't understand young people; they were so ungrateful. But he was satisfied with himself for having carried out his clients wishes to the full. What had happened to his client, what had happened to William Marshall...he didn't give a thought to.

He walked away. No handshake, no good-bye. After a few steps, he stopped and turned around.

'Oh, and like I said, he was very forceful in driving home the need for urgency, so get there tomorrow if you can. Apparently there are two cats to feed.' He nodded his head to check that Jackson had understood, but he was still in a daze. Huw Morris smiled to himself. When Jackson finally regained his focus Huw Morris had blended into the Saturday morning haze, leaving Jackson alone to unravel the impact of what he had just been told.

After about half an hour of fruitless introspection Jackson went back home. His father was sat in the lounge reading the newspaper. His mother had gone out. Jackson exchanged a few meaningless pleasantries with his father, in which the phrase - *what are you doing with your life son?* - was always hidden in his father's words. Finally, Jackson forced himself to ask the question...*Was I adopted?* As soon as he saw the look on his *father's* face he regretted asking it. For days afterwards he was haunted by that look. That hurt look.

Maybe he could have handled it better? Seen it from a different perspective? He mentally rewound and re-worded the moment in everyway possible, but it never allowed the incident to sit more comfortably in his mind. He remembered his father shaking his head before leaving the room. It was then that he realised he didn't want to hear his father's reply. Because deep down in his heart he already knew the answer. And for all their faults, he realised his mother and father, in their own way, loved him and right then he would have taken that uncomplicated emotional arrangement any day. But he knew he couldn't run away from what had happened – from what Huw Morris had told him.

That night Jackson lay awake in bed. He felt a crushing despondency. His birth father, the father he'd never known until two weeks ago, was dead. He tried to make sense of why he felt so sad. Why something so fleeting could cause something so heartfelt. The startling and idiosyncratic fact that he had been gifted his birth father's property was lost in the gloom. Questions collided with questions. Images overlapped images. Thoughts replaced thoughts. Then breaking through his mental confusion his meeting with William Marshall came to the fore. He could see him like he was there in the room. He could hear his words:

Our meeting today. Don't always take things on first impressions.

Soon your life will change.

Sometimes things happen in life for a reason.

They were statements waiting for events to unfold. But now it seemed that whatever it was that was meant to transpire between himself and his birth father was forever lost.

He moved onto his right side.

His thoughts turned to what Huw Morris had said. *Alzheimer's.* Had there been any indication? He wasn't sure. Maybe he'd been having a bad day? Perhaps that's why he'd spoken to him in the park? He'd been confused. Perhaps he wasn't his birth father after all? Maybe it had all been a mistake? Maybe he'd thought Jackson was someone else? He wanted these statements to be true, but he knew they weren't. That he was just trying to find a way out. And then...Jackson couldn't bear to think about it. The suicide. Nothing added up. He felt like he was going round in circles or more accurately spinning in spirals as his thoughts never connected back to one another; like he was trying to make sense out of the nonsensical.

Then, out of the blue, a thought of clarity popped into his head...he needed to go and feed the cats. Tomorrow. It seemed to be the one tangible thing he could act on. He thought back to what William Marshall had said:

Don't forget to look beyond what you see. Because that's where you will find the courage to take action.

He had no idea what that really meant, but for now, going to feed the cats seemed like the best fit.

17

Tawelfan Cottage
2018

Jackson felt cold.

He went upstairs and made himself a cup of tea.

He knew the next part would be the most challenging. Yet, he had no idea why he was making it so difficult for himself. He wasn't even sure why he was so anxious about this part of his past. After all, he lived with *it* everyday. Yet the present was somehow a denial of the past. And now with Detective Sergeant Harry Black on the scene he was deeply worried that his charade would finally be uncovered.

He returned to the cellar, sat back down and took a sip of tea. He felt it warm his insides. He put the cup on the stone floor and then waited. Waited for his mind to take him back to 2003.

18

Stourbridge
July 2003

The day after he'd met with Huw Morris, Jackson woke with a sense of excitement. Gone was the despondency. Gone was the confusion. He was now a man of action. It's what William would have wanted. He'd convinced himself of that. And now, after what Huw Morris had told him, he felt an overwhelming sense of obligation to honour his birth father's words. What had happened, had happened for a reason. And William had said that *things happen in life for a reason*. Yes, it was crazy and yes, it seemed real and unreal all in the same thought. But nothing could detract from the reality that he now had the keys to William Marshall's cottage. The keys to a different future.

The adrenaline was pumping through his veins. His life up to that point had been going nowhere. It was dull. He was dull. He didn't have any real interests. Any real friends. He took the minimum amount of time on choosing his clothes or looking presentable. He wore no jewellery, no aftershave. He had no desire to go to university, yet he had no idea what he wanted to do instead. He had lost himself. He knew that, and now, suddenly, he had been given something that could bring him back to life. And the euphoria he felt completely eclipsed the reality of the situation: his birth father, a man he hardly knew, had gifted Jackson his home, then ended his own life. No alarm bells were sounding because he wanted it more than he wanted to question it. There was hope of something different, something better, something to latch onto, and he wanted to grasp that hope with all his might.

Jackson had passed his driving test shortly after his seventeenth birthday and since then he had been driving his mother's Volkswagen Beetle. He still resided at his parents' house although the up and down relationship he had with his father had recently taken a downswing due to Jackson's disinclination to go to university. Such a decision represented a cross in the box. Not good. But Jackson didn't care. Not anymore. He now had a goal. Something to aim for - the fact he had no idea what it was didn't matter. It was something. That's all that mattered. Of course, he hadn't told his parents what he was doing, what had happened. An explanation could wait until...until he had an explanation.

The drive from Stourbridge to Ludlow took Jackson about an hour and when he eventually found the cottage he realised he couldn't remember any of the journey. His mind had been elsewhere, trying to separate the fact from the fiction, the real from the unreal, the reality from the fantasy.

He parked in front of the property and suddenly the realisation of what he was doing overwhelmed him and he felt panicky. He sat for nearly an hour trying to compose himself. Trying to quieten the deluge of non sequiturs that were pounding in his head. Eventually he found an opening – a space in his mind that allowed him to take the next step. He got out of his mother's car, walked to the door, put the key in the lock, half expecting it not to fit, and…walked into his new home.

****

Tawelfan Cottage (2003)

On entering the lounge he was immediately taken by its authenticity. It had exposed beams, exposed stone and brick walls and bare floorboards. Directly to the left of the front door there was an imposing inglenook fireplace. Diagonally, across the lounge was a narrow staircase. Opposite he could see into the kitchen – compact with a stone floor. He shut the door behind him and took a deep breath. The cottage felt eerie...but he loved it.

The only furniture in the lounge was a table with two dining chairs and one single sofa chair that looked threadbare and forgotten. There was no television. No phone. What shelving there was, was minimalist in its ornamentation.

He wandered around. Each room, downstairs and upstairs, was the same: small and devoid of worldly possessions. It was the complete antithesis of his parents' house, yet, he already felt more at home.

He was back standing in the lounge. He suddenly remembered the cats. He went into the kitchen but saw no sign of any cat bowls or a cat flap. In fact there was no indication that cats had ever lived in the property at all. Another layer of mystery.

He walked back into the lounge. He noticed that under the stairs the wooden floor boards had been taken up and stacked against the wall. He went to take a closer look but paused. On the table was a small box. He wondered how he'd not noticed it earlier. He stared at it. It seemed fairly innocuous, but he still pondered for a few minutes before finally lifting the lid off. Then he waited. When nothing happened he gingerly leaned forward and peered in. His immediate reaction was one of anti-climax. In the box was nothing more than a red poppy.

19

July 2003

Jackson thought no more of the poppy. Yes, it was odd, but everything about the situation was odd. One red poppy sat in a box was just another layer of odd.

He made his way to the stairs. He could see why the floor boards had been removed. There was a trap door. *Leave it*, he said to himself.

He lifted it up.

He peered down into the darkness. There seemed to be a faint light emanating from somewhere inside. He got onto his knees, leant into the hatch and patted the walls; eventually he found what he was looking for…the light switch.

It worked.

He could see that the stairs led to what looked like a cellar. Again he paused, this time to weigh up the potential pit falls of going in. He'd seen the horror films; but maybe the cats had got trapped down there. Reason enough to venture in.

When he stepped off the last step he lifted his head and looked slowly to the right.

A sudden adrenaline surge made his heart freeze. The cellar felt claustrophobic; drained of oxygen. His breathing became shallow. He felt his flight reaction kick in. He ran back up the stairs and headed for the front door. He needed to breathe in the air. To feel the comfort of the wind on his face. And he needed space. Physically and figuratively.

He walked around the driveway in random circles, trying to think, yet trying to avoid thinking. His heart was pounding. What the hell was going on? What was he doing? What he'd seen seemed so shocking as not to be real. He even wondered to himself if he had imagined it.

Gradually he started to calm down. *Focus*, he said to himself, *focus*. The poppy, the cellar. Suddenly a light came on in his mind that was so bright, so distressing, that he had to throw up his hands to shield his eyes from the horror of what he had just realised.

20

July 2003

Jackson had heard about him, read about him...the *Poppy Killer*. But like any normal human being he'd never thought for a moment that his life would ever be touched in any way, shape or form by the *Poppy Killer's* actions. But now he was faced with an appalling and shocking situation.

He'd heard it on the news that a girl had gone missing; a few weeks ago as far as he could remember. The press were calling her the eleventh victim of the *Poppy Killer*. The police were being more coy about it; until a body was discovered, they were still treating it as a missing person's enquiry. But behind closed doors they feared the worst. It had all the hallmarks of a *Poppy Killer* abduction.

It had been front page news but more recently the story had been relegated to the inner pages. Now Jackson had an exclusive. He had found the girl: Alison Marchant. He was sure of it. The poppy on the table, the girl in the cage. It had to be her. He felt sick.

21

Tawelfan Cottage
2018

Jackson snapped out of himself.

He looked around.

He was in the cellar.

It was empty.

He could feel bile in his mouth.

He shivered at the thought of how powerful his memories had been.

He stood up.

He looked down at the half-drunk cup of cold tea that was on the stone floor.

He wondered why he was doing this to himself. But he knew the answer. He was tired of running away from the truth...of hiding the truth. He wanted so much for people to know. For his life to be *normal*; but he knew that would never happen; normal was an option he'd taken off the table years ago. Because the one thought that had never entered his head, in 2003, when he'd stood outside the cottage gasping for air, was to go to the police.

He sat back down.

He knew what came next.

The moment when he first met Alison Marchant.

PART 4

22

West Mercia Police Headquarters
April 2018

Detective Sergeant Harry Black worked in a small office – shabby but police-like in a traditional, nostalgic kind of way. The building itself – Hindlip Hall, Worcestershire – had in a previous life been a stately home and for that reason it was designated a Grade II listed building in 1985.

Since 1967 the Hall has been the headquarters for the West Mercia Police.

Some people believed the 16th century spirit of the hall still occupied the 19th century body of the re-built building and stories of unearthly and mysterious sightings allowed the ghosts of persecuted Catholics to hide in the imagination of impressionable new recruits.

Harry liked the old style layout of the building – lots of small rooms. He hated the modern stations – all open plan, with a cacophony of chatter falling off the cheap panelling.

Harry shared his room with his DI. Other than an incongruous looking hat that Harry kept on his desk - the top hat his father had given him - it was a room devoid of ornaments. Business like: computers, printers, phones, waste paper bins, a white board and four standard issue filing cabinets.

Harry watched DI Trish Bond sit down at her desk and switch on her computer. She briefly looked up at him but said nothing. Harry felt the silent undertone of something as yet undiscovered. He didn't know what it was or whether it was good or bad, but he could feel it. He quickly buried it. Like he always did. He preferred to keep work relationships strictly professional. Not that he had any out of work relationships. That was one magic trick he'd never figured out...the magic of love. He'd never been in love. He'd had infatuations...secret infatuations. But he'd never stepped over the line. It seemed to Harry that love had no rules....that there was no way of knowing what was real and what wasn't real. He'd avoided it, but at the same time it was a trick he knew he would love to learn one day.

23

Kempsey, Worcestershire
April 2018

The next day Harry decided he needed to take a step back. Get a different perspective on the *Poppy Killer* case. So he made the decision to pay a visit to the DI who had headed up the investigation during the final two murders – DI Bob Burnett. In 1999 he had taken over the investigation to a fanfare of optimistically optimistic publicity. His record was unmatched. If anyone was going to catch the killer it was going to be DI Burnett. Five years later in 2004 he retired to the sound of silence.

Harry was in his car. On the way to meet Bob Burnett. His mind was distracted. He thought about his biological parents – he tried to imagine what they looked like. He wanted to feel something, anything, but all he felt was isolation. His mind turned over a page – thoughts of his two siblings came into view. He wondered if they were brothers or sisters or one of each? He wondered if they felt like he did? He wondered...his thoughts were abruptly interrupted by the sight of red traffic lights coming into his conscious view. He managed to break just in time. He took a deep breath, sat up straight and forced himself to focus.
Bob Burnett lived in a small village called Kempsey on the outskirts of Worcester. His house was an Edwardian three-storey semi in a quiet

neighbourhood just off the main road that dissected the centre of the village.

Harry found the house without any problem and a few moments later Bob Burnett was warmly inviting him into his home. Whilst standing in the lounge they exchanged informal *detectivecentric* pleasantries before they got down to business: tea requirements.

Harry's initial thoughts were that Bob Burnett seemed surprisingly untroubled and contented. He could easily have been bitter and angry. He'd had the best record in the force but ultimately his career was remembered not by the full cup of success but by the empty dregs of failure. His failure to apprehend the *Poppy Killer*. The *Poppy Killer* won – ex-DI Bob Burnett lost. There was no way around the truth.

He brought out the tea in two china cups with matching saucers, which while being perfectly acceptable drinking receptacles seemed rather peculiar to Harry. They then sat opposite one another on strangely odd-looking soft padded chairs.

With great aplomb Bob proudly informed Harry he'd been decorating. Harry wondered to himself if, come retirement, it was compulsory to redecorate your house, irrespective of whether it needed it or not. He guessed it filled in the hours vacated by work. As he looked around he was struck by the wallpaper design: vertical stripes of grey and charcoal. It gave the impression that Bob Burnett's lounge had become his prison. Maybe it had?

Harry nursed his tea, gathered his mind, then set about the task in hand.

'So, you know why I'm here.'

Bob nodded. 'I guess you have drawn the short straw.' He smiled but it lacked any warmth.

An odd silence ensued as if neither of them knew where to start.

Harry took a sip of his tea, then looked up at Bob. 'Tell me about the investigation.'

Bob let out a deep sigh.

'It was the biggest manhunt in British criminal history. Bigger than the *Yorkshire Ripper* investigation. As you know, the murders started in 1986 and it wasn't until the third murder that we realised we had a serial killer on the loose. When I took over the investigation, at the beginning of 1999 there had not been a murder for 3 years. There was growing concern that the *Poppy Killer* could strike at any moment. My predecessors – DI Cox – who had taken over from DI Gould, had investigated the case to the best of their abilities but they had come up with nothing.' Bob glanced at his tea. 'I was immediately under pressure to get a result.' He paused. Inhaled. Exhaled. 'When I failed to live up to my billing; when I failed to stop the ninth murder the Home Secretary became involved which meant the chief had a strip torn off him, which meant the chief tore a strip off me. But it made no difference – shouting, getting angry, the blame game; nothing changed, we weren't even close.' Bob picked up his cup and saucer. Harry felt his mind distorting the image, as if Bob Burnett had become a small figure in an oversized chair.

'Harry?'

Harry snapped out of himself.

'Go on.'

Bob held his stare for a few seconds before continuing. 'When the tenth murder happened in 2001 I was already on death row.'

The ex-DI took a sip of his tea.

'I'm sorry to hear that Bob.' He was and he wasn't. 'Please continue.'

Bob put down his cup and saucer.

'We simply did not understand his motives. He never made contact with the press or the police. He was *unprofilable*. He could have been a teacher, an office worker, ex-military, a shop assistant, a politician....he could have been anything or anyone. He simply existed in society.' Bob Burnett got up from his soft padded beige chair and stood in front of the vertically striped grey and charcoal wallpaper. He looked as if he was locked in his own regrets. He scratched his forehead. 'We were never sure where the abductions took place. We narrowed it down of course, the industrial areas seemed most likely, but he was never spotted. The victims just seemed to vanish on their way home. And then, weeks later, they reappeared. Dead. Emaciated. Lying in remote spots, no witnesses. No fucking witnesses Harry...ever. Even with the introduction of HOLMES we never got a sniff of a lead. So no forensic evidence and no psychological profile. How on earth were we meant to find him?' He shook his head. 'The only thing we could hope for was luck. And we never had *any* of that.'

Bob bowed his head, then sat back down and leaned forward.

'Do you know why he stopped.' Harry knew it wasn't a question. 'Because he could.' Bob cued up his thoughts. 'Virtually all serial killers have one thing in common...they can't stop killing. And once they have fulfilled their fantasy, once they have killed for the first time, each subsequent kill needs an extra intensity to maintain the same level of stimulation. That's why they get caught. They become addicted. They crave more and higher doses of their fantasy to maintain their arousal levels' Bob's eyes narrowed. 'But occasionally, very rarely, some don't. *Jack the Ripper* stopped at five. *The Poppy Killer* stopped at ten. And with him...the *Poppy Killer*, each kill, each autopsy was the same. There was never any evidence of violence. Instead he denied them food and water... he dehumanised them. And then in 2001, after his tenth murder, he chose to stop killing. Why? Because *he* was never out of control.'

Harry gazed at his cup. He wondered if Bob felt the same admiration for the *Poppy Killer* that he felt. He wanted to ask him, but he knew he couldn't. He looked out of the window. He searched for the *Poppy Killer*'s face, but he saw nothing. He turned his head and looked into Bob Burnett's eyes. He had the look of a man who blamed himself but wasn't sure why.

A question popped into Harry's mind.

'What about Alison Marchant?'

Suddenly the whole room seemed to go quiet – the background hum of traffic, the birds singing, the wind blowing: it all stopped. And then, as if someone had put a coin in the meter, it all started up again.

Bob made as if he was going to stand up, but stopped himself.

'Alison Marchant.' He nodded his head as if to acknowledge the memory. Then he shook his head and gave a wry laugh.

'The eleventh victim…

'…that wasn't.'

24

'Whatever happened to Alison Marchant?' Bob Burnett seemed to be stuck in his own recollections.

'Bob?'

Bob finished his lukewarm tea, then gazed around the room before re-centering his focus.

'I'm sure you've read the file. She disappeared in 2003. Her car was found in Nottingham and in certain respects her disappearance fitted the *Poppy Killer's* MO...mainly in terms of one minute she was there, the next minute she was gone. And she remained missing for over 50 days before she suddenly turned up at Loughborough Police Station.' Bob paused. Harry motioned for him to continue. 'Our first reaction when we heard she was still alive was that this was the breakthrough we'd been waiting for. That the *Poppy Killer* had finally slipped up and one of his victims had escaped.' Bob shuffled in his seat and took a sip out of his empty cup. 'But as soon as we got there...to interview her...we knew something wasn't quite right.'

Harry looked at Bob inquisitively.

'You know the way he worked. He'd abduct his victims, take them to a place unknown, deny them food, give them hardly any water. Starvation combined with dehydration meant that most of them died within three to four weeks.' Bob's eyes registered the pain of the memories. 'They were all so young, so emaciated. Disposed of like they were nothing. It was heart-breaking. Whoever did it, he was as cold-bloodied as any killer that has ever lived.'

Harry looked down at the floor. He knew he should have felt something for the victims, but he didn't; Alison Marchant was taking up his thoughts.

'And Alison?'

Bob looked vacantly back at Harry as if he was waiting for his memories to reorganise themselves.

'She showed no signs of dehydration and only a mild case of malnutrition. She claimed that she had no recollection of what had happened. Total memory loss.' Bob let out an ironic grunt. 'Selective memory loss more like. The doctors called it delayed post-traumatic amnesia...that it stemmed back to her having an unhappy childhood...a weak mother and an abusive father. The doctors said she had been bottling it up for years; and instead of getting help, she'd created a dreamworld in which she could escape; and for whatever reason the years of bottling it up suddenly exploded and caused her dramatic breakdown...her disappearance, or as it was in her eyes, her escape.'

Harry looked at Bob disbelievingly and the ex-DI knew exactly what Harry was thinking. 'Believe me, we questioned her many times but she stuck rigidly to her story. Or lack of story as was the case. She said that all she could remember was leaving her house and going for a drive. She couldn't recall ending up in Nottingham and parking on the outskirts of the city centre. She said that she must have decided to stop, unaware of where she was. That she just wanted to get out of her car and walk…in whatever direction.'

Harry let that image develop in his mind. He liked the notion of standing at the crossroads, with your future distilled down to one decision.

Bob stood up, walked around the room and sat back down again.

'She was a bit off with the fairies. She thinks she survived by sleeping in deserted barns in the surrounding countryside…living off the land. Collecting vegetables from nearby farmland. Picking apples, berries. Like she was an expert in bushcraft and survival techniques. I mean, *come on*.' There was a hint of redness starting to colour his face – his blood pressure kicking its legs below the surface. 'She couldn't remember where and she said she never saw a soul. We tried taking her to a few secluded barns between Nottingham and Loughborough, but none of them registered with her.' He shook his head. 'It just seemed a pointless exercise…a needle in a haystack. Hell, she probably stayed at some posh hotel – swanning around thinking she was Agatha Christie.'

'And no one noticed her?'

Bob shot Harry a look.

'Never underestimate the public's ability not to notice what is *right* in front of their eyes.'

Harry smiled. A part of him knew exactly what Bob meant.

Bob paused. He picked up his cup and looked at it in disbelief. As if the fact it was empty was a major catastrophe. He sighed, before asking Harry if he would like a refill. Harry declined, so Bob put his cup back in its saucer. Catastrophe over. 'In the end we had to let it go. We had no choice; everything about her story was unbelievable, yet possible. I mean, people have disappeared for a lot longer and turned up alive and well. And, if she had been held by the *Poppy Killer*, what possible reason would she have had for denying it? The whole thing became preposterous, to the point where mental breakdown seemed the only possible answer. How she survived?' He shook his head. 'We'll probably never know.'

Bob reflected on his own thoughts.

'She was a strange one...Alison Marchant. There was something about her that...' He stopped himself. He turned his head as if to find the right words, but then abruptly changed tack. 'How are you getting on with it...the investigation?'

Harry ignored his question and instead got up and walked to the window. Bob twisted around in his chair to face him but Harry had his back to him. He was looking vacantly out into the distance, to the Malvern Hills...the view, a still life arrangement of green rolling waves. The imprint of the *Poppy Killer* a lost shadow in his mind. He turned around. He was feeling weary...wondering to himself if he should pursue the Alison Marchant story any further. He decided it could wait for another day. He was ready to leave, but he had one last question to ask Bob Burnett.

'The poppy...what did you make of the poppy?'

Bob shot a glance at Harry. His throat created a backdraft that sucked a tired smile onto his face.

Harry sat back down.

'The killer's calling card…if you want to call it that. What it meant was anyone's guess.' Harry looked puzzled. 'Look, a symbol can mean anything to anyone. And unless the killer comes forward with an explanation then it's total guess work. Yes, there was one left with every victim…always positioned under their feet, but knowing that led us no further in our investigation.' Harry went to say something but Bob lifted his hand to stop him. 'Yes, we investigated the obvious links...that he could have been an ex-serviceman. We even made this information public. Most of it at least. We kept the positioning of the poppy back. Just so we could weed out the wheat from the chaff. The phones went ballistic. We had more *Poppy Killers* than victims. It was insane. If the damn thing hadn't been so serious it would have been funny. *I'm Spartacus.*' He waved his hands in the air in an oddly idiosyncratic way and gave himself a wry smile. Then his lips straightened.

'You remember what I said earlier…that he was in total control.'

Harry nodded.

'I think that was a key point. He was never an addict. He killed for retribution and the poppy was a symbol of his warped retributive justice.' He briefly looked away. 'I tried telling the chief that and he laughed in my face. He said we're looking for a serial killer not a vigilante.'

Bob noticed a crease in the wallpaper. He stood up and tried to flatten it out with his hand. When he realised it was a pointless exercise he turned back around.

'Believe me, many people spent many hours trying to figure out the meaning behind the poppy; drugs...you name it...but nobody came up with anything that would lead us closer to the killer.' A red breasted robin landed on the window sill. Harry looked at it and wondered if it was symbolic of something; but nothing registered in his mind. He stood up.

'You said you interviewed a significant number of people in connection with the killings. Did any of them raise even the slightest suspicion in your mind?'

Bob gave Harry a furtive look. 'Like I said, there were thousands of people interviewed. Of course, it's possible, as with the *Yorkshire Ripper* case that the identity of the *Poppy Killer* is lying there in the files – undetected. It would be injudicious of me to suggest otherwise. But with no forensic evidence and no visual sightings of the killer, it would have been nigh on an impossible task to have picked him out. And remember, in the end they got the *Yorkshire Ripper* because he was picked up driving around a red-light district with false number plates.' He let out a loud, short, sharp laugh. 'Like I said before, sometimes all you need to catch a killer is good old-fashioned luck.' He shook his head. 'We had none. Nothing. It got to the point.......' Bob stopped mid-sentence, he was back standing in front of his vertically striped grey and charcoal wallpaper. Shoulders slightly slumped, cutting a sorrowful figure. Harry knew he wouldn't finish whatever it was he was going to say, but in truth he knew he didn't need to.

'Thank you,' said Harry.

Bob promptly rebooted himself and walked purposefully over to Harry. He looked at him with compassionate eyes. 'Don't let the *Poppy Killer* get into your head...or before you know it you'll be seeing his face in your dreams.'

'It's too late.' Harry said to himself but carried not a hint of that thought on his face.

'Do you have a plan?' said Bob.

Harry took one last look out of the window. The robin had gone. There was no one there. He sighed.

'Not to let him get into my head.'

Bob gave him a broad grin.

Harry smiled back.

'If you ever need to talk again - about anything related to the case - you know where I am. Good luck with your enquiry.'

Bob held out his hand.

'Goodbye DS Black.'

'Goodbye DI Burnett.'

PART 5

25

Tawelfan Cottage
July 2003

When Jackson ran out of the cellar all he had seen at that stage was a cage with a body in it.

Then, stood outside the cottage, he'd convinced himself it was the work of the *Poppy Killer*. He'd felt sick, but in reality the implications of that thought had not registered. Instead, his outlook had contracted and whatever was to come had been squeezed out of consideration.

He returned to the cellar.

There was an electric heater switched on near the left hand wall. He realised that had been the source of the light he had seen when he first peered into the cellar.

He slowly moved closer to the cage. He could see the face of a young woman. She was covered in blankets, lying supine on what looked like a fold out bed. He just stared at her as if she was some exhibit that had a meaning he didn't understand.

Then he glanced around the cage – he saw a porta-loo and a table with one chair.

He thought he heard the girl make a faint wheezing noise which caused him to take a step back. When no other noise followed he moved slowly forward until his head was just in front of the bars.

Silence.

He thought he could see her breathing but he wasn't sure. There was still colour in her face which he took as a good sign. Suddenly her eyes opened and Jackson felt such a jolt of fright that he almost fell over himself in his backward retreat.

Then he heard a faint voice.

'William...William...is that you?'

He stood rooted to the spot.

Without thinking he glanced around the cellar to see if William was there. The rule book of life had been turned upside down and in that moment anything seemed possible, no matter how bizarre or absurd.

'William...I'm thirsty.'

Jackson ran through the options in his mind. The solution was simple enough but the context was far from simple. When no other course of action presented itself, he ran upstairs. He frantically opened the kitchen cupboards until he found a glass and was relieved to find that the taps were still working. He let the water run for a few seconds and then he moved quickly back down into the cellar. By now the girl was sitting up. She took the glass of water from Jackson and drank it slowly. When she had finished, she carefully placed the glass on the floor and looked vacantly at Jackson.

'William?'

Jackson could see she was confused, disorientated. His mind did a quick calculation. As far as he could remember, the girl – the one the press had labelled the *Poppy Killer's* eleventh victim – had gone missing about 5 weeks ago. He had read about the *Poppy Killer's* modus operandi. That he denied his victims food and water. That he left them to die of dehydration, starvation and humiliation. But the girl in the cage was still alive, yet in Jackson's mind if she had been in there for that length of time she should be dead already. And the way she said *William*...it wasn't in a nasty or fearful way, it was much more sincere and heartfelt.

'William's not here.' Jackson said cautiously.

She tried to focus in on him. Their eyes met. Jackson was taken aback.

She said to him, 'Can I have some more water.'

He couldn't take his eyes off her.

'Please.'

Jackson made his way back upstairs.

This time he found a jug.

After he'd poured the water he stood for a while trying to make sense of things. Without thinking he put his left hand in his pocket. He felt the keys to the house and took them out. Front door, back door, garage, and a key of unknown purpose. He looked at it. He thought of the cage in the cellar. Now he knew.

He returned with the jug of water.

She thanked him.

He watched her while she drank. Even though she was wearing the mask of death, she was the most exquisite girl he'd ever seen. He felt giddy. Confused. Unable to process what it all meant.

'Who are you?' she asked.

In the few minutes since Jackson had first stepped into the cellar he had lost himself. His emotions had poured over the tipping point and there was no turning back. There was no facing the reality that he had been handed a live hand grenade. That he had *inherited* the *Poppy Killer's* eleventh victim. There were no thoughts of searching for the pin, going to the police and defusing the whole situation. Instead he let his mind cultivate a whole raft of twisted trenches and when he had finished he dug in.

PART 6

26

October 2018

No one was surprised when Harry failed to come up with any new leads in relation to the *Poppy Killer* case.

No one blamed him.

Things had moved on.

The press had moved on.

The public had moved on.

It had once again become a cold case

Still open, but buried.

The *Poppy Killer* out of sight.

But for Harry, he was not out of mind.

27

West Mercia Police Headquarters
October 2018

Harry was sat at work. He was feeling a bit out of sorts. His emotions seemed to be locked in a permanent malaise. He looked vacantly at his phone and was somewhat surprised when it began to ring. It was his *friend* Mickey Maguire, the private detective. Mickey had information relating to the wider search Harry had asked him to undertake into his biological parents and siblings. He had traced the agency that had dealt with the adoption. Sometimes Harry wondered why he was doing it. What was driving him? He felt like he was walking through the clouds, never quite sure what view would come into focus next. But always curious enough to keep on going.

One thing Harry had learned about Mickey was that he never got to the point straight away. He always liked to embellish the information he had obtained with specific details on how he'd acquired it. In this instance he was telling Harry how at first the adoption agency had been unwilling to talk. That it was only after he had questioned the ethics and legality of covertly separating triplets at birth; and then thrown in a tabloid press reference, that they had suddenly become very talkative. Harry gave Mickey the praise he sought, and in turn Mickey moved onto the point.

When he'd finished the call, Harry stood with the receiver in his hand, trying to take in what he'd just heard. It seemed unreal. Mickey had found out the name of one of his siblings…Jackson Brown. He tried to think logically; to focus on what to do next. He eventually put the receiver down, then immediately picked it up again and phoned HR to book the following day off.

He looked down at his desk. There was work to do, but Mickey's revelation was affecting his concentration. He opened the file but the words looked blurred. He decided to go and get a cup of coffee. He returned to his desk, took a sip, then with his mind half-occupied he got on with his work.

28

Tawelfan Cottage
October 2018

Harry was on his way to Ludlow to see Jackson.

As he drove along the A443 he thought about their first meeting. He couldn't believe that 5 months had passed since he was last there. He pictured Jackson's face. The look of a man who was hiding something. Now he knew what it was. The question was *why?* Why had Jackson felt the need to deny they were brothers? That's what he needed to find out.

It was mid-morning.

As he pulled up outside the old stone cottage he realised he'd not taken much of it in on his first visit. His mind had been preoccupied. So he took the time to look around. He guessed the cottage was 19th century. It stood in a wooded valley with a stream running adjacent to the house. The cottage looked out across a rugged hillside covered in splashes of yellow gorse and purple heather. It was constructed of what looked like natural Welsh stone, with a slate roof and an old oak front door. The name of the cottage was Tawelfan. It sounded Welsh. Harry liked it. It was picturesque.

He noticed there was a car parked on the drive. Jackson's?

He prepared himself mentally.

Then he got out of his car, walked to the door and rang the bell.

A few seconds passed before the door opened.

'Jackson.' Harry smiled and offered his hand. As he did so, he looked inquisitively into Jackson's eyes. He had seen that look before. That guilty look.

Harry was soon sat down in the lounge taking in the nondescript décor. He was on the plain brown sofa. Behind him to his right was the kitchen and taking up most of the right hand wall was a large open fireplace. To his left he could see the staircase. Once again Jackson was opposite him on the older, shabbier armchair that was positioned to the left of the front door, just in front of the window. No sooner had Jackson sat down than he was standing up again. A woman had entered the room.

'Harry, this is Lisa…Lisa Hopkins.'

Harry stood up and shook Lisa's hand. A switch flicked on inside his head that made his heart flutter. But before he'd had chance to analyse the emotion Jackson was talking again, 'Or should I call you Detective Sergeant Black.' The tone in Jackson's voice indicated it wasn't a question. Lisa quickly intervened, 'Pleased to meet you sergeant…tea?' Harry reciprocated his mutual pleasure in meeting Lisa and accepted her offer of tea.

There was an awkward silence before Lisa returned from the kitchen and placed the mugs of tea on the table. She then retrieved one of the two dining chairs that were stacked up by the stairs and positioned it next to Jackson.

'How can we help you sergeant'? Lisa said.

'Please, call me Harry.'

Lisa smiled.

Jackson shuffled.

Harry guessed that Jackson and Lisa were together, but he wasn't sure.

'I presume Jackson told you that I called round a few months ago?' Lisa nodded.

'I was looking into my birth parents. This was my birth father's last known address. His name was William Marshall.' Harry paused, waiting for a reaction. Lisa acknowledged his statement while Jackson avoided his gaze.

'Last time I was here,' said Harry, 'Jackson told me he didn't know William Marshall. I didn't mention it then because it didn't seem relevant, but on my full birth certificate it states I'm a triplet.' Harry waited to let the impact of his words light up on Jackson's face. Jackson looked at Lisa. Lisa looked impassively back at Harry. Harry continued. 'You weren't entirely honest with me at our last meeting were you Jackson.'

Jackson knew it wasn't a question. He turned his head. 'I…I…I'm not sure…the…'

'When I mentioned William Marshall, back in May, I could tell you were spooked but I couldn't put my finger on why. Now I understand, to a point…you and I are brothers aren't we Jackson…triplet brothers.'

The silence was palpable.

Jackson looked like he was ready to offer his wrists up for handcuffing.

Then Lisa stood up.

'Well, that's amazing news,' she said turning to look at Jackson. 'Isn't it Jackson.' Jackson got up and walked over to the fireplace. He hovered over his thoughts. He knew he would have to accept the truth but the whole truth...that still needed to be protected until he knew Harry's intentions. He prepared a brave face and turned around.

'I must apologise Harry. My mind went a bit fuzzy when you told me William Marshall was your birth father. Of course, I knew immediately what that meant, that we were brothers, but I couldn't understand how. I mean, yes, it's obvious now, although to be honest, I still can't believe it, I mean, don't get me wrong, I believe you, but are you sure?'

'Yes, there is no doubt about it.'

Harry relayed what Mickey Maguire had told him yesterday. That he'd traced the adoption agency. And they'd confirmed that in 1985 Harry Black and Jackson Brown were adopted.

'So why didn't you say anything Jackson?'

'I told you, my mind went fuzzy. You have to realise that I hardly knew him. And when you turned up on the doorstep it just seemed unreal. I needed time to process what you had said. I'm sorry, I should have come clean immediately.' Jackson walked over to Harry and held out his hand. Without delay Harry stood up, gave a faint smile and shook it. Lisa clapped excitedly and shouted 'More tea?'

While she was in the kitchen Jackson asked Harry about their other triplet.

'What's curious,' said Harry, 'is the agency told Mickey that the adoption had only involved twins, not triplets. I'm guessing there could be a lot of reasons for that. Mickey's going to look into it. The agency gave him the name of the hospital where we were born…Worcester Royal Infirmary. So he's going to start there.

Jackson nodded in acknowledgment.

Lisa returned with three mugs of tea. All milk, no sugar.

The tea was steaming; too hot to drink, but Harry picked up his mug regardless. He had something on his mind.

'Our birth father, William Marshall. Tell me about him. Is he still alive? How did you come to be living in this house?'

Jackson glanced at Lisa but she seemed distant. He took a deep breath and composed himself before recounting to Harry the meetings he'd had, firstly with William and then two weeks later with Huw Morris.

When he'd finished, Harry sat for a while in silence trying to absorb what Jackson had just told him: the deed of gift; Alzheimer's; Europe; euthanasia. He felt oddly removed. No sadness, no dejection, just total disengagement, as if Jackson had been telling someone else. He looked across at Lisa who's face had taken on a look of total incredulity. He wondered why, but it was a tired thought.

Jackson shuffled in his chair, looking slightly uncomfortable.

'I'm sorry Harry. I still don't understand why he did it. And now it makes even less sense. I mean, if he was going to do *it* why didn't he gift the property to both of us…or the three of us for that matter?

Harry was desperately trying to force his way through the clouds in his mind.

Jackson stood up and went to the window. He saw Harry's car parked behind Lisa's. He wondered why that seemed significant. He shook the thought away and turned around. 'When it happened, I wasn't in a good place, so I guess I just accepted the inheritance...sorry, the gift...the house. I didn't look too deeply into it...or rather, I didn't want to look too deeply into it. I was afraid that if I did, it would be taken away.' He saw Harry's eyes widen. 'I know...I know, that sounds terrible, especially in light of the fact he ended his own life, but like I said, I hardly knew him. I mean, don't get me wrong, it did make me sad...that he had died and I'd benefited from his death, but what could I do?' Jackson paused to make sure his train of thought was still on track. They all looked at their tea; none of them took a drink. Jackson continued. 'I often wonder why he left it so late...to find me? Maybe it was the Alzheimer's? Maybe it changed something inside of him; that he suddenly felt the need to talk to me. I'm sorry Harry, I don't know what else to say...that's all I know.'

Harry noticed Jackson look across at Lisa as if he was looking for support. Then he moved from the window and sat back down.

'What about Julie Kendrick, our birth mother,' said Harry. 'Did he ever mention her? Is she still alive?' Jackson shook his head. He took a breath, as if he was going to say something, but instead he carried on shaking his head.

Harry picked up his cup.

Jackson and Lisa followed suit.

The quasi-silent sound of tea being drunk resonated around the room.

Lisa smiled to indicate she was ready to change the mood.

'But then two years later *we* met.' She turned her head towards Jackson and he smiled back at her. Harry felt there was something hidden behind Lisa's statement but he let it go. Instead, he blended in with their smiles.

'How did you meet?'

Lisa nodded at Jackson to indicate he should answer the question. She then placed her mug carefully on the table.

Jackson shuffled.

'We were both out walking…not far from here. We were introduced to one another by her collie dog…Dylan.' He looked at Lisa to check she was okay; she'd loved that dog, but he died some years ago. Her face was unmoved.

'He excitedly jumped up at me and from there Lisa and I got chatting and then, in the weeks that followed, we seemed to bump into one another. She'd just moved to Ludlow – renting – so we were both short of friends.' Harry watched as Jackson reached out and took hold of Lisa's hand. 'We just seemed to click and then one day I asked her out. And here we are living together.' Harry felt like Jackson was reciting a well-rehearsed script; he looked at Lisa, who immediately let go of Jackson's hand. 'And now I have a brother-in-law.' she said, and then stood up and outstretched her arms to

Harry who promptly got to his feet and accepted the invitation and the two of them hugged. From the corner of his eye he could see that Jackson looked uneasy.

Harry guessed that Lisa was slightly older than Jackson, but not by much; maybe in her mid-thirties. She was quite petite in stature. And...Harry was struggling to find the right definition in his mind...she was...dream like. As if she was somehow occupying a different space in time. And everything about her seemed to be creeping up on him, disarming him, as if...

Jackson interrupted Harry's thoughts.

'Sorry to bring the mood down, but after your last visit, after you'd given me your card, I went on the internet...it still hadn't sunk in...that you were William Marshall's son...my brother, so I guess I was just trying to search for some answers. And so I typed in your name. First thing that came up was your involvement in the *Poppy Killer* case. Terrible thing he did to those people.' Jackson was fishing. He'd changed tack too quickly for there to be any other reason. Harry knew that...but he didn't know why. His mind was preoccupied; his eyes drawn to Lisa. The way she was caressing her mug close to her chest, moving it gently from left to right. And then...and then he watched as she placed it back on the table so that the handle faced Harry. Had she done that deliberately? Harry wasn't sure, but soon he had convinced himself she had. Was it a signal? He began to toy with different explanations, different meanings in his mind...before he forcefully slammed on the brakes. What was he thinking. He'd only just met the woman and already he was imagining a secret code between them. He shot the mug one last glance before the sound of Lisa's voice allowed him to bury the notion in a shallow grave.

'Jackson, don't be so insensitive. The sergeant...sorry, Harry is here to talk about the two of you; to talk about your father, your mother, your other triplet. You have so much catching up to do.' Harry saw Jackson look at Lisa with daggers in his eyes.

'It's alright Lisa, whether we like it or not the *Poppy Killer* is a source of public fascination.' Harry got up and walked to the window. He tried to think with an uncluttered mind. There was something about Lisa. Something familiar; and yet, something not right. He turned around and looked down at the table. Lisa's mug. The handle. *No*, he shouted to himself and quickly turned to look back out of the window. He switched his thoughts onto Jackson. Harry was sure he was still hiding something, but what? His mind seemed lost. He needed to get away, give himself time to think. 'Unfortunately we are no further forward on solving the case. He wa...' Harry let his words fade, before restarting at a different place. 'I must go. It has been so good to meet you both. I hope *this* is just the beginning.' He reached into his pocket. 'Do you mind if we exchange mobile numbers?' Harry looked at Jackson, then Lisa. When Jackson said nothing, Lisa jumped in, 'Not at all.'

****

Jackson and Lisa sat back down and let the aftermath of Harry's visit gradually fade from the room.

'He'll be back, you know that don't you,' said Lisa. Jackson looked at her. Her words sounded foreign, as if they had been spoken by someone else. He put his head in his hands.

'We'll have to tell him. We'll have to tell him the truth,' said Lisa.

Jackson looked up.

His face had turned pale.

29

Harry
November 2018

Harry was sat at home watching the dying embers of the early evening sun streaming through the lounge window. He lived in a modest two bedroom semi in Barbourne, a much sought after area in Worcester. The location allowed for not only a short walk into the city centre, but also a pleasant stroll down to the River Severn. In addition, it was a fairly simple four mile journey to his office at Hindlip Hall and anything that made life less complicated was fine by Harry.

Apart from a faux leather arm chair the furnishings consisted almost exclusively of Ikea self assembly items which he hated, but his *convenience over all else* approach to décor trumped his dislike of them. He knew the property lacked character but he didn't dwell on it.

As he relaxed in the arm chair Jackson and Lisa entered his mind. They were an odd couple. There was tension between them, a friction that in a strange way seemed to be holding them together. He tried to progress that thought, but nothing developed. Instead his mind narrowed in on Lisa. She seemed…she seemed strangely removed from everything and yet she seemed to have total control over everything. He tried not to think of the mug; he felt a sense of embarrassment for letting himself get carried away.

But she was so captivating, so very captivating...his mind went into an emergency circuit break, bringing Jackson back into his thoughts. He seemed guarded. Harry had seen that behaviour before, in the interview room. Suspects desperately trying not to say the wrong thing, trying to keep to the script. The question in Harry's mind was, what was Jackson trying to hide?

****

The following afternoon, Harry received a call from Mickey Maguire.

In his usual meandering way Mickey told Harry that he'd got through to the Worcester Royal Infirmary - the hospital where Harry had been born - and after gently pressing the receptionist, John, into delving back into the files, he'd confirmed to Mickey that triplets had been born at the hospital on 17th August 1985. He'd also been happy-ish to confirm that William Marshall and Julie Kendrick were the parents. However when Mickey started probing into what had happened to the triplets, he'd come upon silence, followed by muffled voices, followed by John reciting the Data Protection Act, 1998 and then throwing the ball back in the direction of the adoption agency. Mickey didn't push it. Some situations required assertiveness, others, tact and guile, he told Harry, as if the teacher was talking to the pupil. Harry thanked him for his *professional* insight and then Mickey finally got to the point. He'd visited the Bright Future Adoption Agency in person and after what

Mickey described as a slightly irritating and protracted wait they finally revealed the name of his other triplet: Bernard Marshall.

Bernard Marshall.

Why hadn't the adoption agency dealt with Bernard Marshall as well? Harry asked Mickey. *That was the strange thing,* Mickey replied...*they didn't know. They were never informed of what happened to him.* There was a brief silence. *There's something very odd going on with the Bernard Marshall adoption*, Mickey said to Harry citing some form of conspiracy to explain the mystery. But Harry felt more pragmatic. He went through a number of possible explanations in his head, none of which provided a clearer answer. But all of which couldn't be totally discounted. He knew the unknown could play tricks on the mind. Make the unbelievable seem possible. And yet, the most likely explanation was that Bernard Marshall had died. Harry was emotionally unmoved by that thought. If he was dead, Mickey would find out.

Mickey finished by telling Harry that he would be paying the Worcestershire Royal Hospital a visit in person and would get back to him in due course.

Harry stood up. He looked across at his DI's desk. She'd been out all day. He had a vague notion of where she was, but when she'd told him he hadn't fully taken it in. He walked to the window. He wondered how much time he spent staring into empty space. He focused his eyes. Mickey Maguire reappeared in his thoughts. He was an excellent, if not egotistical private detective. And yet, Harry realised how little he knew about him as a person. Tangential thoughts entered his head. Was Mickey happy? He pictured him at home with his wife and kids. Did he have a wife? Did he have kids? Harry was sure he'd mentioned them, but so little of what he said, other than the information he wanted, ever stuck in Harry's mind. There was a knock on the door. His thoughts snapped back into focus. The chief needed to see him. The remnants of Mickey Maguire stayed with him for a few seconds more. He would find Bernard Marshall - dead or alive. And he would find his birth mother. Harry was sure of that.

He glanced at the top hat on his desk and then left the room.

****

Harry was back at home. Alone. Sat in the lounge - the light of the moon reflecting through the window. He was looking at the framed picture that hung on the wall. Bought from Ikea. A mass-produced print of *Picasso's Les Demoiselles d'Avignon.* He would often fixate on it, especially when he was in a melancholy mood.

He wasn't sure why he liked the painting. He wasn't even sure if he actually *did* like it. No, he liked it, but he didn't understand it. But understanding it didn't seem that important to Harry; it's what it represented that was important. What he saw. And what he saw were shapes, colours and images that shouldn't have made any sense, but somehow, somewhere in his mind they did. Maybe it was some innate emotional connection to his adoptive father's magic – the way his father had seemed to alter perspective and make you see what *he* wanted you to see. Was that what Picasso had tried to do or had he wanted you to see what *you* wanted to see? He liked to engage himself in that internal debate but he never resolved it.

The moon went behind the clouds and snatched the light from his thoughts.

He got up and stretched his back. He felt it sometimes, especially in his lower back and standing up and extending and bending his spine seemed to ease the discomfort.

He went over to the window and looked up at the sky. The clouds looked hesitant, as if they were uncertain whether to settle in for the night or keep on moving.

He rubbed his eyes. It crossed his mind that going to bed would be a good idea, but before he'd had chance to convert that notion into action, a stream of thoughts cascaded into his mind.

He felt like he should be feeling more brotherly kinship towards Jackson, Bernard even, but he felt nothing but apathy.

And why did William Marshall leave his property to Jackson. Why?

And Lisa. Oh Lisa. No matter how hard he tried, he couldn't shake her from his mind. She evoked feelings in him that he was unsure of - slightly afraid of.

There was something about her.

But what?

But what?

He looked back at the Picasso print.

Focused in.

The face of the figure at the bottom right. It seemed to grow larger.

Broken, distorted. Unnerving.

He's staring.

Opaque, unformed.

Staring.

Crying out for colour.

Staring.

Drifting.

Dreaming.

Dreaming…

…He sees himself, standing, looking at his dead mother, prostrate, a black and white figure, made starker by the bright red poppy on her chest. Harry totally still, saying nothing. Then he sees his father lying dead on stage. The audience silent, still, as if frozen in time, before he hears an explosion of laughter. Then the stage is blood red with poppies. And then nothing. A wilderness – a vastness of emptiness, before new buds start to appear; and he's looking up at the sky, the bluest sky he has ever seen and then faces, unknown faces start to blossom and then…and then he sees Lisa.

He comes out of his dream.

He stands up and looks around as if he's unsure of where he is. He sees the Picasso print, hanging silently on the wall. He stares at it for a few more seconds before closing the curtains and going to bed.

PART 7

30

Bernie
February 2019

He couldn't remember where or when he'd read about it. It was just a quote that had stuck in his mind. Or at least a version of it had stuck in his mind. That everyone has the desire to kill. But it doesn't mean you're going to do it. It's just a form of escapism. A release. So in Bernie's mind he was just playing out the same fantasy as everyone else. What harm could it do?

Bernie was on his way to work. He could have made more of his life…if he'd got his shit together. But all he'd ever done was shadow box against the injustices that he felt the world was throwing at him. And now his life consisted of the same seat, the same bus, the same time, every working day…

…and the same fantasy.

It was the girl sat opposite. The same girl every morning. A few months ago his usual bus had been cancelled and he'd had to board the next scheduled service. And that's when he first saw her, and immediately something about her registered in his mind. She looked familiar. Not identical to the girl he thought she resembled, but close enough. And from that moment the later bus became his regular service. And as the months went by the differences started to smooth out and now he was sure it was her…it was definitely her.

When Bernie was growing up people used to comment on his eyes; how incredibly pale they were – just a hint of blue that made them stand out. Bernie felt like they were talking about someone else. He couldn't see what they saw. But he did sense it. That strange feeling that there was someone else inside of him - hidden - waiting to get out. He didn't understand it, but then in 1997, aged twelve, his mother took him to the cinema to see Titanic and that's when the penny dropped. He loved that film, the injustices, the romance, the tragedy; he was captivated by Leonardo DiCaprio. He wanted to be like him. He wanted to be an actor.

After that, he was always the first to audition for the school plays. The teachers found him enthusiastic, dedicated, and driven; but increasingly they found his performances lacked emotion, lacked insight, lacked presence. As a result he never got the lead parts and his input gradually moved from front of stage to back of stage.

Bernie was close to his parents. Or more accurately, his parents were close to him. He was an only child. His mother was a librarian and his father was a civil servant. They doted on him. And Bernie both loved and loathed their affection. He needed more. He needed their help, their support, their guidance, their understanding, but all he got was their love.

And sometimes that made Bernie angry.

31

Harry
February 2019

Harry was sat in his office at work.

There was a new case to investigate.

He had been briefed by his DI that morning and now he was looking through the file. Credit card fraud. This did not interest Harry in the slightest. But then again, he knew that it didn't interest any of the other detectives either.

His mind idled.

Lisa drifted in.

There was something about her, something nagging him. And then, without warning, like his brain often did, it connected two seemingly disparate images.

He closed the file on the credit card frauds and made his way to the room at the back of the building. The room was imaginatively called the 'Back Room.' In there were all the old case files that had been stored away. Even though Harry knew that most of the stuff had been digitally copied in accordance with the modern HOLMES IT system, he still preferred the tactile feel of the case notes.

Inside the room he knew exactly where to look…the files relating to the *Poppy Killer* case.

There were no chairs or tables, just filing cabinets, so he laid the *Poppy Killer* files on top of the open drawer and went straight to the section on Alison Marchant – the eleventh victim that never was. He lifted her photo out of the file and looked at it closely. His mind made the necessary age adjustments. There was a match. He put the photo back down. He deliberately cleared his mind. Closed his eyes. Started again. He needed to be sure. He opened his eyes, picked up the photo and waited. There was no doubt about it. It was definitely her…it was definitely Lisa Hopkins.

32

Bernie
2001 - 2005

In 2001 Bernie went straight from school into full time employment. He secured a clerical job at Birmingham City Council, based in the centre of the city, working within the IT team. His parents were happy for him. Birmingham City Council were a good employer. They afforded excellent job prospects...training, security. But his dreams of being an actor were now just fragments of hope in his crumbling mind. Even the jobs he'd previously done in helping with set design had dried up. He felt depressed at being a failure and angry at the people who had made him feel like a failure.

Almost a year to the day after he'd started at the council he moved out of his parents' house and into a rental property. It was a downstairs flat in a converted terraced house in Bearwood, on the outskirts of Birmingham. From his flat it was a few minutes walk to the bus stop and then a short journey along the A456 into the city centre. The property had an old fashioned décor having not been renovated since it was converted into flats in the early 1970's. This suited Bernie – he liked the period look. He hated anything that was trendy or pretentious - like the set designers, producers and actors whom he'd come to despise.

By 2005 he'd saved enough money to buy his first home computer.

It was the new must-have home technology item. What harm could it do?

33

Harry
March 2019

Harry was sitting at his desk.

It was late afternoon.

He'd had an unsatisfactory day investigating the credit card fraud ring that was operating in and around the Worcestershire area. The rumour was that there was an Eastern European gang living locally; that they were using spy cameras to steal bank card data from cash machines, downloading it and then copying the details onto counterfeit plastic cards. Harry knew that to break this gang it would take cooperation from law enforcement agencies from different countries and that the whole process would be time-consuming and require patience and diplomacy. He wondered to himself if it was really necessary. Yes, Harry knew that credit card fraud was a cause of distress and inconvenience to the cardholders, not to mention significant losses to the banks, but he couldn't help but think that the people who'd lost their money would get it back...be reimbursed, and the banks, they could absorb the losses no problem...so why bother? It was a thought that would never have entered his head when he first joined the police force.

As much as he tried to resist it, his mind constantly turned to Lisa Hopkins.

He'd now had time to absorb what he'd found out in the 'Back Room'

That Lisa Hopkins was Alison Marchant.

But what did that actually mean? That's what he was having difficulty getting his head around...her link to the *Poppy Killer* case. Because in reality, there was no direct link. She'd been labelled the *Poppy Killer's* eleventh victim, whereas what had really happened was that she'd had a mental breakdown. Disappeared. So she wasn't and never had been the *Poppy Killer's* eleventh victim. Harry had to conclude that the fact he'd recently met Lisa Hopkins, who used to be Alison Marchant, the girl who he'd read about in the *Poppy Killer* file, was nothing more than a coincidence. Coincidences happen. He understood that. There would be a lot more miscarriages of justice if coincidences were ignored by police officers. And he reasoned it was understandable she had wanted to move on; had wanted to start afresh two years later - rebuild her life after her traumatic breakdown. And it wasn't peculiar that she'd met Jackson – they were both out walking – they had got talking – things like that happen. But despite all his reasoning, something just didn't feel right in Harry's mind. He thought back to his meeting with Bob Burnett. There was something in the way he'd recounted the events of 2003. Something that now sat in Harry's gut. Harry remembered Bob Burnett's unfinished sentence: *She was a strange one...Alison Marchant...there was something about her that....'*

That what? Harry kept asking himself. And the harder he tried to silence the doubts in his mind the more he thought the girl he was falling for, the girl who he couldn't get out of his mind, could, after all, have been the *Poppy Killer's* eleventh victim.

He looked up and noticed his DI was looking at him. She held her stare. It felt surreal. And for the first time he could remember he noticed the woman behind the detective. Her short curly brunette hair. It was old fashioned in some ways, but she made the style look natural. Her square jaw. It was the feature that defined her face. It created a wide, toothy smile, that caused her eyes to tighten. At first he'd thought it unattractive. And yet, as he looked at DI Trish Bond, he was taken aback by how striking she was, and it made him realise how superficial his initial impression had been.

She asked him if he was okay; she said he looked troubled. For a moment Harry thought her words sounded distorted, as if he was having an hallucination. He quickly regained his composure, assuring her he was fine.

Shortly after, she left the room. Harry tried to remember the last time his DI had asked after his well-being. He couldn't remember. He wondered if he was losing his mind. First Lisa, now Trish. His life seemed to be out of kilter with reality. The world seemed to be a different place - people were different; the way he felt was different; what he wanted in life was different. He wondered if he was reaching a turning point. That perhaps he was becoming a more emotionally responsive person.

He needed to return to Ludlow.

But first he needed to phone Lisa. He wanted to ask her something about the events of 2003.

34

Harry
March 2019

Harry was about to head off to Ludlow. The date had been arranged a week ago…he'd phoned Lisa. As he drank his tea he thought about their brief conversation. He remembered how his heart had seemed to come alive when she'd answered her mobile, when he heard her voice. She had seemed genuinely pleased to hear from him…cheerful, upbeat. That was until he got to the reason for his call.

'I was looking through the files again yesterday. The Poppy Killer files. Specifically about the events of June 2003…about Alison Marchant.'

The sound of silence amplified Harry's words.

'Lisa?'

'You must come here…talk to us both.' The warmth had gone from her voice.

'Does Jackson know?'

'Yes.'

'Everything?'

'You must come, next week. Saturday, 1100am.'

35

Tawelfan Cottage
March 2019

On his way to Ludlow Harry made a conscious effort to put Jackson and especially Lisa to the back of his mind. He knew it would be foolish to try and pre-guess what might happen; that he would need to respond to things dynamically, think on his feet.

As he drove through Stockton on Teme he encountered a brief shower and the hypnotic movement of the windscreen wipers seemed to flip his mind back to Jackson and Lisa. When he arrived at the cottage – to a bright blue sky – and parked up, the sudden cessation of the wipers acted as a trigger, tipping his mind back to the present. He wondered to himself how long he'd been driving in the sunshine with his windscreen wipers on?

But he didn't have the time or the inclination to think about the answer.

When Lisa answered the door she greeted Harry enthusiastically. Jackson, who was behind Lisa adopted a more cautious, reserved welcome. While they all stood in the lounge, there was a brief round of shallow, inconsequential conversation, before Harry walked over to his *usual* seat and gestured for Jackson and Lisa to sit opposite him.

Lisa made an offer of tea, but it didn't seem to fit the mood.

Harry looked around, focussing on nothing in particular, but at the same time noticing the absence of anything on display to indicate Lisa and Jackson were a couple. No photos; in fact the room was devoid of anything that could have remotely been called romantic.

He looked at them both.

It was time.

****

After Harry's last visit, Jackson and Lisa had discussed, argued and agreed to disagree on what they should do next. They knew that Harry would return. He was a detective; he'd been reinvestigating the *Poppy Killer* case. It didn't take a quantum leap of imagination to conclude that he would eventually figure it out…that Lisa was Alison Marchant. So when Lisa took his call last week and he said he'd been looking into the events of June 2003 she knew he'd made the connection.

There were a lot of factors starting to interlock, but the one detail, the one crucial detail that remained outside the interlacing rings was the fact that William Marshall, Jackson's father, Harry's father, was the *Poppy Killer.* Only two people in the world knew that fact. And it could have remained that way – if they'd wanted. But Lisa wanted to bring Harry in – square the circle. She trusted him. And besides, it wasn't just a subjective feeling. She supported her argument with the objective truth. The *Poppy Killer* was Detective Sergeant Harry Black's birth father. His brother was dating the last victim of the *Poppy Killer*. What else could he do once he knew the truth but bury the information. It would be too explosive for him personally to do anything else. Jackson wasn't so sure, he wanted Lisa to keep to her original story. That she'd had a mental breakdown. But if she had to, then just tell Harry half the truth…that yes, she had been abducted by the *Poppy Killer*, but she had been blindfolded. She never saw where he took her or what he looked like. And then for reasons unknown he let her go. There was no need to tell him the whole truth…the real identity of the *Poppy Killer*. But Lisa was worried that by giving him only half the truth it would leave open the possibility that he would announce a major breakthrough and re-open the investigation, totally oblivious to the Pandora's box he was about to unlock?. And then the press would hound them, especially Lisa, who would be vilified for not having told the truth in the first place.

Jackson wasn't convinced. But his circumspection was driven more by a lack of trust for Harry. He didn't know why he felt that way, it was just a feeling, but ultimately, whatever his feelings or opinions were, they very rarely had any weight in terms of the end result. Lisa always got her way. He wasn't strong enough to stand up for himself or to argue forcefully for his point of view. He was malleable. He knew that and so did she.

So they ended the argument in silence. An impasse. Which meant the decision - on what or what not to tell Harry - came down to Lisa.

What Lisa had not told Jackson was that Harry had fallen for her. She had seen it in his eyes; heard it in his voice. She was certain of it. That's why she wanted to tell Harry the truth. It would draw him even closer to her – give her more control.

****

Harry turned to face Lisa. He'd run through this moment a thousand times in his head. How to word the question. In the end he'd decided there was no point in rehearsing it; that nothing would ever sound right. Instead he would just let it spill out.

He looked at her straight in the eye. 'You were the eleventh victim *weren't you Lisa…Alison.* The eleventh victim of the *Poppy Killer.*'

36

There was a three-way exchange of looks - the atmosphere amplified by the deafening silence.

Jackson motioned to respond first but Lisa cut him off.

'You are right Harry, I *was* Alison Marchant.'

Jackson's heart sank. He could tell just by Lisa's tone of voice, by her posture, that she had decided. That she had decided to tell Harry everything.

'And yes, I *was* abducted by the *Poppy Killer*...and...I remember everything.'

She stared directly at Harry, not even glancing at Jackson. She was surprised at herself, at how easy the words had come out. And she felt much better inside; as if she had been carrying an injury and by confessing to Harry, it had somehow helped heal the wound.

'Stop!' They both looked at Jackson in surprise. Jackson turned to Harry. 'Lisa knows my feelings on this matter,' he said. 'It's not that I don't want to tell you Harry...I do...well...I do and I don't. You see, there's far more to it than you could ever imagine and even though you're my brother we hardly know each other. Lisa and I have no way of knowing how you will react.'

Harry looked at Lisa who gave him a faint nod of her head as if it was an established code in their own private club. She then turned to look at Jackson. He sighed. 'You don't understand…this thing…it's bigger than both of us, bigger than all of us.' Jackson's tone carried a hint of aggression. He got up forcefully from his seat and strode towards the cupboard doors under the stairs. His heart was pounding. 'But you know what…I'm tired of hiding. So if Lisa wants to tell you everything then fine.' He moved to open the cupboard doors.

'*Jackson*.'

He stopped.

There was a tension in the air. Harry weighed up his options. Lisa's admission that she *had* been abducted by the *Poppy Killer* was such a bombshell that it felt like her words had imploded in on themselves. Yes, it needed to be discussed but Harry was aware that whatever happened to Lisa in 2003 could be a minefield of mental distress if unleashed without the proper care. He would need to tread very carefully. Allow her the space to let it come out in her own time.

'Look,' he said, 'as far as I know the only crime you have committed is withholding information. He paused. 'Of course, I would like to talk to you about what happened. Why you denied it? What you remember; how you escaped. But it can wait…until you're ready.'

Lisa and Jackson exchanged glances, surprised at Harry's understated, restrained response.

'You look surprised.'

'You're a copper.'

Harry let Jackson's pithy words settle in his mind. He wanted to be certain he was doing the right thing.

Ten years ago he would have taken Lisa straight in for questioning. He would have demanded to know everything...everything she could remember about her abduction, about the *Poppy Killer*. But things had changed, this wasn't just about the *Poppy Killer*; it was about his feelings for Lisa and the more he thought about it, the more convinced he was that he *was* doing the right thing. He liked that feeling – that he was putting Lisa first, ahead of his own personal ambitions. It felt different; he felt different; it felt good.

'Yes Jackson, I'm a copper, but I'm not here with my detective hat on. I'm here to find out the truth. And if the truth takes me with you then so be it. Sometimes you have to change things; change what you do; change who you are; for better or for worse; you just have to do it.'

There was an odd sense of drama in the room as if they were actors in a stage play in which all the characters' hidden secrets were gradually being revealed.

Lisa ad-libbed her lines. 'I admire your candidness, your frankness Harry. It's how I'd hoped you'd be. But I wasn't certain. In fact, I wasn't even certain what I was going to do today, what I was going to say, but now we've started, well, I guess there's no going back.' Lisa looked down at the table and stared for a while at the place where her mug of tea would have been. Then she slowly lifted up her head. 'But now...I think it would be a good idea to pause things, wait a little...like you suggested Harry. Prepare ourselves for what is to come. Let's meet back here next week. Lisa got out of her seat and stood in front of Jackson. 'It's the right thing to do.' She said to him. He nodded as much in resignation as in agreement. She turned to face Harry. 'Harry, thank you for your understanding. I trust you, but you must do one thing for me.' Harry remained passive. 'You must take time off work. What we are going to tell you next week will shock you to the core. You will need time to think things through. Will you do that for us...for me?'

Lisa repeated her clandestine nod.

Harry agreed, lost in her power.

Lost in the power of Lisa Hopkins.

Lost in the power of Alison Marchant.

37

Alison Marchant
Early June 2003

Alison doesn't remember how she got there…the cage.

She remembered being happy. Playing hopscotch under the moonlight.. Lost in her own thoughts – fantasising about her dream man. Feeling a sense of expectation. And then…and then, she was looking into his eyes.

The eyes of the *Poppy Killer*.

And all she felt was relief.

At first she was denied food and given only a minimal amount of water. She felt terrible but she never felt afraid.

Then, as the hunger and the thirst gradually subsided she started to feel more positive about things, as if she was accepting and then warming to her own fate.

She had been hiding for too long, unable to make sense of her feelings - the emptiness, the aching, the loneliness – feelings that had burnt a hole in her soul. But now, as she lay between the four walls of the cage she was finally starting to understand things. She felt free of her restraints and for the first time in her life she experienced an ethereal connection with herself. As if she had been released.

And the weaker she became the more euphoric she felt.

Then, one day - she wasn't sure when it was or how long she'd been down there, in the cage, in the cellar - things started to change

He brought her a glass of water.

And as time went by...food.

She wasn't sure why at first. She just accepted it.

And slowly but surely a routine was established.

Every morning he would come down, open the cage door and handcuff her to the bed. He would then return with food and water, empty the waste reservoir of the porta-loo, change the bedding and occasionally put out new clothes for her.

He never spoke.

And not once did she ever feel the need to ask him *why*?

Then, one afternoon - or was it the evening? - she wasn't sure - he brought down an old wooden chair and sat just a few feet away from her. Their lives separated only by the bars of the cage. And he talked to her. Guarded to begin with. Then gradually opening up.

And the more he talked to her, the more she felt like he appreciated her. That he didn't think her weird. And that was important to Alison. She wanted him to like her.

****

One day, William brought a folder with him.

He placed it on the floor and sat in silence for a while.

Then, as if an invisible clapperboard had suddenly snapped, he started to talk about his father.

'My father was a poet, a war poet. Not a famous one. Not even a great one.' William stared straight through Alison as if he was looking at the visions in his head. His voice was neither proud or despairing.

'He never got over the war. Whatever happened to him, whatever he must have seen - he never talked about it. But he hated the country he came back to.'

William picked up the folder.

He re-focused on Alison who had now sat up, attentive, engaged.

'Poetry was his voice. Let me read you one.'

The Red Shoe

On the battlefield, under the gloomy morning light
A red shoe lay still, so beautiful and bright
A patent leather reminder of their time together
For the unknown soldier and his Cinderella

The touch of colour, so strikingly red
Silent against the layers of the colourless dead
To reach out and to hold...to romanticise
Such beauty that rises above the genocide

I hope one day that I will get to tell her
That she was every soldiers wartime Cinderella
That her shoe was alive in this horrible stagnation
Where sanity required an insane imagination

She walked on the battlefield – the girl in the shoe
She laughed and danced under the sky blood blue
Her heart so free in her fine red slipper
She lit up the front with her sparkling glitter

And I try to picture the face that fits the shoe
When I realise it's everyone and everything I knew
Muslim, Catholic , Christian or Jew
They would all fit into the bright red shoe

British, French or even German too
They would all fit into the bright red shoe
Peace, love and the dreams we hold true
They would all fit into the bright red shoe

But no Fairy godmother will grant our wishes
No prince will bring us gifts and riches
So I pick up the shoe...the lady's shoe bright red
And wait for the whistle...then the orchestra is dead

Alison didn't know what constituted a good poem; all she knew is how she felt...alive. She could have been anywhere: on top of a mountain; drifting in the pacific; it didn't matter where she was, as long as she was in that moment with William.

He looked up.

'He was a good man...but...but things got to him. People got to him. The new generation...' William shook his head, '...no respect.' His head movement slowed. 'Eventually he lost respect for himself.'

William closed the folder, got up and took a few steps towards the stairs before pausing. He looked back at Alison.

'He fought in the war and then he fought himself.' William took a deep breath. 'In the end, he had the look of a man who'd lost both battles.'

New memories filtered into William's mind prompting him to return to the wooden chair; he stood behind it with his hands resting on the backrest.

'We existed – me and him – he...he wasn't a great communicator.' William looked at the folder in his hand. He held it up. 'This was his way of communicating.'

He walked towards the bars.

'You see Alison.' The tone of William's voice had changed as if he'd distilled all the feeling out of it. 'He was like a stranger to me. And then...one day we were on a roof top...'

He reached into the folder, picked out another poem and sat down.

'This was the last poem he ever wrote.'

Blinded

I dug my trench to fight for the fare of liberty
Now I starve on the leftovers of my dignity
I walked and crawled on fields now poppy red
Sown on the seeds of the slaughtered dead

So bitter sweet the sound of the bell that rang
Silent bullets amplifying the voices that sang
And in the ghostly trenches I buried my pride
To blow on the wind to the English countryside

Now I, blinded of heart, can no longer tell
If there's really a heaven or just a hell
Every downward slope an upward climb
Each daily task an empty mime

Nowhere to run, no key for my chain
Just total despair to feed on my pain
No more can I dream, no more can I give
Defiled is my soul of the will to live

A tear fell from Alison's eye.

She glanced at William. For a moment it looked like his spirit had left his body and he was just an empty shell. Then, as if in a trance, he carefully placed the poem back in the folder.

He shuffled in his seat.

'I could have saved him. That's what he wanted. To reach out to me. To release all the emotion he'd been bottling up for all those years.'

As William fixed his stare on Alison she watched as the colour of his eyes disappeared before her.

'He said some stuff before he jumped. It didn't make any sense at the time. It was only later, when I read his poems that I realised he'd been quoting lines from his own work. And you know the one thing that sticks in my mind. He said *this will make you stronger*.' William stood up abruptly, he held both palms out to his side, tilted his head back and looked up to the heavens. 'Is this what you wanted? Am I stronger?' Alison was transfixed, still lost in the moment. He looked back at her. 'You know what I felt when he jumped.' Alison remained motionless. '*Nothing*, that's what I felt when he jumped...nothing. I said nothing. And I felt nothing. All I could hear was the sound of screams, and I remember when I heard them that they sounded so inconsequential...as insignificant as the sound of the traffic.'

William sat back down and looked vacantly at the wall.

Ten minutes later, he left the cellar.

****

The more William talked to Alison the more his words became her oxygen. And she breathed in his hurt. Felt his pain. Understood his anger.

But more than anything she fed on his honesty. Because in Alison's mind the fact he was confiding in her meant he had feelings for her. And what reinforced this more than anything, what made this an irrefutable truth, was the day he absentmindedly called her *Julie*. She didn't mind. It made her feel special.

He'd mentioned Julie before…revealed emotionally censored snippets of their life together. She can't remember when. A few days ago? Maybe last week? She had no sense of time - where it began or how quickly it was going.

Now she felt humbled…humbled that she reminded him of his Julie. She thought about her own identity; about that vague feeling she'd had of connecting with herself. Now she wondered if it was more than that, that maybe she was connecting to whoever William wanted her to be and that her own identity had long been forgotten?

38

Julie and William
Saturday, 17 August 1985

William loved Julie…in his own way.

She was different – someone he could relate to.

Up to a point.

She had an indefinable vulnerability and fragility that reached out to his heart.

She was petite, her face was delicate. And her individualistic beauty was for his eyes only.

They talked, laughed and made love. And in those moments he saw the world in all its colour. People, animals, trees, buildings, the moon, the sun, the stars; they all looked different…brighter, more alive, more visible.

Julie was pregnant.

It wasn't planned.

For a moment she thought things were going to be different, that the gods were smiling upon her. That having a child would make her feel better – would make their relationship even stronger. So she drew pictures in her imagination…of the two of them together with their baby. But they were rough sketches at best and most of the time she couldn't make out what she'd drawn. The only real clarity she felt was that it wouldn't last, that the joy she felt when she was with William was just a short ferry ride between the dark shores of loneliness and unhappiness.

So the day she was told the news...*you're having triplets,* Julie cried. She didn't think of the babies, she thought of William. Her vague images of their future happiness together now extinguished. Taken away from her. And all she felt was a wedge between their love - three wedges - and her anxiety, her apprehension, her fear, grew exponentially.

When she told him the news he took the information in his usual way - with emotional detachment. But she could tell he was unsettled.

Julie went into labour prematurely...as if she had wanted to rid herself of the babies early. To return to *normal*. To return to William. The caesarean birth - one month before her due date - was carried out without significant complications. At least that's what the obstetrician initially thought.

It was Saturday, 17 August 1985.

Julie never saw her three sons.

The babies were classified as being of a low birth weight and were immediately transferred to the Neonatal Intensive Care Unit; part of the Maternity Department of the Worcester Royal Infirmary, which was the nearest hospital to her home in Redditch that had a maternity ward.

Just a few hours after the triplets were born she developed a one in one hundred thousand complication that was so acute that severe bleeding and clotting was quickly followed by cardiorespiratory collapse.

When she felt the sinking feeling, that her life was slipping away, she experienced for the first time an inner contentment. The peace of mind you can only get when you know that life can no longer harm you. She thought of William's cottage, just the two of them, in front of the log fire. And then, in the setting hours of Saturday evening, she closed her eyes, took her final breath and died. She did not put up a fight. Her tragic Hollywood love story had ended.

Amniotic fluid embolism was the official medical term written on her death certificate. An incredibly hard condition to diagnose and after a thorough investigation the doctors and the midwife were totally exonerated of any responsibility.

William felt crushed.

But he immediately hid the tragedy away.

It went into a sealed box in his mind.

He didn't want to have to think about it.

He organised the funeral, and returned to work.

He told no one.

Two days after Julie died he contacted a number of adoption agencies, and after speaking to all of them at length, he chose the Bright Future Adoption Agency, primarily because of their *flexible* approach to the process.

For William, to have his sons adopted was a simple decision. Neither he nor Julie had any family: no children, no brothers, no sisters and their respective parents were dead. Most significantly, he had no desire to raise the children himself.

He was advised it would be easier to find separate parents for the babies, because of the difficulty in placing more than one child in a single household.

Soon after, he met the parents whom the adoption agency had identified as the most suitable to adopt his sons.

A month later he signed the adoption papers.

He was very clear on his instructions to the agency. His sons were never to be told the true identity of their birth parents. His only request was to receive a photo of each of them, once a year on their birthday.

He did not say goodbye to his sons. Julie had not been given the chance and he saw no reason why he should be given the opportunity.

It was three months before William visited Julie's grave.

The world around him was now darker, less alive, less visible than it had ever been.

He stood motionless in front of her gravestone.

He thought of his mother…of her funeral.

A lady who was visiting the grave opposite looked at him…she felt uneasy. She had never seen such disturbing looking eyes before.

The breeze briefly picked up.

He looked down one last time.

A place in his head played a silent movie of him and Julie together…happy. Then his mind screamed out loud and the image faded…

…and his mind went pitch black.

For a moment he wasn't sure where he was

Then…

Clarity.

That feeling inside.

There was no other way. Life had signed him a blank cheque. Life had given him permission to do whatever he wanted. And what he wanted was retribution; for his father, for his mother, for Julie, for everything.

The following year on 7th June 1986, he started to pay life back.

39

The Cellar, Tawelfan Cottage
Late June 2003

He could see it in her eyes.

'You're different from all the others.'

The sound of William's voice floated into Alison's semi-conscious mind. She stirred.

'The others; they were all spoilt. Blamed their predicament on everyone and everything but themselves.'

Alison rubbed her eyes.

'It was always the same: shock, to denial, to anger, to pleading, to depression to acceptance. All the time they would cling on to the pathetic belief that what was happening to them simply wasn't fair. It wasn't their fault. But you…you are different.'

Alison slowly sat up. She saw William standing close to the cage, his eyes were piercing, yet distant.

'You have always accepted things.'

He walked round to the old wooden chair.

He could feel it in his heart.

At first he'd tried to resist it. He'd felt like his mind was playing tricks on him. His love for Julie was in a sealed box. Had it somehow come back to life? Escaped?

And then something clicked. And just like that, it happened….he was in love…in love with Alison.

Not love in the traditional sense. It did not grow, fade or fluctuate. William's version of love was much more binary: there was life with love and there was life without love; like two parallel lines, never meeting, but never far apart.

Alison was a similar age to Julie, the same green eyes, the same shoulder length reddish-brown hair, the same individualistic smile, the same delicate face. But there was a difference. Two differences ...two *big* differences: her guile and inner strength. Traits that drew William to her in a way that Julie never had – he was less protective, more open. But despite this, he knew they would never be able to do the things he and Julie had done; that he and Alison would never get to laugh, never get to make love, never get to be with one another.

And there were limits, places he wouldn't go, subjects he wouldn't discuss.

Like the occasion when she'd asked him about Julie...about her death. William's reply had been short and emotionless: S*he died shortly after giving birth.*

What Alison had really wanted to know was what had happened to the baby, but she could tell by his face that the subject of Julie's death was strictly off limits. And Alison hadn't wanted to press it any further because she'd been worried that she might have said the wrong thing and accidently revealed to William that she already knew Julie had died giving birth.

40

The next day when William brought Alison some food and drink she was surprised when he didn't handcuff her to the bed.

Instead, he asked her to step back to the rear of the cage, before placing the tray on the floor.

She then watched as he walked out of the cage and sat down on the old wooden chair, gently rubbing his hands on his thighs.

She glanced at the open door – she felt slightly uneasy.

Then, as was his manner, without any preamble and without any context, he began to talk.

'My mother worked in a bar in Birmingham. Her weight ballooned after the death of my father and…and the drunken revellers…they mocked her…mocked her for her size.' His eyes suddenly seemed lifeless. 'She went into a deep depression; stopped eating. I watched her waste away before my eyes. In the end she even refused water. She…' William's face soaked up his pain until there was nothing left to see…his words abandoned, his mother locked away.

Alison stood up. She wanted to hold him, hug him; she yearned to make things better for him.

William got to his feet and walked towards the cage.

'Do you know what you've done?'

Alison looked confused. She shook her head.

William's eyes dipped and in that moment she saw something in him that she'd never seen before – a look of forlornness.

He rested his head on the bars. 'I never expected this. I never expected to feel this way, not again. Not after Julie died. I…I only ever wanted to feel the hate. It stopped me from feeling the pain. But now…' He walked around to the open cage door. 'but now, this is different…I couldn't save Julie…but I *can* save you.' He extended his hand. 'I will do whatever I can to help you.' She looked at William expectantly. 'But you must realise that things will never be the same for you…not after this. You are different; special; and this, you and me, we are different. You must always remember that.'

Alison stepped forward to his outstrechted arm and in that moment, as she took hold of his hand, she felt an incredible surge of adrenaline. As if she had finally been liberated.

They looked into each others eyes. No words were spoken.

Slowly his grip weakened, then he released her hand and stepped back.

'I am growing weaker and you…you are growing stronger.'

He shook his head.

'You must eat. I have things I must do.'

He locked the cage door, turned around and walked a few steps before turning back.

'The two of us…we could…'

Whatever it was he was going to say wilted and died.

Then Alison watched him leave.

She thought for a moment. She talked to the empty space he had just occupied. She thanked him for saving her. For treating her as an equal. For freeing her from herself. Because for the first time in her life she felt a sense of self-worth. That she mattered to someone and that she was finally being accepted for who she was.

She lay back down and turned her head towards the stairs; then she closed her eyes and let her imagination escort her to her slumber.

41

Tawelfan Cottage
July 2003

William sat upstairs on his favourite sofa chair...his only sofa chair. He looked around at the emptiness in his life.

He knew his mind was in turmoil.

Thoughts entered his head unannounced. The people he had killed. He was surprised. They were meant to be dead memories. Consigned to the sealed boxes in his mind.

There was a time - before Julie died - when the thought of killing was just that...a thought. An unformed feeling. It just hid inside of him. After Julie died it welled up like a natural spring. As if it was meant to be. It replaced love and eventually it drowned out every other emotion. Until he felt nothing. Then he could live, carry on in society. Carry on as if Julie had never happened. Carry on as if all that was happening, wasn't happening.

But now, Alison had peeled back the layers of nothingness. She had revealed feelings in him that he'd not felt since before Julie died. But there was a difference: the dark clouds that had descended after her death...they were still there. And he knew they would never go away, that he would never again see the world like he had done with Julie...that he would never again feel that wonderful sense of normality.

He sunk into the sofa. He felt tired...tired of being the *Poppy Killer*, tired of being William Marshall. His eyes started to close. He drifted into a semi-conscious state before waking up with a start. He sat up straight, snapped out of his malaise and refocused his mind.

He had things to do. A solicitor to see.

42

Tawelfan Cottage
July 2003

'The two of us...we could...' Alison repeated these words a thousand times in her mind. And a thousand times she imagined a different meaning.

Three more days passed.

William seemed preoccupied. Less talkative. More fragile. Whatever he had on his mind, she wanted to help him. She wanted to reach out to him and give him strength.

Then, on the forth day he came down with enough food and water to last her a week.

He didn't say why.

After he'd given her the tray he locked the cage door and extended his left arm through the bars.

She stood up and took his hand.

He stared into a space that only he could see.

Then suddenly his eyes bore into her.

'I know how you did it.'

She instinctively took a step back. Then bowed her head, uncertain of what she should say.

He paused, there was a profoundness to the silence.

He squeezed her hand.

'It doesn't matter; I mean it matters, but I get it now. I admire you for it.' His tone was softer.

Alison looked at him – incredulity etched on her face.

He gave a wry smile. 'You're clever, very clever. You must use that. You must be ruthless. It will help you survive.'

Alison's thoughts raced ahead of one another before she felt an incredible longing in her heart. A longing for William to say *'us'...it will help 'us' survive.*

William's head twitched.

His mind was tracking randomly.

'Did you like my father's poetry?'

Alison nodded.

William scanned the cellar as if he was looking for his father's image in the rustic brick walls.

'He tried to be different...he didn't want his poetry to appear precisely formed or perfectly schooled. He wanted it to be real, but he never found his own voice; just echoes of the poets he didn't want to be.' William sighed. 'And then his peers cast vitriol on his work. They said his poetry was unbalanced, unstructured, pretentious, amateurish. But you know what, if they could have seen my father on that rooftop, that day in 1950, they would have known. They would have understood. It was all those things because he wanted his poetry to fail. To have succeeded would have destroyed the only thing that, in the end, made any sense to him...failure. Not just the failure of his own life, but the failure of mankind.'

She felt his grip tighten.

Alison could no longer hold back; she had to tell him.

'William...I love you.'

For a moment she was surprised by how the sound of her own voice seemed to fill the whole room.

William stopped.

He looked up.

He smiled.

There was a long silence; they both stood motionless. Then William let go of her hand, turned and sat back down.

He took a slow and deliberate breath.

'I should have said something to my father. I didn't get it for a long time. I just...' He looked at her as if she wasn't there. 'But something stopped me.'

He stumbled between thoughts, before his mind went off on another tangent.

'There is a phrase...that there is nothing either good or bad, but thinking makes *it* so.' He let the expression sit for a while. 'But the phrase is wrong. It's not thinking that makes *it so*...it's life. Life makes *it so*. Life makes the devil as real as flesh and blood; as real as the moon, the stars, the sun. And life, nothing else, gives you a reason to kill.'

Alison's mind was skipping around in fleeting, random patterns. She tidied her bed to try and bring some order to her thoughts.

'We have each other...life has brought us that. Isn't that enough?' she said.

William looked up. There was something detached about his face. Emotionless, yet full of meaning. He shook his head.

'You don't see it do you.' He straightened up. 'Have you ever looked in the mirror...the side mirror, when you were driving – there was nothing there so you pulled out. But then you had to swerve violently to avoid a collision because there was a car in your blind spot that you hadn't seen. That's where the devil sits all the time, right next to you, in your blind spot. There but never seen.'

Alison moved to the bars.

'William, I need you.'

He stood up and moved towards her.

'You cannot beat *it*.'

'*What*...what William, what can't you beat?'

'Life. You can't defeat life Alison, all you can do is bargain with it.'

He stretched out his hand.

'Look at me.'

Alison looked empathetically into his eyes and took his hand.

'What do you see?'

She gently shook her head, unsure of how to respond.

He frowned.

'After Julie died I saw things with such clarity. What I needed to do. How I was going to do it. It all made perfect sense. And that's the thing with anger, it's the most natural of instincts.' The furrows in his brow seemed to widen and then narrow. 'People think you can release anger, you can't, you can only feed it. And the more you feed it, the more it wants. And anger loves solitude, it thrives on it. Solitude asks no questions, it does not judge, it does not seek to distinguish between right and wrong. It does not give you false hope...people do that. They make you want things that you know are impossible. That is what you have done.' There was a hint of compassion on the edge of William's voice. 'You have made me look at myself and there is no way out. I cannot turn back and I cannot go forward. If I did nothing, that would destroy me and yet, if I did what I wanted, that would also destroy me. So what am I to do? Maybe I can't save myself, but I *can* save you, Alison. *That* is my clarity.'

Alison tried to look inside his words. But she couldn't find a way in, so instead she dismantled them.

'We *can* save each other William. We *can* be together.'

William shook his head. Gave a faint smile.

'There was a moment when I thought that might be true, that somehow, someway, there could be a future for us. But I know it's not possible. We could never be together. Life would never allow it.'

Her eyes welled up.

William released her hand, walked over to the brick wall and leaned against it with his head down.

'But....'

William spun round and cut her off. His eyes darkened.

'Look at me...this is what you need to see....the *Poppy Killer*...do you understand...do you *know* what that means?'

'William, you need to pull yourself together. You're not making any sense.'

He laughed out loud. 'Alison...Alison.' He stared at her intently. 'Look at us...there *is* no sense; there never has been and there never will be.' William turned and stared at the wall. 'I don't want you to see the *Poppy Killer*, I want you to see William Marshall, but how can I undo what I've done...I can't. I can't put out the fire that I started...that they started...I didn't start it.' William stood as if he'd set off some chain reaction in his mind. Then, just as quickly, he regained control. 'But now...'

She saw him say something to himself - she tried to pick the words from his lips; it sounded like *it's useless*; or was it *unless*, she wasn't sure and before she'd had chance to let the moment sit in her mind, her attention was deflected to the sight of William walking towards the stairs

Alison's heart cried out.

'When will I see you again?'

He stopped, made a half turn and lifted his head.

Alison reached out to him but his face had lost its intensity.

'Whatever happens, just remember...when you leave here...be yourself; be the person you have become; the person you are now. Because there is no going back. Not now, not after this.' His eyes briefly glistened. He stared into the middle distance...before whispering...'I love you.'

As the soft tones of his last words fell into the gloom, Alison looked down at the tray – all the food. She no longer felt hungry. Instead, she felt a strange mix of elation and despair. She'd heard him, it was faint, but she'd definitely heard him say the words...*I love you*. But, at the same time his words - *we could never be together* - kept spoiling the moment. Surely he couldn't have meant it – they'd find a way; she believed that without reservation. But the tray…all the food. What was he thinking? What was he planning? She slumped on the bed and wrapped herself in the blanket. Her heart suddenly felt empty and she was gripped by a terrible feeling that she would never see him again. She tried to dismiss it, hide it, override it, but as she drifted into a deep sleep the feeling had taken root and when she woke up a few hours later, cold and alone, it had grown into a crushing sense of sadness.

43

Tawelfan Cottage
Sunday, 13 July 2003

She wasn't sure how long it had been. She felt confused. Sad. He'd not been down. Not for ages.

Her food had run out and she'd drunk the last of her water. She was drifting in and out of consciousness.

Sometimes she thought she heard someone, that it was William, but it must have been her mind playing tricks on her.

She didn't believe that William had deserted her. That he'd left her for dead. He loved her. He'd had an accident. It was the only thing she could think of to explain why he'd stopped coming down.

She sat up and tried to focus. She looked around the cellar. Apart from the old wooden chair, there was just the electric heater by the right hand wall, isolated on the stone floor, providing warmth. When she'd been well and she'd felt happy, she'd looked at the light of the heater for hours...in a trance...her mind glowing. She'd be with William, in the cottage, just the two of them. He contented. She looking after him...in control.

She lay back down, closed her eyes and wrapped herself in her thoughts - it helped her not to feel so sad.

And alone.

Then one morning she thought William had returned – that he was standing in front of the old wooden chair.

She felt confused. She delved into her mind.

Was she dreaming or was it real?

She turned her head and looked again. She was sure it was real. It was William…right there. Her heart missed a beat, while simultaneously her brain registered a doubt.

44

2003

At first, Alison thought William had come back for her; that they would be together after all.

But something felt wrong; her mind felt disorientated. He looked different. Younger. Maybe it was the dim light? Maybe it was a dream? Maybe she was delirious? She called out to him, but he didn't answer. He just stood there as if he was in a trance.

She asked for water.

He left and returned soon afterwards.

'William?'

'William's not here,' he whispered.

This time she got a better look at him. She knew straight away. The weeks she'd been sat listening to William, absorbing every detail of his face. She could tell the resemblance immediately.

She asked for more water.

She needed time to think.

Over the next few days Alison received regular meals. It was always the same routine. He would gingerly open the cage door, place the tray on the floor, lock the door and then leave.

Every other day he would nervously tie her hands to the bars while he emptied the toilet and changed her sheets. He would also leave her a bowl of hot water, soap and a towel so that she could wash herself.

Slowly, she started to regain her mental and physical strength, and she was able to look at her new *companion* with a clearer eye. There was something about him – he seemed more timid than William. A follower, not a leader. He had never once sat down on the old wooden chair…where William had spent many hours talking to her. It was like he was afraid of her. She laughed to herself at the thought of her new jailer being afraid of *her*, but then, she gradually came to the realisation that it was true.

****

It was the fourth or fifth day, she wasn't really sure. She felt stronger. Ready to talk. As usual, he placed the food on the floor, locked the door and walked away.

'You're his son aren't you?'

He stopped. Slowly turned around and bowed his head.

'I'm sorry. I…I don't know what to say. This…' He glanced at her before lowering his eyes. 'You…it…it doesn't seem real…I'm sorry…' He looked up. Alison could see the confusion on his face.

'Don't be afraid.' The irony of Alison's words were lost in the moment.

'What's your name?'

He seemed to take an eternity to answer.

'Jackson…Jackson Brown.'

She smiled at him. She felt sorry for him. *She* felt sorry for *him*. She let out another silent, dry laugh. He seemed bewildered at his predicament. She sensed he was more in the dark than she was.

'I'm Alison. Please...sit down.' She gestured at the old wooden chair.

Jackson looked at the chair, pondered for a moment and then, lost in his own trepidation, sat down.

'Jackson,' she said.

He sat motionless.

'Look at me Jackson.' He tilted his head up, but his eyes remained lowered.

'Jackson.' This time he looked up.

'You need to talk to me. Tell me why you are here. Tell me what is going on.' Jackson stared blankly at her.

'Jackson.'

He shook his head as if trying to unblock his thoughts, before standing up and pacing around the cellar. Then, as if he'd found an opening in his mind, he sat back down and took a deep breath.

'About three weeks ago I was sitting on a bench in Mary Stevens Park...'

Jackson proceeded to tell Alison exactly what had happened. Firstly, his encounter with William Marshall. Then, what Huw Morris had told him a fortnight later: that William was his birth father; the deed of gift; Alzheimer's; Europe. He told her how, after his meeting with the solicitor, he'd arrived at the cottage the day after to feed the cats. No cats, just the Poppy. Then finding Alison in the cellar; the realisation: the *Poppy Killer*; the eleventh victim. And then not knowing. Not knowing what to do.

When he'd finished she lay down on the bed and looked up at the ceiling. She was numb with shock. She felt devastated. William was dead. It couldn't be true. She felt the strength sap from her body.

Lost in her despair she slowly turned her head to look at Jackson. He looked so forlorn, so vulnerable, so afraid. She watched him shake his head. She could see he was genuinely daunted by the predicament his birth father had landed him in. And William was definitely his birth father....there was no doubt about it. She'd seen the facial similarities immediately. Not in Jackson's eyes or mouth, but in the smaller detail. And there was something else she'd noticed about him: he only ever glanced at her; he never held his eye contact. She knew what that meant. She just had to decide what to do about it.

All of a sudden he got up, made an apology and left. As she watched him leave she recalled the one occasion when she'd asked William about Julie's death. He'd seemed put out. As if the question had been an affront to him personally. And then, when she'd enquired about the baby...the look on his face...it had obviously struck a nerve. And now she knew why, now she had the answer...he'd had the baby adopted.

Maybe he'd had no choice? She wondered how he must have felt. Clearly the whole thing tipped him over the edge. What did he say? *Life, nothing else, gives you a reason to kill.* A chill went down her spine. She looked at the halogen heater, glowing by the wall. She tried to find some answers in the shadows but all she ended up doing was tying herself up in knots with questions that only William could answer: *Why Jackson? Why his son? Why had he gone to see him after all this time? How did he know where to find him?* Nothing made sense. She could hear his voice…*Look at us…there is no sense.* 'But there was.' she said to the empty cellar. 'You and I made sense. But this, your son, what am I meant to do?'

His words kept flashing in her mind.

Maybe I can't save myself, but I can save you.

We could never be together. Life would never allow it.

Be yourself; be the person you have become…there is no going back.

You must be ruthless. It will help you survive.

I love you…

'I love you too,' she said.

She sat for a while.

She felt strange. Hours passed. The broken pathways in her mind were reaching out to one another. Signals were being sent. Constructs were been formed…uncensored possibilities shepherded by the vividness of her imagination.

Then, without prompting, William's voice shouted out at her…*unless.*

Unless.

That was it.

She sprung to her feet.

Unless he could find a way of destroying the *Poppy Killer.* She grabbed the bars of the cage and shook them. 'He's alive.' She shouted. 'He's alive.' It was the *Poppy Killer* who was dead. The *Poppy Killer.* All that was happening, all his plans, they'd all been done so he could finally rid himself of the *Poppy Killer.*

Her mind was racing. Jackson, his son, he was just a guardian. Someone to look after her until…until what? Until when? She wasn't sure, but it didn't matter. The important thing was that he was still alive. And the more she played with that notion the more she truly believed it. She'd not come this far to give up so easily on William. She needed to take control in order to survive…in order to be with William again. That's what he would have wanted…and that's what he would have expected.

She sat back down on the bed. The rustic brick walls seemed more vivid. As if the brightness of her thoughts had heightened the colours of the surroundings. All the doubts in her mind had gone. All the sadness, the emptiness had dissolved. She thought back to the day when she'd suddenly found a focus for her emotions…a focus for her life. She remembered the rough sketches she'd drawn in her head…that grew into her machinations. She'd had to stir them, play with them, mould them to fit the ever changing landscape, and even though things hadn't worked out exactly as she'd planned, she had new hope; a renewed determination to see things through to the end.

She wrapped herself up in the blanket and let her mind paint pictures of the future…of her and William together.

She could not hear the deafening denial that was playing out in her head. To Alison, what had happened to her when she was growing up...that was bad; but everything she was doing now...that was good. It was that simple. And William had told her, it's not thinking that makes things real, it's life. And now, it was Alison's turn to use *life* as a reason for her actions. *Life* owed her and now *life* was going to pay.

45

2003

For a brief moment, for a brief few seconds, when he'd first stepped into the cellar, when he'd first seen her, Jackson had tried to resist the way he felt. A faint, barely perceptible signal had told him that the whole thing was perverse, warped, sick. That he should do something. But instead, he'd just stood there and stared at her. And in that moment, without realising it, he'd erected a barrier to his rational thoughts. A barrier that would prevent him from going to the police; a barrier that would prevent him from seeing the truth. Because now, the only truth that mattered to Jackson was she was the most beautiful woman he'd ever seen; he couldn't take his eyes off her, and yet, he found he was unable to look her in the eye; unable to control his emotions; unable to stop himself from falling in love with her.

And with that love came his failure to understand that Alison Marchant was not a normal woman. Her mental health struggles had been allowed to grow unchecked. Her imagination had been allowed to flourish unrestrained. She was a woman for whom the world was a place to escape from, a place to manipulate.

For Jackson, the world, his world, was now a place that involved Alison. He could see no further than Alison. And the more he talked to her the more he began to accept things and the more the outside world seemed to fade from view.

And slowly but surely his ability to perceive the difference between right and wrong disappeared from sight altogether. Alison Marchant had been locked up by the *Poppy Killer* for over a month – the *Poppy Killer*...his birth father...the murderer of 10 innocent people; and she was still locked up - yet she was acting as if everything was normal, that everything was going to be okay. Jackson should have done something...anything.

Anything but nothing.

46

2003

He now accepted why William had come to see him…why he'd left him his property. Alison had made it seem okay…natural – he was his father…a kind man. She had turned the monster that had been the *Poppy Killer* into the victim that was William Marshall.

Any deeper insight by Jackson into how his birth father had found him or what had really been going on inside William Marshall's head was suppressed by Alison.

In truth, Jackson was out of his depth. He lacked the mental strength to deal with things. To navigate the tricky waters he was in. All he could do was hang on, let things unravel and hope for the best.

So Alison had taken the helm. And now she had Jackson in the palm of her hand. She knew that. He knew that. In truth, she'd known it from the very beginning – the way he'd looked at her…hesitantly…love-struck. And they both knew that things couldn't go on the way they were. That things had to change. So she devised a plan. A plan that would make the impossible seem possible.

****

It had been twelve days since Jackson first discovered Alison.

It was time.

Time to bring Jackson in on her plan.

He was sat on the old wooden chair.

Alison's food lay untouched.

Jackson looked at her as if he'd done something wrong.

She stood up and walked to the bars. She held out her hand.

He sat there, unsure of himself.

She nodded for him to stand up.

He gave a faint, hesitant smile, before slowly standing up and taking her hand.

He felt like his fingers had shrunk.

His heart was thumping uncontrollably in his chest.

She had Jackson exactly where she wanted him.

She looked him in the eye. He bowed his head. She felt at ease with the thoughts that were simmering in her head.

'We can be together Jackson. You and I. I know it's what you want. It's what William would have wanted.'

Jackson's heart stopped.

Alison had made her move.

She was now ready to tell Jackson her plan.

47

Tawelfan Cottage
March 2019

Harry had listened attentively to Lisa's account of the events of 2003. Lisa of course, had only told Harry an edited version of the truth. Snippets of facts, recounted with her usual candour; about the abduction; about William Marshall; about meeting Jackson. It was as if she had been recalling a drama that had been based on true events but she'd changed some of the scenes and incidents to suit her narrative.

Harry shuffled on the plain brown sofa; Jackson sat motionless in the shabby armchair. They looked at Lisa sitting upright on the dining chair. She looked detached, other-worldly.

Three full mugs of tea sat abandoned on the table.

There was an anxious uncertainty in the air. Like three friends that were really strangers, entering into an unknown task...not sure of how they should react.

Some time passed. No one was certain how long.

Then simultaneously they all motioned to say something, but interrupted each other.

Silence returned.

Lisa stood up and walked over to the window. Now Harry knew the shocking truth: that William Marshall was the *Poppy Killer*. She looked over at him...his face looked strained. She looked at

Jackson…he was sat facing away from her, but she could sense his drawn, vacant eyes.

She turned and stared out of the window, up to the clear colourless sky. She was confident that Harry would defuse the impact of what she had told him; that he would think things through and quickly realise he had no other option but to absorb the truth and bury the information.

Harry stood up and walked to the fireplace. It seemed impossible. Beyond belief. And yet, all he felt was weariness. As if what he'd heard had drained him of his emotional filters. He tried to force himself to face the reality…about the *Poppy Killer*, but instead his thoughts turned to Lisa and William. Her devotion to him. He'd read something about it – the Stockholm Syndrome. He made a mental note to look it up when he got back home. Out of the corner of his thoughts he saw Lisa turn around and their eyes met. Harry was taken aback by the look on her face…ethereal bordering on possessed. He tried to clear the image from his mind, but it was attacking him from all sides.

Her eyes softened and she gave him the faintest of smiles. He was caught in her web. He tried to smile back but instead he looked across at Jackson. He looked gaunt and pale. As if Lisa had eaten into his soul and left nothing more that the endoskeleton. He wondered if the same fate awaited him. Because all he wanted now was to be wrapped in her silk threads. And the truth didn't seem to matter so much. *Shit*, he said to himself and tried to throw away those thoughts…but they came bouncing back with force.

Trapped in the chaos of his mind, his birth mother suddenly came into view.

He tried to imagine what she would have been like, but then sadness filled his heart.

'Did he say anything else about our birth mother?'

Lisa shook her head. 'I'm sorry Harry.'

Harry acknowledged her sympathy. He looked around. The whole room seemed oddly out of perspective.

He reached inside of himself – searching for a focus.

'Tell me about the plan.'

Lisa nodded, as if she'd been waiting for the question.

'I knew, if we were to be together we would have to put distance between us. Dismantle what we had and then re-build it at a later date. No one knew why I'd disappeared. No one knew about the cellar or how Jackson had found me. No one knew the identity of the *Poppy Killer*...except Jackson and myself. In fact, no one knew anything. All I had to do was come up with a convincing explanation for where I'd been...why I'd disappeared. And that was simple.' Lisa allowed herself a half smile.

'So I returned to civilian life suffering from amnesia. Of course, to start with, everyone thought I'd been abducted by the *Poppy Killer*. They didn't know what to say. *Poor thing is so traumatised she's completely blanked it out.*

But it wasn't difficult to fool people. I'd had an unhappy childhood. And the doctors, they were so *understanding*...they faithfully joined the dots and called it post-traumatic amnesia. That I'd been bottling it up for years.

'As time went by people started to believe me. Either that or they stopped caring.

'And that detective…Bob…Bob Burnett I think his name was. He was so pliable. Eventually he even believed my story about sleeping in a barn…living off the land. At least that's what I think I said; amnesia allows you a great deal of latitude in how you weave or don't weave your story…what you can remember and what you've forgotten.' Lisa spun round and gazed out of the window. She watched the trees – silent and statuesque; like time had stood still. She let out a deep sigh.

She turned back around.

'They never saw through the façade. They thought I was mentally ill. Which was fine by me. William would have been proud of me.'

She sat back down and put her hand on Jackson's thigh.

'Then all we had to do was sit and wait.' She smiled at Jackson who returned the gesture minus the confidence.

'Two years later, I announced to my mother and the few friends I had left that I was going to start afresh; start a new life. No one was surprised. In fact, I think they were relieved. Relieved not to have to make an effort to say the right thing.' She paused. Picked up her mug of cold tea, looked at it and placed it back down on the table. 'I was renting a flat at the time. Close to my mother.' She gave a half shrug as if that information wasn't important. 'To start with I pretended to look at a number of locations...before settling on Ludlow. I fell in love with the place. The river, the castle, everything; it was easy to convince people. Then I found a flat to rent in the town centre. I left my job. I changed my appearance and I started using my middle name and my mother's maiden name. Lisa Hopkins. And the rest you know.'

Harry reached for his mug, swirled it in his hand and watched the tea come to rest. He then moved over to the window.

Lisa got up and moved to where Harry had been standing, by the fireplace.

Jackson remained seated. He looked up at Harry and nodded in support of what Lisa had said. That was his job.

Harry thought about Lisa – about her abduction.

'How was it that you came to be in Nottingham on the night of the abduction?'

Lisa turned and looked at the fireplace. She didn't want Harry to read her face.

'I guess that having a mental breakdown *was* part of the truth. I just got in my car and drove off. I didn't really have a destination in mind. I just wanted to get away. For no reason in particular. And out of pure chance I ended up in Nottingham late at night. It was a clear sky, so I fancied a walk. I just happened to be in the wrong place at the wrong time.' Lisa smiled to herself. 'But as it turned out it was the best thing that has ever happened to me.'

She remained with her back to Harry and Jackson.

Harry looked at Jackson who immediately looked away.

'But he killed *ten* innocent people,' said Harry.

Lisa spun round.

'He was a good man, a great man. But he allowed himself to become possessed by hate and anger. It turned him into the *Poppy Killer*. But you must understand, he wasn't like that all the time. He was Jekyll and Hyde. Outside of those dark moments he was well respected and liked. That's why no one ever suspected him. Like I said, he was a great man.' Her eyes narrowed in on Harry. 'So the question is…how do you judge your father? As an evil man or a good man?'

Harry knew that Lisa was being delusional. And he knew he should challenge her. He turned and looked out of the window. The leaves on the trees were faceless. The whole landscape seemed grey and sombre. He desperately tried to rouse the detective inside of him, but nothing came to the surface. Maybe it was the pure bizarreness of the whole situation. Maybe it was because there were a million responses he could have given, a million questions he could have asked, and yet not one response, not one question leapt forward in his mind. The only certainty that presented itself was that he was sure Lisa wasn't telling him everything; there was more to her abduction than she was letting on.

He would come back to it another day.

The cellar popped into his mind.

He pointed towards the doors under the stairs.

'Can you show me?'

Jackson nodded.

48

March 2019

Lisa, Jackson and Harry stood at the foot of the stairs, in the cellar of Tawelfan cottage…reflecting.

Lisa thought of William; Jackson thought of Lisa; and Harry thought of the *Poppy Killer*…and then Lisa.

At the far end of the cellar, by the wall, Harry noticed an old wooden chair. He moved towards it. In front of it he could see four small holes in the stone floor that had been filled in. He calculated that the area made by the holes formed a square of approximately 50 square feet.

'The cage?'

Harry turned and looked at Lisa - she nodded. He felt a sense of anti-climax. All those years the police had been looking for the *Poppy Killer's* lair and it came down to a simple cage in the cellar of a remote stone cottage.

He glanced around - apart from a single light that hung in the middle of the room, there was nothing else other than the wooden chair and an old electric heater. There were no windows – just the four brick walls that were showing signs of salt deposits and giving off a slight musty smell. The stone floor was bare and menacing.

A tingle went down Harry's spine.

He turned to face the far wall.

He stared deep into his mind.

'I used to think I could see the *Poppy Killer*. In my imagination.' He zoned in on the wooden chair. 'How could I have known that what I was really doing was searching for the face of my birth father? I don't know, it sounds ridiculous, maybe I'm reading too much into things, but it felt like I was reaching out to him.'

Harry shook his head. His mind jolted.

He took a deep breath and turned back around.

Who was Harry Black? He wasn't sure. He glanced at Lisa. All he knew was that he felt different. Not just because of what Lisa had told him, but because she *had* told him. Trusted him. And because of that, even though everything about the situation should have sounded alarm bells, he was refusing to listen to his own voice of reason. He knew what he wanted and everything else would have to wait.

They made their way back upstairs.

'You were right to tell me.'

Lisa looked at him appreciatively.

'And you were right to trust me. This is no longer a police matter. This…' Harry fixed on the cellar door. '…what happened…this is now between the three of us.'

He gave them a brief nod.

He looked down at the three mugs of cold tea; there was something oddly symbolic about them. An image flashed into his head of The Three Little Pigs and the Big Bad Wolf. He almost let out a faint laugh but dismissed the thought before it had chance to flourish.

He moved to the front door.

'I took your advice and booked a few days off work. I must go back home...think things through.'

He opened the door and stepped out onto the gravel path. He could sense their eyes on the back of his head. He stopped and turned around.

Lisa gave him a faint nod of her head. Harry hoped he understood the meaning behind it.

But in truth...he didn't.

On the way back Harry thought about Bernard Marshall, his other triplet brother. He wondered how Mickey Maguire was getting on with his search; he thought about phoning him, but decided against it. He wondered what his brother would make of things. How he would handle the truth about his birth father. He questioned whether he should even tell him. Of course, he knew that all his reasoning, all his internal debating, would be irrelevant if Bernard was dead. He glanced at his phone again, but instead, he continued on his journey home and let thoughts of Bernard Marshall fade from his mind.

49

Bernie
2010

Bernie had an antagonistic mix of personality traits: he was driven, but he lacked confidence; he was extrovert on the inside, but shy on the outside; he wanted to be himself, but he couldn't face himself; he was angry, but all he wanted was peace of mind. This cocktail of characteristics, of emotions, meant he was always fighting himself. He found it draining. That's why he needed to find a way of escaping it.

His home computer.

The Internet

What harm...........?

Why do some thoughts come into your mind? Bernie wasn't sure. But one Saturday night, alone, randomly surfing through the pages on the World Wide Web he suddenly thought of a name. Maybe it was a symptom of how he felt inside. But something in his mind shone a bright light on the *Poppy Killer*.

He did a Google search: it produced over 30 million hits.

He immediately clicked on the link at the top of the page. Then the one below it...and the one below that...and the one below that...it wasn't until 4.00 in the morning that he finally turned off his computer and went to bed.

Over the following weeks and months he became obsessed with the *Poppy Killer,* as if the *Poppy Killer* somehow held the answer to whatever it was he was looking for. He needed to let go…let go of himself – he knew that. But the more he stripped away the veneer the more he heard a distant voice in the far reaches of his mind – a lonely child crying out for recognition and acceptance; reaching out to anyone who would understand him – but no one ever did.

It was during one of his *Poppy Killer* searches, when one page linked to another that linked to another, that he came across an article entitled, *The Poppy Killer's Eleventh Victim?* It talked about Alison Marchant – her disappearance. How at first – when she'd gone missing – it was assumed, mainly by the press, that she had been abducted by the *Poppy Killer.* However, when she reappeared, 8 weeks later, she was diagnosed as having suffered a severe mental breakdown: delayed post-traumatic amnesia. The article questioned the medical diagnosis, presenting the argument that she could have been suffering from some severe and extreme form of Stockholm Syndrome; that her vague memories of sleeping rough were her way of protecting the identity of her captor.

Bernie read the article over and over again and the more he devoured it the more he became convinced that the *Poppy Killer had* intended to kill Alison Marchant – that he *had* intended her to be his eleventh victim.

And that something must have gone wrong.

50

Bernie
2010 - 2018

For months, years, Bernie trawled the internet searching for anything and everything on Alison Marchant.

He wasn't sure why. It was like he had taken a wrong turn down a dark alley and instead of turning back he just kept on walking, further and further into the darkness – not knowing where he was going.

And with each passing year, the *Poppy Killer* and the mystery behind the *eleventh victim* occupied more and more of his thoughts. He wanted it all to be real, not just words on a screen.

And the more he let *him* in, the more he felt like he had an innate connection with the *Poppy Killer*. He didn't know why – it was something he couldn't explain. It was just there – that feeling. Maybe it was his way of punishing himself? Virtual self-flagellation for all his perceived failings. A way of taking his mind off his own desires, his own frustrations, his own battles.

And the days melted into one another and passed virtually unnoticed.

Then one day he saw her on the bus...Alison Marchant. The *eleventh victim*.

51

Harry
March 2019

When Harry got back home he sat, lost in the darkness.

Alone.

Hours passed before he eventually stood up and turned on the light.

His mind gradually attuned to the brightness.

Four big questions began to rebound in his head; four key questions that needed to be answered.

First he decided to focus on the question of Lisa. There was something he needed to look up.

He went over to the desk and turned on his computer. He logged onto the Internet and did a Google search for Stockholm syndrome.

Harry had heard of it. He had a vague idea of the condition…that a hostage can develop a psychological attraction towards their captor. But Lisa's fixation with William Marshall…it seemed to go way beyond anything he had ever known, way beyond the normal parameters of a psychiatric illness or disorder.

He clicked on Wikipedia. It stated there were four key components that characterised Stockholm syndrome: *A hostage's development of positive feelings towards their captor; no previous relationship between hostage and captor; a refusal by the hostage to cooperate with the police; a hostage's belief in the humanity of their captor when they cease to perceive the captor as a threat...because the victim holds the same values as their aggressor.*

Harry mulled over what he had read. Lisa's behaviour could certainly be attributed to one if not all of the key components of Stockholm syndrome, but then again it may have had nothing to do with her behaviour.

He tried to remember what Lisa had said. He dug deep. Forcing her words into his mind. She'd been snatched off the street, abducted by the *Poppy Killer*, and yet, not once did he ever remember her mentioning that she'd been frightened, that she'd felt fearful for her life. And the way she'd sat, the tone of her voice, it had all felt wrong. He tried to resist the thought, but it was too strong - *had she wanted it to happen*? He recalled what he'd just read, that hostages can develop a psychological attraction with their captor - it was as if Lisa had come with her attraction already in place. He knew it was a ridiculous thought. He remembered what she'd said about that night, the night of her abduction, that *having a mental breakdown was part of the truth.* He shook his head. Perhaps he was seeing something that wasn't there, that the whole episode was a mental breakdown after all. And because of her breakdown, by pure chance, she'd ended up on the streets of Nottingham, the night the *Poppy Killer* had been there. In fact, it had to be pure chance, because what other explanation could there possibly be? And yet, it still didn't feel right.

He stood up and walked into the kitchen, his mind turning over all the time.

The kitchen was small but functional.

He loathed it, but he no longer cared.

He thought about her plan…returning to Jackson in 2005, as if she was treating Jackson as a way of connecting back to William…keeping his spirit alive. Perhaps that's all Jackson was to her...a link back to William? He questioned in his mind whether Lisa actually had any feelings for Jackson at all – maybe she was just stringing him along? She was definitely the dominant force in their relationship. That was clear to see.

He turned on the tap.

He watched mesmerized as the water ran down the sink.

He thought of Bob Burnett. He wondered if he should go round and see him again? Bob hadn't mentioned Stockholm syndrome, but he was sure it would have been considered as a possible explanation for Alison Marchant's behaviour. But there had been no mention of it in the file…that was perplexing.

He went back on the computer. He quickly found a small number of articles that matched his specific search criteria: "*Alison Marchant*" and "*Stockholm syndrome.*" Mostly dating back to 2003. The majority of the articles had questioned the medical diagnosis of delayed post-traumatic amnesia, but none of them had come up with any evidence or proof to substantiate their counterclaims. He imagined what it would have been like for Alison Marchant in 2003 - the media circus following her reappearance. He knew the press made no allowances for a person's mental state; *press freedom* and *in the public's interest* always overrode individual considerations. Harry thought about how that must have been for Alison. The press espousing all manner of unsubstantiated theories. The police doubting Alison's explanation. And sat in the middle, Alison, with the truth. Her truth.

He scrolled down a few more pages. He found a literature review of the condition, dating back to 2008. It stated the majority of Stockholm syndrome diagnoses are made by the media, not by mental health professionals. He pondered. Was Stockholm syndrome something that only the media had labelled Alison with? Had the police dismissed the theory? That could explain its omission from the file. But what did it really prove? Then he was hit with a damning thought. What was he *really* trying to prove? That Lisa was complicit in someway or was the real truth that he was trying to find excuses for her behaviour?

He suddenly felt a chill run down his spine.

The sound of running water filtered into his consciousness.

He went back into the kitchen and turned off the tap.

He decided against making himself a cup of tea, instead he went upstairs.

He turned on the bathroom light. He stood as if he was unsure of what to do next, as if he'd forgotten the reason he'd gone into the bathroom in the first place.

He walked over to the mirror. Looked at himself. But he refused to see anything other than his own reflection. He refused to acknowledge to himself that he was minimising the truth and maximising the delusion. And all the warning lights that were flashing so bright in his head - he was finding ways around them. Just by the power of Lisa.

But what was it that Lisa had over Harry? He wasn't sure he could explain it. Because the problem for Harry was he had no idea what was going on inside Lisa's head. He had no idea what plans she had and if they included him. All he had was the look she'd given him, the nod of the head, the knowing smile, the positioning of the mug. But that was enough.

He turned around, switched off the bathroom light and walked into the bedroom. He felt lost. Confused. His birth father had been a mass murderer, why wasn't that bothering him more? Why wasn't he doing something about it? Why was he so uncertain of what to do next? Then he remembered something his adoptive father had once told him: *before you know what to do, you have to know what not to do.*

He shook his head and sat on the bed.

He thought back to what he'd read on Wikipedia. The last component of Stockholm syndrome: *The hostage ceases to perceive their captor as a threat because the victim holds the same values as their aggressor.* His mind ticked over what possible meanings that could have in relation to Lisa.

But nothing made sense.

He let out a long, deep sigh.

He was going round in circles. Faster and faster.

He needed something to hold on to, because deep down he knew he was reaching out for the one thing he shouldn't be – Lisa. And in doing so he was losing a grip on everything else.

He pulled back the duvet.

As he started to undress, he heard his phone. He reached into his back pocket and stared at it.

He let it ring for a moment…fixating on the name lighting up the screen. He tempered his eyes. Tried to think. For a split second he thought about not answering, regain some control, but he knew it was no use, that he was only fooling himself, that he wouldn't be able to resist it. Resist Lisa.

He slid the green button across.

52

Bernie
2018

Bernie was a creature of habit.

And for him, habits formed very quickly.

It was 7th November 2018.

He had missed his usual bus.

Or to be more precise, it had been cancelled.

This was something that caused him great irritation. It didn't matter that the sixty or so people who usually caught that particular bus were also inconvenienced. The bus was cancelled specifically to annoy him. And it churned in his stomach.

When he got a seat on the next scheduled bus he had worked himself into such a lather that at first he didn't notice the woman sat opposite him. But, as he calmed down something about her registered in his mind.

He held on to her image all day at work.

When he got home that evening he went straight to his computer. He typed in *The Poppy Killer's 11th Victim?* He clicked on the article. Half-way down the page there it was, the photo he was looking for, the photo of Alison Marchant taken in 2003.

He peered closer at the screen. He stared at the photograph for so long that his eyes started to diverge, creating a 3D-like image of her face – the face of the girl on the bus. He wasn't a hundred percent certain...that the girl on the bus was Alison Marchant. But he was pretty sure it was her...and he so wanted it to be her. But he would need to make sure. He'd never seen her on his usual bus before, so tomorrow he would catch the later one. Maybe, just maybe, that was her regular bus?

And the next morning, when he boarded the bus...there she was.

And the next day.

And the day after that.

Most times he got to sit opposite her. Sometimes she even acknowledged him with a faint smile.

And, when he was sure it was safe to do so - when she had her eyes closed - he would stare at her face. Just for a few seconds. Sometimes longer.

He felt like he was in a different world, away from the realities of day to day life.

And, as the months passed, the girl on the bus gradually became the girl in the photograph. Until the day his mind was made up - fait accompli - it was definitely her. He'd found her. Alison Marchant.

For days afterwards he was beside himself with exhilaration...firing on adrenaline. He felt like he'd found the Holy Grail. However his external persona continued to run at the same speed. So no one would have noticed his state of internal excitement, least of all the girl on the bus. He was very good at hiding things. Keeping himself to himself.

As the buzz gradually wore off, the question that entered his mind was, *what shall I do next?* He wasn't sure. Well, he had an idea: to imagine that he was the *Poppy Killer* - finish what the *Poppy Killer* started. Play the game. Put his head in the lion's mouth and see how far he was willing to go.

It was just a bit of fun.

What harm could it do?

****

In March 2019 he bought a DVD. It was a film he'd been wanting to watch ever since it was first released at the cinema in 2017. He had intended to go and watch it that year, on the big screen, but he hadn't felt up to going alone.

It was a sequel and he loved it with even more passion than the first film. It reminded him of how he'd felt when his mother had taken him to see *Titanic* in 1998, how he'd come out of that film with a purpose. How he'd fantasised over Leonardo Dicaprio. And now he had someone else to fantasise over: the villainous lead character.

He put the DVD back in its case.

He sat for a while looking at the blank screen of the TV.

A plan was racing through his mind.

A plan where he could play the lead role.

He went over to his computer and logged on.

He needed to research options.

Buy things.

He felt a calm, detached joy – like it was a dream that he was creating and perceiving simultaneously.

He was too much in the moment to realise he was allowing his emotional self to race ahead of his rational self. And besides, he didn't want to spoil things by engaging in another internal battle with his conscience.

He felt free.

Then he heard it…the distant voice...the lonely child.

And for a moment he felt afraid.

53

Bernie
2019

Bernie was sat in his flat.

It was Friday afternoon.

Mid May, 2019.

He was a nervous wreck.

He'd been off work all week.

Putting the pieces of his plan together.

On the Monday he'd started the ball rolling.

On the Tuesday he'd ordered the accessories he needed.

And today, Friday, he'd been waiting. And waiting. At home. Patiently at first, then impatiently. He looked at his watch. It was 4.55pm. His stomach was churning; he hadn't eaten. Between 8.00am and 6.00pm they'd told him. He looked at his watch again, then he started pacing around the room, sitting down, then pacing around the room again – a routine he'd done a hundred times already that day.

Then suddenly, he jumped with fright. The doorbell rang.

It was the following morning…6.25am.

He didn't bother getting dressed. Instead he nervously made his way from the bedroom to the lounge. He was thinking about what he'd done the previous evening. Had he dreamt the whole thing? He wasn't sure. He wasn't even sure if he was dreaming at that moment. He opened the door and closed his eyes, as if he was a child on Christmas

Day. When he opened them, there she was, with her painted eyes, standing in the corner...*Alison Marchant*...the girl on the bus.

PART 8

54

The Letter
June 2019

It was headline news – across the world. Everybody was talking about it – in the offices, bars, clubs and at home. Everyone was talking about the *Poppy Killer*. That the *Poppy Killer* was going to strike again. On Saturday, 7th September 2019.

The police had received what appeared to be a credible letter. At first they'd been reluctant to inform the press before a proper analysis of the letter had been undertaken but an internal leak had forced their hand.

The chief had spoken to DI Trish Bond and she was to lead the investigation. She had concerns about it, as the exact nature of the investigation was still to be made clear. In all the time the *Poppy Killer* had operated he had not once contacted the police or the press. He was a faceless, voiceless, serial killer. And yet now, after 18 years of inactivity he had decided not only to contact the police but also announce when he would strike next. It just didn't add up. It had to be a hoax, a fake...another *Wearside Jack*...a misfit pretending to be the *Poppy Killer* and doing nothing more than perverting the course of justice.

The chief shared DI Bond's disquiet but such was the media and public pressure that the Force had to be seen to be doing something.

She was sat in her office. The *letter* in front of her. Forensics had already drawn a blank.

It was printed.

Impossible to trace.

Posted from Birmingham.

Impossible to narrow down.

Ridiculous.

But impossible not to take seriously.

DS Harry Black entered the room. He nodded at DI Bond and sat down.

She looked at him. He was so hard to figure out...so hard to understand. He'd alienated a lot of fellow police officers – he didn't want to join their club or enter into the office banter or go to the pub. But more than that he didn't want to adapt to the challenges of modern policing. He preferred to follow his instincts instead of the rule book. He was old school. But modern policing was much more accountable. Much more visible. Social media was everywhere. That meant it was more difficult to operate on just pure gut instinct. Policing was now about consistency. It was about gaining the trust and confidence of the public. And most importantly, policing was now about working within the law.

Yet for all his shortcomings DI Bond felt empathy for DS Black. She respected him. And more than that, she knew, deep down that he respected her.

The fact she was a woman and had been made a detective inspector at the relatively young age of 38 had ruffled a few feathers. Most of the antagonism had been casual, hidden sexism. Less in your face, but equally debasing. She could have complained, but she rose above it. And Harry...he'd never engaged in any of it.

He had his eyes down; she watched as his head gently swayed – the tiniest of movements as he typed up a report. She wondered about his life, what he did when he was off-duty. She wondered if he had a girlfriend? He never spoke about things like that. She wondered...then one thought triggered another and before she'd had chance to fend it off the notion entered her head that in some inexplicable way she actually liked him.

She'd never been in love. Ironically she was born on Valentine's Day in 1979 but she'd never gone looking for romance. In fact, she'd always fought against it. She would wait for it to come to her - that's what she said to herself. And in any case, her job gave her the excuse not to love...it helped fill the void.

Inevitably, some people considered Trish Bond a cold person. Not unsociable or hard to reach like Harry, but guarded. She'd recently turned 40. But she didn't have a party, just a few drinks after work; she was back home by 9.00pm.

Back home...alone.

He looked up and caught her eye. She looked down at the *Poppy Killer* file that was open on her desk. She picked up the *letter* that was sat next to it.

'What do you think?' She held up the *letter*.

Harry sat up in his chair.

He'd prepared his mind. He'd obviously been briefed about the *letter*. And yesterday he'd heard that his DI would be leading the investigation; so he was expecting to be brought in on it. Therefore he had no other option but to play the whole situation with a straight bat. Put to the back of his mind what he knew. Respond to his DI's questions without any hint of circumspect.

He looked at the *letter* in DI Bond's hand and then he looked at the file on her desk. He felt an odd sensation ripple through his body. He knew that very few officers went into the *Back Room*. That all the information had been digitally copied and was available to view on-line. So seeing the file on her desk made him feel something that he couldn't explain. As if she was a kindred spirit.

'The *letter* contains classified scene of crime information,' he said. 'Details that have never been released to the press before. If it is a fake, then someone must have hacked into the file.'

Trish Bond nodded. She knew that was a possibility. The West Mercia police computer was linked to the Police National Computer...the PNC. A hacker using a Perl script could have searched for blank passwords. If a computer on the police network had been left with its default password active, then it would have been possible to enter the site and see highly confidential information. Including the confidential file on the *Poppy Killer* murders. Of course, the network was thought to be secure. It could only be hacked if an officer had failed to log-out of the PNC properly. Every officer had been made aware of that imperative...to log-out properly. But sometimes the pressure of work could give rise to potential lapses in memory.

She placed the *letter* back down on her desk

'I've got the guys in IT doing a check on whether there has been a breach of security. Probably hear back from them next year.'

Harry smiled.

Trish smiled back.

Harry straightened his lips.

'If it is genuine, then what?' he said, his gaze briefly shifting to the left before refocusing on Trish.

DI Bond's eyes hardened. In recent years, the press and the public had turned the *Poppy Killer* into a cause célèbre. Part of the folklore. The morbid target of public fascination. An infamous figure who was never caught. It was presumed he was dead – what harm could it do? What harm could it do to the ten dead souls... innocent, voiceless, victims - consigned to helpless bit players; unwitting participants in the *Poppy Killer's* rise to fame.

'We have nearly three months.

'Until we hear otherwise, we have no *choice* but to treat it as genuine.'

Harry nodded, but he felt that it may have come across as an unconvincing gesture.

He forced his mind to re-group. But he knew he was struggling.

'It still puzzles me,' he said. 'If it is genuine then why send it? Why broadcast the date of his next strike? It carries so much risk. It's so *un-Poppy-Killer-like*.'

'Maybe he's lost his mind?' Trish let out a short ironic laugh at her unintended satire. 'Perhaps he didn't want to die anonymously. Serial killers normally seek notoriety for their crimes. Maybe he suddenly felt the need to be appreciated - have one last hurrah before he died? Who knows. Trying to understand the mind of someone like the *Poppy Killer* is nigh on an impossible task.' She noticed that Harry was looking slightly awkward. 'But of course, you know that already, don't you Harry.'

Harry gave Trish a mock smile. Did she know something or was she referring to his previous involvement in the case? He was starting to lose his mental discipline. Deviating from the strict mindset he had set himself. Now he was having to really battle to stay focused. He felt like he needed to get out of the room.

'For now, let's just concentrate on the date…the 7th September…coordinate a response with the other forces. Work with the press…try to flush out whoever it was that sent this *letter*,' said DI Bond.

DS Harry Black nodded. He then stood up and walked towards the door.

'DS Black.' Harry paused. He looked at his superior officer. 'If you need to talk…'

Harry stared vacantly back at her. Then he opened the door and left the room.

Trish Bond sighed. She turned and looked at the top hat on his desk. Something was troubling him…something was not quite right. Something that sat aside from his normal unorthodox, detached attitude. She couldn't put her finger on it. Even a professor of non-verbal communication would have been hard pressed to have unravelled Harry Black's body language, but something was definitely amiss.

55

Harry
June 2019

Harry was driving in his car. He had no destination in mind.

A part of him was still back in the office…the look on his DI's face etched into his mind.

He felt at odds with himself.

He knew *the letter* was a fake.

It had to be.

The Poppy Killer was dead. He heard those words in his head, but they sounded unconvincing, like there was something sitting behind them – something that turned the full stop into a question mark.

He didn't like having to hold back from Trish Bond, he felt like he was deceiving her. But he'd made an agreement with Jackson and Lisa that the identity of the *Poppy Killer* would remain between the three of them. Not that he had much choice. Revealing his true identity would create unfathomable destruction. And although the police would never admit to it in public, it would cause them untold embarrassment. Not satisfaction for having solved the case…just embarrassment that one of theirs was the killer's son. That riled Harry a little.

He suspected his DI would be more understanding, more sympathetic, but he respected Trish Bond too much to drag her into his chaotic world. So he would carry on with the deception, but he wondered how long he could keep it up…having to act normal in front of his colleagues, in front of his boss, when he felt anything *but* normal.

He looked at the road ahead. He was on a quiet country lane unaware of how he'd got there or where it led. He didn't mind, he just carried on driving…thinking.

He wondered if DI Bond had noticed…noticed that something wasn't quite right. Yes, he knew he was good at hiding stuff, but he also knew she was an outstanding detective and that she could pick up on things. That's why just over an hour ago he'd left the office; he'd felt like he was losing a grip on himself.

When he'd got to his car he'd sat for a while and thought about what Trish Bond had said to him…*if you need to talk*. There was something about Trish, something about her that seemed to be gaining momentum inside of him. Something he couldn't define. Just a feeling.

But he wouldn't allow himself to consider the nature of that feeling. Because…

Because the dominant force in his head, in his heart, was Lisa Hopkins.

Ever since March when she'd phoned him and told him she had wanted to meet with him, his life had been a blur. As if he was living it without any conscious control of its direction.

They'd met the next day. She'd suggested the town. He'd suggested the rendezvous place. A café located under the shadow of the Great Malvern Priory. Modernity shaded by medieval blackness.

And it was in that café as he looked across at Lisa that he realised without a doubt in his mind that he'd fallen in love with her. *This is what love must be like*, he'd thought to himself. That feeling of being afraid of nothing. And yet, being afraid of everything.

And as they talked, there was no other place where he would rather have been. And that's when it all started. Or to be more accurate, that's when she started it...the affair. Although, he'd been the one who had turned the flirting into a serious proposition. And yet, she'd been the one who had taken the lead...started the playful banter. In fact she'd led the whole thing; toyed with him until he had nowhere else to go but to submit to his own emotions, his own longings, his own weaknesses. Lisa had played out the whole scenario with such ease that she'd even managed to look surprised when he finally plucked up the courage to ask her out – to be his girl.

And Jackson? He'd not even entered their thoughts - as insignificant in their consciousness as the other people sat around them in the café, enjoying their coffee. Still life paintings...background scenery to the main event. Faceless symbols of the need for human beings to be together...to be anonymous.

After they'd left the café, they'd walked for a few minutes before she'd paused to face him. She gave him that look, not just any look, but a look that Harry would remember for the rest of his life. A look that created a total connection within him. A look that left nothing untouched.

She asked him to hug her. And in that moment, as they embraced and then gently kissed, he felt that everything that was Harry Black was slipping away and was being replaced by a version of himself that he didn't know...a version of himself where the boundaries to his emotions were unknown. And what he was capable of, how he would act, was also unknown.

And when Lisa had suddenly broken off their embrace, Harry had been blinded...totally oblivious to what Lisa was feeling; because in that moment propping up all of her thoughts, all of her visions, all of her emotions, was William...William Marshall.

Since then...since March, they'd been meeting, discreetly...when the situation allowed.

But always in the background...the background of Harry's mind was what to do about Jackson.

Then a few days ago he received a text from Lisa. She wanted to meet with him the coming Monday 17th June, 2019 at the café in Malvern.

She was ready to tell him the truth....

...the truth about Jackson.

56

Bernie
June 2019

Bernie turned on the TV.

He'd had a bad day at work.

His yearly appraisal was in two months time and he'd had a run in with his boss in the IT department. He'd accused Bernie of trying to access confidential files within the council. Bernie denied it, said there must have been a mistake. But they had evidence. Disputable evidence in Bernie's mind, but he hadn't been in the mood for a fight, so he'd had to accept a formal reprimand. He felt like he was being victimised. That his boss had it in for him. Bernie detested him. He was such a prima donna.

It was 6.00pm. The news was starting.

He felt wired. The day's events were still raw in his head.

And so he could feel it in his bones - that something on the news was going to affect him.

He listened.

The main headline.

The *Poppy Killer*.

The *letter*.

The date.

Saturday, 7th September 2019.

He instinctively looked at his watch.

He turned off the television and carefully placed the remote control on the armchair of the settee.

Then he sat in silence.

He felt uncomfortable in himself.

He thought about last night. He'd tried to blank it out but it was no use, he had to face it. *Christ, what was I doing*, he said to himself. He'd stayed on the bus…all the way to her stop…he didn't want to think about it…what he might have done.

He looked over at the girl standing rigid in the corner - *Alison Marchant*. He went and stood next to her. He gently stroked her hair.

'What *are* we going to do now?'

Her painted green eyes stared back at him.

He walked over to the mirror. The man in the mirror shook his head. Bernie's eyes started to well up. *What a piece of work is man!* He said to the stranger staring back at him. His quiet, melancholic voice, barely audible.

He suddenly spun around and looked at *Alison Marchant*.

'Why that day of all days? Why September 7th? A life created, a life extinguished. Is that what it is? Have I no choice in the matter? Have I got to do it – have I got to finish what I started last night?'

He looked back at the mirror.

'What have I done? What have I become?'

He sat back down and thought about his life. The sadness of it hidden behind the ironic smile of his mild mannered office persona. He thought about his mother and father. He wondered what they would say? Whether they would understand his actions? Whether they would put a comforting arm around him and tell him that everything was going to be okay? Because that's all he wanted. He wanted to be loved for the person he was. He looked around, searching for something, but unable to muster the heart to see anything. For a moment he felt like a child. He stood up and walked slowly into the bedroom. He didn't undress, instead he just curled up under the duvet. He felt lost and alone.

What have I done? What have I become?

57

Jackson
June 2019

Jackson stared in disbelief as he read the BBC headline news on his laptop.

The *letter.*

He deliberated for a moment.

The *Poppy Killer* - William Marshall - was dead. The *letter* had to be the work of a nutcase - a wannabe copycat. End of debate.

He closed his laptop.

He went up to the toilet, not because he needed to go, but because he wanted to distract himself.

William Marshall was dead. Why did that sound wrong? Like saying a plant has died, while all the time you still hope it will regrow. That the green leaves will reappear.

Had he really gone to Europe?

He stared at the cistern.

William Marshall.

Had he planned it all?

He went back downstairs to the kitchen. He stood by the sink...motionless...looking out of the window, at the patchwork of greenness.

He was suddenly overcome with a deep sadness for his birth father.

He saw the faintest reflection of himself in the glass. Enough to see the guilt in his own eyes...that he'd never really thought of him as his father. In fact, he'd never given him much thought at all. As if he'd been protecting himself from the truth…that his birth father was…had been the *Poppy Killer*.

How does a person deal with that? The murders. He let out a slow breath. It was a question he didn't want to have to face, let alone try and find the answer to.

He turned on the tap.

He watched the water flow.

He let his thoughts empty down the plughole.

He walked back into the lounge, checked his laptop was off and looked vacantly at the wall.

The *letter* - it had to be a hoax.

Move on.

Not yet.

He reached for his mobile.

He spoke to Lisa.

She told him they needed to speak to Harry.

He phoned him.

Harry chose the location.

They arranged to meet on Tuesday, 25th June 2019.

58

Harry
Tuesday, 25 June 2019

Harry was on his way to Stourbridge.

A couple of weeks ago he'd received a call from Mickey Maguire informing him that he'd found out where his birth mother, Julie Kendrick was buried.

At first Harry had been surprised to hear from him. With everything that had been going on in his life it had slipped his mind that he'd phoned Mickey to tell him that his birth mother was dead, and that he should be focussing his search on where she was buried or cremated.

Mickey had done well - if finding his birth mother's burial place could be considered in those terms.

Harry noted down the address and thanked his *friend*.

Mickey was apologetic for not having made progress on the burial place of William Marshall or the whereabouts of his triplet brother, Bernard Marshall, citing *the bonkers workload* as his excuse. Harry was aware that Mickey was hiding his frustration - that he was annoyed with himself. Because the one thing he knew about Mickey Maguire was that he hated dead ends. He would never have admitted to it - reaching one - because a dead end to Mickey meant failure...and failure in his eyes represented the beginning of the end for him as a private eye. His reputation would be in tatters, and then what would he do? It was the only thing he was good at. The only thing he knew.

Harry told him not to worry, that he had full confidence in him. And he did. Mickey appreciated his words.

Shortly after his call from Mickey two weeks ago, Harry received a call from Jackson requesting that he, Harry and Lisa meet up. They agreed a date a fortnight hence on Tuesday, 25th June. Harry suggested Stourbridge Cemetery as the meeting place. The place where his birth mother - their birth mother - was buried.

A few days after speaking to Jackson, Harry received the text from Lisa asking to meet up...at *their* café in Malvern. They'd met on Monday, 17th June. Now he knew the truth...the truth about Jackson.

****

Tuesday, 25th June 2019

He was half an hour away from the cemetery, driving on the B4190, just past Bewdley.

His thoughts turned to what Lisa had told him about Jackson. He found it hard to believe; he'd not noticed it himself, but Lisa was so convincing. And he wanted to help her, support her.

Romantic images of their future together briefly interrupted his flow. He forced himself to snap out of it and returned his thoughts to what she'd said about Jackson. She'd asked Harry not to say anything to him. Harry had reluctantly agreed, but he knew it was going to be hard to pretend to Jackson that he didn't know about the other side to him…his darker side.

59

Tuesday, 25 June 2019

Harry was nearing Stourbridge Cemetery and Crematorium.

He could feel the anticipation in his heart. He was about to visit his birth mother's grave; he was about to see Jackson in a new light - Lisa's light; and he was about to meet Lisa. He thought about which of those scenarios was causing him to feel such anticipation - but he knew the answer before he'd even posed the question…Lisa.

He stopped at a set of traffic lights just off the Stourbridge ring road, about a mile from the cemetery. He stared at the red light as if willing it to change colour, not because he was in a rush, but because he wanted a symbol, any symbol, something to tell him he was doing the right thing. He counted them down in his head…5, 4, 3, 2, 1…still red. The same thing again…still red. The lights seemed to be taking forever. He gave up on the idea and instead he looked away. A few seconds later he heard the driver behind him honking his horn. Green light. As he continued on his journey he found that his mind had switched to William and Julie and to what Lisa had said about how they'd first met at the Grange Comprehensive School in Lye, near Stourbridge.

He assumed that's why William Marshall had chosen to have Julie Kendrick buried at the

Stourbridge Cemetery - because it was near to where it had all started for them. A reminder. A way in which he'd been able to feel closer to her when he'd visited her grave. Closer to the memory of when they'd been together. Happy.

As he neared his destination he could see that the grounds to the cemetery sloped downwards, and he was taken by the stillness of the white gravestones juxtaposed against the moving dark clouds. On the near side of the grounds was the site of the crematorium building, which he'd read was once used as an old chapel. Harry parked adjacent to it.

The first thing that struck him was the vastness of the cemetery. The gravestones were lined by a guard of honour made up of trees that looked like pines and yews but Harry wasn't certain. As he made his way to the path that cut through the centre of the graveyard, he could see that there were earthen graves, woodland graves, child graves, traditional graves and cremated remains graves - in fact there were graves as far as the eye could see. But what caught his eye the most was Jackson, waving, at the far end of the cemetery - furthest away from the crematorium building - and standing next to him was Lisa. Within a few minutes he had joined them both...at the site of his birth mother's grave.

For a brief second Harry locked onto Lisa's eyes. She gave him a look that both lifted and dampened his spirits.

He tried to process what Lisa's look had really meant, but then from the corner of his eye, he could see Jackson looking at him.

He watched as Jackson's eyes darted over to Lisa, before he did a half turn and pointed.

'Look at the inscription.' Jackson said.

Lisa moved away and stood in the background.

Harry focused on the gravestone.

Julie Kendrick
Born: February 15 1962
Died: August 17 1985
Age: 23

There were no other words.

Harry was struck by its formality. Its lack of sentimentality.

He felt odd. He tried to force himself to feel some emotion. His birth mother had died shortly after giving birth. William had revealed to Lisa that much and the date on the headstone confirmed it. She had died so her triplets could have life. So *he* could have life. He should have felt something. But he felt nothing. She had become just a name. A name that was as cold in his heart as the inscription on the gravestone.

He wondered why he'd come, why he'd chosen the cemetery to meet Jackson and Lisa. It had seemed like the right thing to do, but now it seemed like an empty gesture. And all he'd ended up doing was exposing a side of himself that he'd rather not have seen. The stony, selfish side.

He shuffled around in his thoughts.

He decided to search nearby.

No sign of a grave for William Marshall.

He glanced around. Hundreds of gravestones; earthly reminders of the only certainty in life. Too many to search.

Jackson and Lisa joined him.

'No sign of William Marshall?' said Jackson.

Harry shook his head.

'Where do you think he's buried? Has that private detective friend of yours come up with anything yet?'

Harry let Jackson's words settle in the dust.

He turned away and looked up at the breaking clouds.

'There are many ways he could have done it. Many places he could have gone. And his body, his ashes, they could be anywhere. It would take a miracle to find him...to find out what happened to him.'

He turned back to look at Jackson. He saw Jackson glance over at Lisa, who he noticed in his peripheral vision was looking at him. He watched as Jackson's face changed from a look of confusion to a look of fear. Fear that arises when a person feels insecure...threatened.

Lisa walked away to look at another grave. She had closed her ears to any talk of William Marshall's death. She was floating off into her own vision of reality.

'So to answer your question,' said Harry, 'Mickey's still making enquiries...including the whereabouts of Bernard Marshall. I'll let you know as soon as I hear anything.'

Jackson was now looking at Lisa's profile as she looked down at the dilapidated gravestone that was in front of her.

Harry walked back to his birth mother's grave. Jackson followed him. Lisa joined them. They each took one last look at the headstone before heading back to their respective cars.

As they neared the old chapel, Jackson suddenly stopped.

'Wait. *The letter*. I almost forgot. *The letter* sent to the police.' He zoned in on Harry. 'The *Poppy Killer*. We know it can't be true. He's dead. It has to be fake. But...but we must talk about it...the *letter*. I want to know what you think. What the police think.' His eyes looked pleadingly at Harry.

Harry looked at Lisa who nodded.

'You're right,' said Harry, 'let's go and have a cup of tea.'

Jackson jumped on the offer. 'The café in Mary Stevens Park.'

Harry pondered for a moment. 'Fine, I'll see you there.'

60

Tuesday, 25 June 2019

By the time they had made the short journey to Mary Stevens Park the last of the cirrus clouds had drifted away and it had turned into a fine sunny morning.

They parked in the car park situated near the main entrance before walking the short distance to Mary Stevens Coffee Lounge which was located in the middle of the park.

When they got there they found that the café was humming with the pre-lunch crowd and at first it looked like they wouldn't be able to find a table - inside or outside. However, two elderly ladies *suddenly* stood up and waved at them to indicate they were leaving. Lisa gratefully acknowledged their signal and they made their way over to the corner table. The café had a nice lodge feel to it – a compact, functional interior that created an ideal ambiance for drinking tea and chatting. Harry appropriated an additional seat and at the same time ordered the tea from the counter.

When he returned they all glanced around to assess the privacy of where they were sitting. Then they looked at each other and agreed non-verbally that as long as they kept their voices down it was sufficiently private to talk.

To start with they chatted aimlessly as if to test the strength of their non-verbal agreement.

Then, when the tea arrived, a silence fell over the table.

Harry let the tea brew before pouring.

Jackson could no longer contain himself.

'It's a fake. We know that, but why are the...' He instinctively looked around before lowering his voice.'...why are the police treating it so seriously?'

Harry leaned forward.

Lisa and then Jackson mirrored his action.

He picked up his cup and rested his elbow on the table.

'Needless to say, everything we discuss today remains between the three of us.'

They both nodded.

Harry reciprocated.

'The *letter* included crime scene information that has never been released to the public. Stuff only the killer could have known.' Jackson shuffled in his chair. Harry gently rotated his cup in his hand and watched the tea swirl around. His own words floated back into his mind. *The killer...the killer.* It was as if he was someone else...not their birth father. Like the two of them had become separated. Had Lisa done that - separated the two? He tried to think, but nothing made sense. He wondered if they were all in denial? Lisa coughed politely. Harry returned to his train of thought. 'We're looking into whether there could have been a breach of our cyber-security, but as yet nothing has been found.'

Jackson jumped in. 'That's it...that has to be it...someone's hacked into your network.' He looked imploringly at Harry. Harry remained impassive. He looked across at Lisa. She took a sip of her tea.

'Supposing the *Poppy Kil...*' Lisa checked herself. '...supposing *he* had an accomplice, someone we know nothing about?' She quickly shot Harry one of her looks before honing in on Jackson. 'None of us know for sure. I only ever saw him in the cellar...' She whispered the last word. '...and Jackson only met him once...in this park.'

Jackson was getting agitated. He picked up his tea, gulped at it and then put it down as if the taste had surprised him. 'This is insane.' Lisa motioned for Jackson to keep his voice down.

'We all need to be vigilant,' she whispered. 'Until we know more about this *letter* we will have to be careful. If someone else *was* involved then this person has always stood in the background...until now. Why now? Perhaps he knows about us?' She gave Jackson a concerned look.

The warm air, the hot tea, his insecurity, were all conspiring to raise his body temperature and tiny beads of sweat were exuding through the pores of Jackson's forehead.

Harry remained straight-faced.

There was a contemplative pause as the convivial chatter of the other patrons engulfed their space.

Jackson suddenly jerked upright, snatched at his tea and spilt it in the process.

'I've got it.' He put down his cup and shot an excited look at Lisa, before turning his gaze on Harry. 'Our brother...Bernard Marshall.' He tipped his empty cup at Harry as if to confirm he'd solved the mystery.

Harry refilled it. Jackson looked around. Everyone was deep in conversation – tiny microcosms of life.

Harry shook his head. Then he thought for a moment.

'It's possible Jackson. But unlikely. He's the same age as us. Too young to be an accomplice, but maybe William confided in him before he...' Harry looked at Lisa and tailed off his words. 'Maybe he knows. Maybe he's been bottling up the information for all these years. Maybe he's gone insane. Maybe he knows about us, maybe he doesn't. I could go on and on with the maybes. Like I said at the cemetery, Mickey Maguire is looking into his whereabouts. So let's just be patient. There's over two months until September 7th...plenty of time for things to unravel themselves.' Harry paused to let his words sink in. He re-stirred his tea.

'Am *I* in danger?' Lisa said.

Jackson let out a short high pitched grunt. He flicked out his hand to pick up his cup as if was a nervous affliction.

'I don't think so.' Harry threw Jackson a scolding look before his eyes softened onto Lisa's. 'I mean, yes, it's possible someone has found out your real identity. There was no reference to Alison Marchant or the eleventh victim in the *letter*, but it would be wrong of me to dismiss that as a possibility...that some sicko believes you escaped from...*him*. That he is going to finish off what the *Poppy Killer* started.' Harry mouthed the final three words. 'I've been in the force long enough to know that you should never discount any possibility, no matter how remote, until the truth is known.'

Jackson slammed down his cup. The surrounding chatter abated. Harry and Lisa turned and smiled reassuringly at the other customers and immediately the background prattle resumed.

'I'm sorry Jackson, but Lisa needs to know. It would be wrong of me to wrap her up in cotton wool and pretend everything is fine. Someone sent that *letter*, someone who knows things. The question is…who and why?'

Jackson gave an ironic shake of his head.

'You need to be strong,' said Lisa to Jackson, 'you need to be strong for me. I need you.' Jackson looked like a lost child. Harry put his hand on his shoulder. 'Look, it could be something, but it's most probably nothing. Nine times out of ten…more than that…ninety nine times out of a hundred, something like this; like this *letter*…it's the result of some harmless crackpot who just wants his 15 minutes of fame. I'm sure it won't be long before we discover the police files were hacked into and then we'll apprehend the perpetrator in no time. So I would forget about thoughts of Bernard Marshall or some deranged accomplice.'

'But before you said that…'

Harry raised his hand to cut Jackson off.

Jackson looked unconvinced but, with a helping smile from Lisa he regained a degree of composure and finished his tea.

Harry settled the bill and they leisurely made their way back to the car park.

Standing by Harry's black Audi A4 they said their goodbyes.

As Harry watched them walk back to Jackson's Skoda he thought about Lisa, about their affair. It had been a struggle to hold things back. Talk as if nothing was happening. Yet he had the feeling that it had been a lot easier for Lisa.

He looked up at the trees, at the birds.

He wondered why Jackson had been getting so agitated. Why the identity of whoever had sent the *letter* was so important to him? And then a thought hit him so hard that it seemed to make the birds scatter from the trees. Jackson was afraid that the *letter was* genuine. That the *Poppy Killer*, their father *was* still alive – because if that were true, then it would be the end for him and Lisa. Then an unseen, seemingly implausible thought slammed into that one. If William Marshall *was* still alive, then what would that mean for *his* relationship with Lisa?

His trance like state was broken by an apologetic dog walker reprimanding her King Charles Spaniel for jumping up at him.

He patted *Rufus* on the head and reassured his worried looking owner that everything was fine.

Then he got into his car and sat for a while. *Some people's lives are so simple*, he thought to himself. He envied them…that state of being.

His mind fixed on what Lisa had previously told him about Jackson. *The truth about Jackson,* as she'd put it. That she thought he would do anything to keep her. That he was capable of much more than Harry could ever imagine.

Harry had seen a glimpse of his anger in the café. Although, if he was being totally honest with himself, it had seemed more like paranoia than anger. And in reality, based on his experience, he didn't think Jackson posed much of a threat to Lisa. But she seemed worried. Not just about Jackson, but about the *letter*. And that created an unhealthy urge in Harry to exaggerate her concerns. Envisage that she needed him, so that he could reach out and protect her.

But he knew he would have to play things by *her* rules. How had she put it last Monday when'd they'd met in the café in Malvern. *Let me manage him…I'll control the situation…I'll use the power of love.* He'd seen some of that earlier, when she'd told Jackson she needed him. It hadn't been easy for Harry, to hear her talking to Jackson like that, but there was something about the way she'd said it that made him think it was nothing more than a holding statement. Something to calm him down. He wondered what game she was playing. Yes, he was willing to play things by her rules, but what exactly *were* her rules? He tried to envisage different scenarios, but he knew it was a futile exercise. Instead, he tried to think of things about Lisa that would settle his mind, something that would stop him from constantly wondering what was going on. Nothing. She was so hard to figure out. One minute vulnerable, the next minute in control. It crossed his mind that maybe even William Marshall had succumbed to her spell.

He looked down at the steering wheel. He knew it was wrong…the way he was feeling, the way he was thinking, the way he was acting, the way he was letting himself be steered. Maybe he could still avoid it? Avoid whatever pain there was in store for him. But he knew it was too late, because in order to do that he would have to avoid Lisa…and that was something he couldn't do. Not any more.

He glanced across to the park one more time, he noticed in the distance the lady with the dog. It triggered the memory of what he'd been thinking of at that moment when *Rufus* had jumped up at him. The *letter*. The damn *letter*. He took a deep breath. He tried to make sense of why the *letter* was making everyone so nervous. Then he smiled to himself for even having considered the possibility that William Marshall could have been a threat to his relationship with Lisa. He's dead. He has to be.

His mind was just in the process of starting to relax when his thoughts suddenly froze. Lisa. She had put forward the accomplice theory; she had asked whether she was in danger; but she did not once put forward the possibility that the *letter* was real. Surely she must have considered it? If she had, then she'd given no indication of the fact. Why hadn't she voiced at least a faint hope that it could have been sent by him, that *he* could still be alive? It was as if she knew…she knew that it hadn't been written by William Marshall. Which could mean only one thing…that Lisa had written it. He slammed on the brakes to that thought. Now *he* was getting paranoid.

As if paranoia was infectious. He trusted Lisa. He had no choice. He trusted her. Almost.

He stared back at the steering wheel.

Then he started the engine and headed back home.

61

Jackson
Tuesday, 9 July 2019

Jackson first noticed it two weeks ago when they'd visited Julie Kendrick's grave. The look. The look that Lisa had given Harry. It was etched into his psyche as brightly as his insecure mind could paint it.

He'd tried to rationalise it, but his irrational side was stronger…telling him that Lisa was adept at hiding things, an expert, and his thoughts had rebounded randomly and uncontrollably causing his stomach to churn with the bile of insecurity.

It had happened so many times before, that terrible doomed feeling that he was losing her…losing Lisa. But she'd always pulled him back from the brink. Her demeanour would change. She would show him sensitivity. He would even sense an air of vulnerability.

And recently…the last few days, it had happened again - she'd been different. She'd been fretting about the *letter*? They'd hardly spoken about it since Mary Stevens Park. He'd wanted to bring it up but he'd been afraid that it would worry her. That she would accuse him of being insensitive. Of not understanding. And if truth be known he had been worried about it at first - that it would somehow threaten him and Lisa. He'd even played with the notion that the *letter* had been sent by his birth father - William Marshall. That he hadn't gone to Europe after all. But eventually he'd dismissed that belief and now he wasn't that bothered who'd sent the letter. That was Harry's problem. In fact he viewed the *letter* as a godsend. Because Lisa was looking afraid. Afraid of what might happen. And now he was starting to believe - again - that she really did need him. His emotions had swung manically back to the positive side. To the thoughts he'd had on and off for the last 16 years: that it was meant to be. The deed of gift; finding Lisa; William's words...*sometimes things happen in life for a reason*; *you must learn to grasp the nettles with the same consideration and care as you would hand pick a rose.* He must have been referring to Lisa. It had happened for a reason...it *was* meant to be.

62

Lisa
Barbourne, Worcester. Tuesday, 9 July 2019

Lisa was sat in Harry's lounge.

Harry had gone out to get a take-away.

Chinese.

She looked around at the non-descript décor.

At the grotesque Picasso print.

Then she closed her eyes.

William entered her thoughts.

Whatever happens, just remember...when you leave here...be yourself; be the person you have become; the person you are now. Because there is no going back. Not now, not after this.

She knew what he meant. All his words had been assigned a special meaning years ago. A meaning that had allowed Lisa to believe whatever she had wanted to believe.

Now she felt a warmth in her stomach.

Her plan, as much as she ever planned anything, was coming together - the seeds of which were planted shortly after she'd first met Harry.

She'd immediately seen something in him that had reminded her of William. It was his persona. It wasn't a firm connection. Harry didn't have the presence of his natural father, but it was enough for Lisa to feel closer to William and anything that brought her closer to him was worth having. And so Harry was worth having. It was as if he was helping to keep his memory alive...keep William alive. Just like Jackson had. But now Jackson had served his purpose. She still needed to manage the situation - press the right buttons at the right time - make sure he played his part. But his time was limited. It was just a matter of when, not if.

And Harry - he was performing his part admirably. He was clearly mentally and physically stronger than Jackson...

...She smiled to herself...

...Yes, he was stronger...but just as pliable.

She looked back up at the distorted shapes and forms on the Picasso print. The horrible twisted face of the woman on the right. It reminded her of an image she thought she'd buried. But she knew it would never go away.

She stared angrily at the print. She owed the world nothing. She believed that without reservation.

A sound erased Picasso from her mind - the front door was opening. She stood up.

William's words returned to her thoughts.

I will do whatever I can to help you. But you must realise that things will never be the same for you... You are different; special; and this, you and me, we are different. You must always remember that.

From a young age she'd known she was different. But after William she had the confidence to *be* different. To survive. And now, it was the only way she knew how to live. The only way she could get through life. She wasn't to blame. It was life. William had taught her that. Life makes it *so.*

She glanced out of the window and into the imaginary portal that connected her with William and she mouthed the words…*I love you.*

Then Harry entered the room.

63

Lisa and Jackson
Ludlow. Wednesday, 10 July 2019

On the outskirts of Ludlow there are 3 car parks owned by the Forestry Commission. The Vinnalls car park; the Whitcliffe car park and the Black Pool car park. They are linked by the Climbing Jack Trail which creates a challenging circular walk of about 9 miles. The trail takes in the majority of Mortimer Forest and there are a number of vantage points on route offering up amazing views of the surrounding country side.

Tawelfan cottage was situated not too far from the Whitcliffe car park and this morning Lisa and Jackson had set out to walk the full length of the Climbing Jack Trail.

They'd been strolling for just over an hour and Jackson could hold back no longer. He'd been waiting for Lisa to bring it up, but the conversation up to that point had been about inconsequential things. He needed to know.

'How was last night?'

Lisa's body language maintained a perfect cadence.

'It was fine, it was good. The usual stuff…I drunk the wine while Hannah told me all her troubles; and all the gossip from First Class. It was enjoyable…in its own way.'

As far back as Jackson could remember, certainly soon after she'd returned to Ludlow in 2005, Lisa had been seeing her old work friend from her days at Children's First Class Catering in Birmingham. Of course Jackson had had his suspicions - he'd looked up her name, Hannah Wasserstein, and she did exist and she did still work at Lisa's old workplace - but short of following her every move, he'd had no choice but to trust her. So, as he half glanced at her, he accepted she was telling the truth – about spending last night with her friend. After all, she'd been doing it for so long now – visiting Hannah and staying overnight – that if it had been an affair he was sure he would have found out by now. She would have given something away. But then again, she was so damn good at hiding things...he stopped himself, then berated himself...why did he always have to end things on *but then again*. He was starting to think his own thoughts were like a broken record. He was tired of himself. Tired of hearing the same old doubts in his mind. He just wished he could settle on something. Be relaxed in his thoughts. He made a pact with himself that he would never think that way again. A pact he'd made on countless occasions before.

Lisa slowed down.

'It's so beautiful up here Jackson.' She reached out and held his hand.

Jackson felt a jolt to his senses.

'It's not been easy...you and me. It's not been easy since...' she paused. She playfully rocked their arms back and forth. 'Do you remember when we met, here on this walk, in 2005. We'd planned it so well.'

Jackson smiled.

'Well, you did most of the planning.'

'But it went like clockwork. The police never suspected a thing – that I was returning to the place where I'd been held.' She gave Jackson a knowing smile, then pointed up ahead. 'Look, the rendezvous point. It's not too far from here.' Jackson could see the path ahead, the one that led to Black Pool car park. They had met just a few yards from the information board. Jackson smiled at the memory, then turned and kissed Lisa on the cheek.

As they proceeded on their walk, the memories of that day in 2005 continued to flood his mind. Leading up to it he'd been full of trepidation. Full of negative thoughts. That Lisa's plan would never work. Could never work. And yet on the day itself, he'd felt totally energised. The excitement, the adrenaline. He'd never felt so alive.

He looked to his left. There was a field awash with bluebells. For some reason the violet glow of the bluebells set off alarm bells in his head. He desperately tried to fight them back, but they had to be heard.

'Have you heard from Harry?'

Lisa looked lazily at Jackson and then out to the sea of bluebells.

'Beautiful aren't they?'

Jackson stopped.

He turned round and looked Lisa in the eye.

'Lisa, have you heard from Harry?'

Lisa shook her head.

Then, she skipped on a few paces.

'Isn't nature wonderful.'

Jackson watched her go ahead. He felt her words drift by his ears. He couldn't believe he was doing this to himself. Allowing thoughts of Harry, of *that look,* back into his head. What about the pact he'd just made with himself. He could feel the self-loathing building up inside. He'd got over it, he was past it. Why was he letting it ruin things? Why was he letting it get between him and Lisa? He had to stop it, but he couldn't help himself...whenever he felt things were going well, it made him even more paranoid.

'I...I...need to ask you something about Harry...I...'

She floated back over to him and put her forefinger on his lips.

'Come on.'

They walked in silence for another half a mile before Lisa suddenly stopped. She looked out to the Shropshire Hills.

'I miss him.'

Jackson felt almost paralysed with panic.

'Who?'

'Dylan.'

Jackson looked out in the direction that Lisa was looking. He felt stupid, embarrassed, for immediately thinking the worst. That she was about to say she was missing William or Harry or some unknown person that she'd had some unknown affair with. He felt so frustrated with himself. Ever since he'd first *found* Lisa – in the cellar, so weak and helpless – not a day had gone by when he hadn't wished for more inner strength. But he had always felt second best, firstly to his birth father, then to his own insecurities. He knew he could never be like William Marshall – nor did he want to be. But he wished, sometimes, that he could make it go away…whatever it was that was inside of him. He'd been so close to asking her about Harry and what did he have…what did he really have to go on…nothing. Fortunately the moment had gone. He felt relieved.

Jackson turned to look at Lisa, but she carried on looking straight ahead.

Then, as if Dylan had suddenly vanished from her mind, she took his hand and they carried on walking.

After ten silent minutes she suddenly stopped and looked into his eyes.

'Jackson.' His heart jumped. 'I'm afraid.' Vulnerability swept over her face. She took hold of his other hand. 'I know you're trying to be strong for me, but whatever's happening; whatever's going to happen…I feel so helpless.' Jackson was desperately searching for the right response. Searching for the words that would comfort her; make her feel protected. But his mind went blank. So instead he let go of her hands and embraced her. He held her with all the passion his helpless body could muster.

'Jackson.'

He stepped back.

Lisa swept her hair.

'How do I know you won't just leave…leave me? Alone. How do I know that?'

Jackson shook his head.

'That's ridiculous and you know it. I'd never leave you.'

'How do I *really* know that? How can I ever be sure? How can I know for certain that our bond will never be broken?'

Jackson laughed ironically.

'Well, there's always marriage, but I know you'd never consider that.'

'Was that a hypothetical statement or was that a proposal?' Lisa said, in a playful voice.

'Don't tease me Lisa. Not about that. You know nothing would make me happier.'

'So, was it a proposal or not?'

Jackson looked out to the landscape, but the view had been consumed by his thoughts. He looked back at Lisa and sighed.

'Okay, yes it was.'

'Well, ask me properly then.'

Jackson thought about shaking his head, but something stopped him.

'Okay...Lisa, will you marry me.'

****

Thursday, 11 July 2019

Jackson still couldn't believe it. Of all the things he thought Lisa would want to do in her life...getting married would have been last on his list. In fact, it wouldn't have been on the list at all.

And yet, there he was 24 hours later phoning Harry to tell him the news.

'That's great Jackson. I'm really pleased for you.' Harry said in a flat, seemingly unsurprised tone.

A part of Jackson had hoped to hear the sound of disappointment in his voice.

'I'm still in shock,' said Jackson.

'Please send my congratulations and best wishes to Lisa.'

His voice sounded so formal. Perhaps he *was* disappointed?

'She's here. Do you want to speak to her?'

'Not now Jackson. I'm snowed under at the moment.'

'Oh, okay, I understand.'

'When's the wedding?'

'Well, that's the thing.'

'Go on.'

'Lisa was feeling vulnerable. Afraid of what might happen on September 7th.'

'I'm not sure I follow.'

'She didn't want to feel afraid. She wanted to be in control of her emotions...not let some faceless person...some sick...' Jackson paused...as if to hold back on whatever he was about to say next. He could feel Lisa's eyes on the back of his head.

'Whatever…anyway, she wanted to look forward to the day, not dread it. So, this morning, while I was out, she phoned around…on the off-chance that she might find a venue that was free at short notice – that had had a cancellation. And would you believe it, she managed to get St Laurence Parish Church…it's in the centre of town. The date had come free only yesterday. Apparently the groom…' Jackson shook his head. '…that's not important. What is important is that the date has been set…September 7th.'

There was silence.

'Harry?'

'That sounds great Jackson. I wish…..'

'There's one other thing.'

Silence.

'I want you to be my best man.'

Continued silence.

'Harry?'

'Of course…of course…that's fine, no problem Jackson. I mean, I might be busy that day. With all that's going on, but I'm sure I'll find some time to break off from work.'

'It's at….'

'I must go now Jackson. I'll catch up with you soon. Send my love to Lisa.'

Jackson stared at his phone for a while then turned to Lisa.

'He sends his love.'

She stood up, walked over to Jackson and gave him a kiss on the cheek.

As she left the room Jackson felt his insecurity flooding back into his veins. There was something wrong.

It had been Lisa's idea to ask Harry to be his best man. At first he'd questioned it, but he could hardly have refused. He had no real friends of his own. And why should he be worried? His suspicions about the two of them had all but disappeared. He was sure of that…almost sure…not that sure at all.

The damn voice was back. Annoying him. Pounding inside his head.

It was just a little thing. A little big thing. It was Lisa's request…Harry's response. It had all seemed predetermined.

As if it had all been planned.

PART 9

64

St Laurence Parish Church, Ludlow.
Saturday, 7 September 2019

The Reverend Thomas Kingsley stood at the altar looking out to the Lady Chapel. He glanced at his watch. It was 4.00pm. He looked down at the names on the card he had placed in front of him. Lisa Hopkins and Jackson Brown. He took another look at his watch and shook his head. The previous wedding - the 1.00pm service - had gone like clockwork. Like normal.

As he focused his stare on the empty wooden pews he tried to recall the faces of the bride and groom. In the far reaches of his mind he vaguely remembered meeting Lisa Hopkins. But no face appeared. Perhaps alarm bells should have sounded. Normally, before the wedding day, he would meet the couple to talk about the ceremony; however, every time a date had been arranged the bride, Lisa, had phoned to cancel the meeting. Sickness, working away, she needed to look after her elderly mother, excuse after excuse. And when he'd phoned to ask her about the choice of hymns, music, bible readings, she'd simply replied, *you choose reverend*. But it was not unprecedented...not entirely. He'd known it happen before. Sometimes it was for superstitious reasons - the bride didn't want to step foot inside the church in the weeks leading up to her wedding. But they would normally discuss things over the phone. But with Lisa, when he *had* managed to speak to her, she had sounded distracted, like there were more important things on her mind.

Thomas Kingsley had excelled at Theological college and had shone during his time as a curate. As a result he'd quickly risen to the position of Rector and in 2016, aged 38, he was assigned to St Laurence Parish Church in Ludlow.

He'd been conducting wedding ceremonies since 2014 when he was in the second year of his curacy. And he'd never had a 'no-show' or an incident of any kind. They'd all gone very smoothly. He sometimes wondered if the marriages themselves had gone as smoothly. But unless he happened to know the bride or groom he had no way of knowing.

He glanced back down at his watch. 4.12pm. Something was definitely wrong.

He made his way to the office.

Josephine, his personal assistant, informed him that no one had phoned. There was no explanation for their absence. He asked Josephine to phone Lisa Hopkins's contact number and while she did that he looked at their booking form.

He was normally good with faces. A gift he was grateful for. Because it was an integral part of the job. People liked being recognised – called by their first name. It made them feel special.

He centered his mind. Eliminated all extraneous noise. Faces. Faces.

'No reply,' Josephine said.

He let her words settle in his short term memory without acknowledging her. An image appeared - grainy at first, then becoming slightly clearer.

'Did you hear me?' Josephine asked.

Thomas turned and nodded before returning to the picture he had in his head. The picture of Lisa Hopkins. By herself. He was reasonably sure of that. He had no recollection of Jackson Brown. And since that meeting, both himself and Josephine had only ever spoken to Lisa on the phone. Yes, he should have suspected something. But suspected what? He dug deep to that first meeting, the one and only meeting, when he'd met her in person, when she'd made the booking. There was a vague yet distinct memory that she had seemed incredibly focused, bordering on consumed. Not the excitedness that a bride would normally exude when booking their wedding.

'Is there anything else you need me for?'

Thomas Kingsley looked up. 'No thank you Josephine, you can go now.' He watched as she put on her coat, and made her way to the door, muttering something under her breath.

He smiled to himself, before putting Lisa's and Jackson's booking form back in its folder. He then returned to the Lady Chapel.

He looked up at the stained glass window above the altar. It never ceased to impress him. But at that moment he felt a sadness inside...that the plans and dreams of Lisa and Jackson had become grey and colourless.

He went and sat on one of the wooden pews.

He looked at his watch one last time - It was 4.30pm. He knew there was no point in him remaining in the chapel.

He returned to his office.

Walked around.

Gathered his thoughts.

Then he suddenly stopped.

There was a knock on the door.

****

'I must apologise Vicar. We've been waiting outside the church. Hoping he would arrive, but he's gone missing – the groom…he's disappeared.'

Thomas Kingsley was stood at the far end of the office.

'It's Reverend, but please, call me Thomas. And you are?'

'My apologies Reverend…err…Thomas…I'm Harry…Harry Black. I was…am, the best man. I think the wedding will have to be cancelled.'

'I see. That is very sad news.' He looked at Harry empathetically. 'My thoughts are with the bride and groom. It must be very distressing. I'm sure he'll…' He stopped as if to correct himself. 'The wedding can happen another day, the most important thing is that the groom…Jackson Brown I believe his name is…is found.'

The Reverend moved to his desk.

'Thank you.' Harry said. 'That is very understanding of you.' He looked around, as if unsure of what to say next. He gesticulated towards the door. 'I must go. The bride. Like you said…she's very upset…it's such a shame. She'd been so happy when she'd managed to book the chapel at such short notice, after you'd had the cancellation. I'm very sorry Reverend.'

Reverend Kingsley nodded. 'Please, no need to apologise Harry. I appreciate you letting me know.'

As Harry reached for the door handle he heard Thomas Kingsley call his name. He turned around and saw him looking down at his desk. Then he looked up at Harry.

'There was no cancellation Harry. Lisa Hopkins made the booking last November.' The Reverend shrugged his shoulders.

Harry stared back at him, nodded, then turned around and left.

65

Saturday, 7 September 2019
11.00 am

Half an hour had passed since Harry had arrived at Tawelfan Cottage.

Jackson had been busying himself with empty tasks while Harry had been sat on the sofa chair looking straight through Jackson.

The conversation up to that point had been flat and strained.

Jackson was finishing polishing the table that was positioned in front of Harry. He looked up at him.

'Thank you for coming Harry.'

'You've already thanked me a dozen times. Why don't you sit down Jackson.'

'I've got too much to do.'

'What…what have you got to do?'

'It's my wedding day for Christ's sake…I've got loads to do.'

'Jackson, sit down. We need to talk.'

Jackson stopped. He threw a shape of defiance – then he looked at Harry and begrudgingly sat down.

There was silence. The atmosphere was awkward. Like they were two strangers in an empty room. Then their eyes met.

'Have you heard from her recently…Lisa?'

Harry shook his head.

Jackson looked away. 'I've not seen her for a week,' he said. 'She's been staying with her friend. An old work colleague, the one she's bringing to the wedding. She's not even been answering her phone.' Jackson stared down at the table. 'Said it would do us good...to be apart before the wedding.' He shook his head. 'She's very good at that...very good at getting her way.'

Harry stared at Jackson.

Jackson looked back, but his thoughts were clouding his vision.

'Do you think it's odd...our wedding?' said Jackson.

Harry remained expressionless.

'All those years of being dead against marriage, then suddenly, after the *letter*, she seemed almost un-Lisa-like in her enthusiasm. Like she'd...' Jackson stopped himself as if he knew it wasn't appropriate to say what he was going to say. Instead, he repeated his opening line. 'I mean, that seems odd to me, don't you think?'

'She's been through a lot,' said Harry.

Jackson shook his head, stood up and then immediately sat back down.

'And she books a room big enough for 40 guests, then decides she only wants to invite two people. I mean...what's that all about?'

Harry looked at the empty table in front of him. He noticed a mark on it that Jackson had missed.

'Maybe she doesn't like to be around large groups of people? Maybe it would panic her? Like I said, she's been through a lot.'

Jackson let out an exasperated laugh.

'You seem to know her better than me.'

Harry gave Jackson a firm, unyielding stare.

Jackson huffed.

'I've not even told my parents. She didn't want me to.'

Harry could see the hurt in Jackson's eyes but he quashed any sympathy that may have been rising inside of himself.

'Two witnesses; that's all you need. It will still.....'

Jackson interrupted Harry.

'I feel so bloody inadequate. Ever since...' He paused to try and regroup his thoughts. '...she seemed so vulnerable. I thought I could help her, protect her. But...' He shook his head. '...I'm not so sure...I'm not sure of anything these days. Lisa said *we* should take control of things. You know, in terms of the *letter*, but...it seems...I don't know...like *she* has taken control...and I'm...I'm just a bystander at my own wedding,' he got up and walked to the window. '...my own wedding for Christ's sake.'

Jackson stared aimlessly out into the distance. Suddenly Harry's words floated into his mind.

'I'm sorry Harry, you said we needed to talk. Is it about that stupid *letter*? Have you finally found out who sent it?'

Harry gestured for Jackson to sit back down. 'It's about our brother...Bernard Marshall.'

Jackson sat back down.

66

Lisa. Barbourne, Worcester
Saturday, 7 September 2019. 11.05 am

Lisa was sat in Harry's front room. She disliked his house. All modern and predictable. She imagined the estate agent showing Harry around. The bullshit: *Bespoke development; versatile and generous accommodation; successfully combines contemporary living with period charm; landscaped communal gardens.* In other words: general issue construction of interlocking soulless building blocks sharing a small garden with people you dislike.

Harry had told her he'd bought the house because it suited his needs…it was uncomplicated. He had wanted something he didn't have to think about. Functional he called it.

She felt almost claustrophobic in it. She'd never felt like that when she was in the cage…in the cellar.

She thought back to that night – the night she was abducted by William Marshall. She liked to think that what happened to her was an act of serendipity. The unexpected outcome of her spontaneity. And yes, there was some element of luck to it…she'd had no way of knowing the outcome. But had it been done without premeditation?…she knew that bit wasn't true. She had plotted the whole thing…she had made the journey especially so she could walk that route. Planned spontaneity. She let that phrase settle in her mind. That's how it was back then…everything - planned or unplanned - was so compulsive. A compulsion stoked by the fires of her obsession and fanned by the shadows of her mind. A far cry from how she viewed herself now...controlled, focused. But that night...had she really expected it to turn out the way it did? Or had she just hoped it would? Because when she woke up in the cage, in the cellar, she felt...she felt a sense of relief; like the wait was over; as if a part of her life was over; and she could finally start to let go of the past and get everything - everything she had suppressed - out of her system. Like a form of therapy. An extreme form of therapy. And William...he was to be her therapist, her lover, her father figure, her saviour...in life or death.

She returned from her thoughts and went into the kitchen. *Fully fitted. Stylish. Fully integrated.* She detested it more than any other room in Harry's house. It was so annoyingly *unfunctional*.

67

Bernie
Saturday, 7 September 2019. 11.15 am

Bernie was at home – lights dimmed, curtains shut.

Standing in the corner of the lounge was a mannequin. Dressed to look like the woman on the bus – to look like *Alison Marchant*. Long auburn hair; striking painted green eyes; faint red lips; a long brown silk bohemian dress.

He put his head in his hands and tried to escape from his thoughts. But he couldn't.

He sat for almost an hour. He kept asking himself…*what was I thinking? What was I doing?* He tried to reason with himself. Doesn't everyone have the desire to kill, even if it's just for the briefest of seconds? That's all it was…a fantasy. The mannequin was just a bit of fun. A way of satisfying his fantasy without it getting out of hand.

But it *had* got out of hand.

He shook his head.

Had he really followed her last night? Again. The girl on the bus. The girl who looked like Alison Marchant, *had* been Alison Marchant…for a while. But, deep down, he'd always known that she wasn't. That all he'd done was allow himself to believe something that he knew wasn't true. And yes, he had followed her. All the way to her house this time. But for what reason? He didn't even want to think about that. He didn't want to have to face that scary feeling…when you're unsure of yourself. Unsure of what you might have done, or what you might do. But he had to face it. Because he'd imagined it...going round to her house and killing her. Yes, he'd imagined it. And he'd practiced it. On the mannequin. The mannequin he'd bought especially for that purpose. The mannequin - his companion, his foil. And then...last night...he'd attempted it. *Stop!* He shouted to his inner voice. *I did not attempt it. I was just testing myself...to see how close I could get to the edge. But what if you had done it? What if you hadn't pulled yourself back. What if you had killed her?* He put his hands to his ears and screwed his eyes shut. He was feeling sick. He couldn't understand how he'd got to this point. It was sending him crazy. He suddenly stood up and went over to the wall opposite the sofa and turned up the lights.

He looked across at the DVD he'd watched twenty times before, maybe more - *Paddington 2.* He pictured Hugh Grant - the actor. He pictured the character he'd played - *Phoenix Buchanan* - the main antagonist. The washed-up actor who had lost his way...a lonely, sad and bitter figure who talked to his mannequins because they were the only *people* who understood him. He looked across at his own mannequin. Suddenly, it seemed like a lifeless, pitiful figure. He tried to understand his own feelings. Maybe he should despise Hugh Grant...because in *Phoenix Buchanan* he could see himself. Maybe he should loathe him, hate him...but he couldn't. He adored him.

But now, it was useless, he knew that. He'd let things get out of hand. He could have ended it - his obsession with the *Poppy Killer* - but it had become like a drug, a way of escaping from himself, and once he was hooked he couldn't find a way of stopping it. He'd let his mind go to places that it should never have gone, and now he'd hit rock bottom.

He'd had enough.

He had relentlessly, year after year, placed brick after brick on his shoulders, letting them build up, constantly fighting against their increasing weight, until he could no longer withstand their force. He had let himself be crushed by himself and now he had no more fight to give. He wanted it to end. He wanted it to end before it was too late. Before he could no longer stop himself. And yet, he knew, in his heart of hearts that everything he was thinking, everything he was feeling was not really him, that somewhere under the rubble there was the real Bernie. But right at that moment, in the maelstrom of his own emotions he could see no other way out, but to end it. End his life.

68

Harry and Jackson. Tawelfan Cottage
Saturday, 7 September 2019. 11.15 am

'I had a call yesterday from Mickey Maguire. The private detective.'

There was a coldness to Harry's voice. Something oddly non-contextual. Jackson searched his face for any sign of emotion but it was empty. It made him realise something…that in the short time he'd known Harry there had been a change in him. A darker, colder side had surfaced. He thought back to himself - how he'd changed, or more accurately how Lisa had changed him; from insecure to needy to paranoid. Well, maybe not changed him, but brought out the worst in him. And now he could see signs of paranoia in Harry, much more hidden, much more controlled, but it was there. He wondered if Lisa had somehow got to him as well, that maybe there *was* something going on between them, but that thought was quickly snapped shut by what Harry said next.

'Our triplet brother is dead. He died on 17th August 1985.'

69

Saturday, 7 September 2019
11.15 am

Jackson was trying to comprehend the cold directness of Harry's words.

'He died at birth? Christ, he never had a chance in life,' said Jackson.

Harry looked at the door under the stairs.

His mind was elsewhere.

'But there was no grave when we visited the cemetery. It was just...'

'He was cremated. Maybe William scattered his ashes in the wind? That's what Lisa thinks. That he wanted him to be free. Not buried in the ground. I don't know Jackson. We'll probably never know.'

Jackson felt for Bernard, his brother, but he felt more sorry for himself. The whole atmosphere was wrong.

'It's terrible news Harry, but why tell me now? Why now, on my wedding day? Couldn't it have waited until tomorrow, or next week, or next month?'

Harry got up out of his seat and turned his back on Jackson.

'I'm sorry if our brother's death has dampened your spirits Jackson but I thought you would want to know right away.'

Jackson stood up, his eyes fixed unerringly on the back of Harry's head.

'But you thought it best to tell Lisa first – you said you'd not seen her.' Jackson's imagination lit up. Thoughts of his brother's death lost in the bright light.

'I spoke to her Jackson. On the phone. I'm the best man...remember. That's what the best man does. He acts as the liaison officer between the bride and groom. She was the one who suggested I tell you today.' There was an ominous antagonism to Harry's voice.

Jackson moved towards the fireplace, then to the stairs and then back to the fireplace. Trying to think. There was a growing feeling of unease welling up in his mind. He looked around for something to latch on to. Something to break the mood.

'Do you like the suit?' Jackson pointed at the light blue 2-piece single-breasted fully lined wedding suit that was hanging on the far wall. In the buttonhole was a red poppy. 'I hope it fits. I gave them the measurements you told me, but you can never be sure. You should have come with me.'

Harry turned and looked. Then he shifted his stare back on Jackson.

'Why the poppy?'

'Why not? It's a form of remembrance. I thought it would be a nice tribute...to our birth father.'

Harry thought about the words *nice* and *tribute.* He let them sit in his mind. Unprocessed.

He moved towards Jackson who quickly side stepped him and moved to the window.

'Do you know something Harry. I'm getting married today, yet, I feel like an imposter. I haven't heard from Lisa for a week and now this – you and me – it's like I don't know you.' He exhaled deeply. 'Christ, I hardly know myself these days.' The tone of his voice was a mix of incredulity and rising fear.

Harry looked through Jackson. He thought of how insignificant he appeared against the light of the window.

'You know this is a sham don't you Jackson.'

The look on Harry's face implied it wasn't a question.

Jackson was startled. He turned around to try and hide his anxiety, but he knew it was too late.

'Don't look so shocked. Lisa told me everything.'

Jackson spun back round.

'Meaning?'

'That *you* sent the letter. *You* sent the *letter* telling the world that the *Poppy Killer* was going to strike again, because *you* wanted to scare Lisa.'

'What!'

Dark thoughts ate into the dimming light of Jackson's mind.

'*You* sent the *letter* so that *you* could protect her. Control her. You made her feel vulnerable, helpless. She found a copy of it - a few days before your spurious engagement - on your laptop. It made her frightened. Frightened of what you might do. So when you asked her to marry you, out of desperation, out of fear for her own safety, she said yes.'

They now stood facing each other, separated by nothing more than their own delusions.

'That's ridiculous Harry and you know it. If I *had* written the *letter*, which I didn't, I'd hardly keep a copy of it on my computer.'

'Our IT people found no evidence that the files were hacked. And we've eliminated everyone at the force who had access to them. That leaves only two people who could have known that the killer always positioned the poppy beneath the feet of his victims: you and Lisa. And it wasn't Lisa who sent the letter.'

Jackson couldn't think straight and instead of trying to defend himself, he tried to deflect the blame.

'What about the *Poppy Killer*, our birth father, William Marshall. He could have sent the letter.'

Harry sighed. He looked across at the wedding suit hanging on the far wall.

'The *Poppy Killer* is dead. He died in 2003. Sixteen years ago. Christ, when will you stop deluding yourself.'

Jackson's eyes widened.

'*Deluded*. It's not me who's deluded Harry. This whole thing…you…me…right now…this is deluded. I mean, really…you don't know anything do you. For one thing, it was Lisa who brought up the subject of marriage. I just followed her lead.'

'Isn't that what you've always done Jackson…follow her lead.'

Jackson shook his head.

'And what are you doing now Harry - whose lead are you following.'

Harry felt a jolt in his heart that stirred his anger.

'The pretence is over Jackson, she's told me everything…your sudden bursts of anger. She was afraid of what you might do…if she didn't…'

Jackson jumped in on Harry - his face turning red.

'Harry, you have got it all wrong. You heard her in the café. She said she needed me.'

The power of love sprung into Harry's mind. Had he also become powerless to Lisa's spell? It was a thought he could neither answer nor dismiss.

'She *said* what she thought you wanted to hear.'

Jackson was almost incandescent with disbelief.

'And what bursts of anger Harry?...I've never...' Suddenly a shocking realisation went through Jackson's mind.

'You knew didn't you...all along. You've been in on this right from the start. When I phoned you to tell you the news. To ask you to be my best man. It was like you'd been expecting the call. I knew there was something wrong and now...'

'She phoned me, Lisa phoned me a few hours after she'd agreed to marry you. She was in a state. In tears. She didn't know what to do. So we talked. That's when we decided that she would suggest to you to ask me to be your best man. So I could deal with things.'

'*Deal with things?* What does that mean?'

'And then the next day you phoned...so yes, I knew.'

Jackson moved closer to Harry. His steps felt unbalanced. His mind unstable.

'Harry, this is meant to be my wedding day, you are meant to be my best man, what the *fuck* is this all about?'

Harry looked around at the exposed beams...the exposed stone and brick walls. A thought entered his mind...what if Jackson *was* telling the truth...what would it mean? But thoughts of Lisa quickly overpowered the question.

His eyes zoned in on his faltering, desperate brother.

'You've lost. You never deserved Lisa. You inherited her. She stuck with you because she had no other choice. Now she has a choice and she's chosen me.'

Jackson's mind crumbled into the rubble of his hopes. He let out a distorted laugh – crazed, panic stricken sounds.

'You and Lisa.' He shook his head violently. 'I knew it…I knew it. You and her…' tears started to well up in his eyes. 'She's got to you Harry. She's taken control. She always takes control. She…' Jackson checked himself. Lisa's face flooded his mind. He suddenly realised what he was saying. That he was blaming her. And then the unimaginable reality of the situation hit home…he was losing her. He wiped his eyes. 'I love her.' He forced himself to stare into Harry's eyes. 'And you're wrong about me, I would never do anything to hurt her.'

Harry let Jackson's words wash over him.

He remained impassive.

Jackson's emotions were see-sawing violently. His wedding day had descended into chaos. Lisa, his bride, was having an affair with his brother and she'd lied to Harry about him.

The whole situation was madness.

Then suddenly a light bulb went on in his mind. Maybe Harry was unstable? Maybe he was making the whole thing up so that *he* could have Lisa? Lisa's words sprung into his mind, as if they had been waiting their turn to be loaded. She'd told him, last month, that she thought Harry was a troubled soul. But, at the time, instead of asking her what she'd meant, he'd felt relief. As if her words proved that she wasn't having an affair with him.

He felt a fragile resurgence of his self-belief.

He straightened his back.

'Lisa needs me. It's our wedding day. And quite frankly Harry, right now, I don't believe a word you're saying.'

He had hoped his words would weaken Harry's resolve, but he stood firm.

Harry reached into his pocket.

He held out his mobile.

'Fine, phone her, phone Lisa, ask her yourself.'

Jackson stared at Harry's phone as if it was a dagger.

He wanted to reach for it, but something stopped him.

He felt cornered

'It's over Jackson. She doesn't want to marry you. You lose.'

Harry's face fixed in on his own words.

Jackson could feel his emotions spilling over the tipping point.

And suddenly, without warning his nervous system defaulted down to its basic instincts…fight or flight.

He lunged at Harry.

70

Saturday, 7 September 2019
11.30 am

The scuffle was intense but brief.

Harry was much more capable of handling himself and he soon overpowered Jackson...securing him with an armlock.

He looked around the room. He saw what he was looking for hanging on the far wall.

He took Jackson down to the cellar, sat him on the old wooden chair and using the necktie from his wedding suit, he tied his wrists behind his back.

Jackson's posture slumped, the pressure inside his head felt intense. Like gravity was pressing down on him.

Harry stood close to him.

They were both sweating.

Harry noticed a wound on his own wrist - it was inconvenient more than debilitating, something he could easily hide.

Jackson watched as Harry dabbed his wound with a handkerchief. It felt like it wasn't really happening, that it was somehow all in his imagination.

A desolate silence engulfed them both.

The future seemed to be waiting, listening, as if weary...fearful of what might come next.

Jackson tugged on his restraints. There was some give.

He looked up at Harry.

'This is insane.'

Harry looked away, his mind unchaining itself from what had just happened.

'She's playing with you Harry.'

Harry straightened up and jumped on Jackson's words.

'You're a leech Jackson. A parasite. You attach yourself to people and then try and squeeze them dry with your clinginess.'

Jackson shook his head.

'You're wrong Harry. I'm the one who's had all the blood sucked out of me. And you will be next.'

Harry's eyes bore down on Jackson.

'Why do you always blame someone else for your own failings?'

'I'm not blaming anyone. I wouldn't change a thing. Lisa is my life and for every second I have been with her I am grateful.'

Jackson saw Harry staring at him disbelievingly.

'You will find out soon enough Harry. That you will do anything for her. That you will forgive her for anything.'

Harry scoffed. 'She doesn't need forgiveness. You're the one who's lost it.'

He momentarily turned his head. Jackson's remark - *you will do anything for her* - was lighting up his mind. He tried to dim it.

'Do you know that she told me she thought you were a troubled soul.' said Jackson.

Harry re-focused. He gave him a wry smile.

'You're the troubled one Jackson.'

Jackson continued to work on the necktie.

'No Harry, I can see it in your face.'

Harry moved over to the brick wall and leaned back on it.

'She's been with *me* all week.'

Harry let his words eat into Jackson's mind.

'You had her but you drove her away. Now it's my turn.'

Jackson shook his head and then lowered his gaze to the floor.

'I love her Harry. I have loved her since the moment I first saw her.'

He looked up.

'If I can't have her, if I can't be with her, then there is nothing more for me.'

Harry moved forward. He searched for the coldness in his heart. It was there, but it felt…it felt strangely disingenuous. He knew he couldn't harbour such a conflict, that he had to remain strong…he had to remain cold-hearted.

'We are brothers, triplets; yet, we are as far apart as two people can be.'

Harry walked towards the stairs.

Jackson shouted out.

'You love her. You love her…don't you Harry.'

Harry paused and turned.

'Yes Jackson, I do and I will be with her for the rest of my life.'

Jackson locked onto Harry's eyes.

'You're wrong Harry, you and me are more alike than you can ever imagine.'

Jackson watched his words create an unconvincing smile on Harry's face.

Harry turned away.

'What are you going to do now Harry? Leave me here to die?'

Harry stopped in his tracks and turned around.

'It's for you to decide what to do with your life Jackson. You're on your own now. Lisa is coming to live with me. The wedding is off.'

Harry started to climb the stairs.

'She'll get to you Harry. Do you hear me! She'll get to you!'

Harry stopped on the final step.

'I'll be back later. Use the time to think about your life Jackson. The two of us will forever be tied by William Marshall but, after tomorrow, we shall *never* see each other again. And you will never see Lisa again.'

The cellar door closed and gave way to a ghostly silence. And in that moment Jackson felt a cold shiver run through his body. Like the ten dead souls of William Marshall's victims had possessed him; each one screaming - devoid of their humanity.

Jackson shouted out ...'No!'

The sound of his voice fell silently onto the cold stone floor.

71

Saturday, 7 September 2019
12.00 Noon

Jackson had freed himself from the chair.

He'd been surprised at how easy it had been...considering Harry was a copper...but the way he'd tied the necktie had allowed for a lot of give.

He remained seated.

Harry had left the light on, making the cellar seem like a dimly lit tunnel.

He tried to see through the clouds in his mind. But they were darker and more dense than they had ever been before.

He thought back to the time when he met William Marshall, the *Poppy Killer*. *The Poppy Killer*! He winced. He wondered what his life would have been like if he'd never met him. All the dominoes that would still be standing. Instead, his life had been a chain reaction of events that had culminated in this moment: detained by his brother, on his wedding day, in the cellar of his father's old house...the cellar...the *Poppy Killer!*...he winced again. Why had he chosen a poppy for the buttonhole? *Remembrance...tribute*. He laughed ironically to himself. He stood up. He suddenly realised how chaotic his thinking had been in recent weeks...months...years.

He thought about going back upstairs. There was no lock on the trap door. And he doubted if Harry had covered the hatch.

He wondered if he was still there. Sitting alone in the lounge. Then he thought about what Harry had said...he was wrong. He would never scare Lisa. He would never harm her.

Oh Lisa, he said to himself, *what have you done*? *Look at me...on our wedding day. Why did you say those things to Harry? Why did you tell him that I'd sent the letter.* He wrestled with himself. Then suddenly his mind stopped. *Unless*. *Unless*. He wanted to shut the thought out, but the notion kept getting stronger....unless Harry was right...that Lisa *had* said and done all of those things so she could be rid of him.

Oh Lisa.

Why had she never said anything to his face? Why had it all been so...so clandestine? He couldn't understand it. And yet, a part of him knew the answer. The answer he had always refused to believe. That hidden, deep below the surface, far away from where anyone could see, was the true Lisa. The Lisa that needed help – professional help. Perhaps it should have been glaringly obvious in light of what she'd been through and how she'd behaved in 2003. Since 2003. But she had the ability to dismantle your thoughts and your beliefs leaving you unsure of yourself...unsure of what you once believed to be true.

Lisa.

It seemed that life to her had become a game. A game in which it was impossible to read her moves. Impossible to know what was going on inside her head. Impossible to predict what she was capable of.

A game, in which all you could do was hold on and hope for the best.

But this time...this time, Jackson knew he was finally losing his grip.

He'd often suspected her of having an affair. Affairs even. She would suddenly change jobs for no apparent reason. She would stay with an old work friend – a friend Jackson had never met. His train of thought was interrupted...until today...he was meant to have met her today...Hannah someone. At the wedding. He felt a terrible emptiness in his stomach. His thoughts went back to his suspicions...why had he never questioned her? Why had he never confronted her? He knew the answer...that he was afraid of losing her...of pushing her away. That his distrust may have given her cause to leave him.

And so, if he was guilty of anything, it was his obsessive love for Lisa. A love that had made him a prisoner to his own actions and thoughts.

He had invested all of himself in her and now he realised with chilling clarity that without her there was nothing left of Jackson Brown. Nothing left to save.

He walked to the middle of the cellar.

He no longer wanted to play the game.

72

Saturday, 7 September 2019

Jackson
12.35 pm

Jackson looked up at the lightshade.

He looked down at the necktie resting on his lap.

It was long enough.

His mind had shrunk to one simple thought. One simple solution. One simple action that would take away the agony in his heart.

He was tired of fighting…fighting himself, fighting Lisa, fighting Harry, fighting life.

He did not want to face the reality of what Harry had said.

That he had lost. That Lisa was no longer his. That she would not be coming back to him.

He had nothing left to give. No desire to pick himself back up.

He was ready.

He took the chair and placed it under the light shade.

Bernie
12.35 pm

Bernie took the rope out of the bag. The rope he had purchased that morning. He looked around the room for a place to tie it to. His eyes stopped at the hanging ceiling light. The fitting looked sturdy enough. He could tie the rope above the light shade onto the solid brass chain that was suspended from the ceiling. He gazed pensively at the light. It had three glass shades that were housed in three curved arms, that made it look like a small chandelier. He'd never really noticed it before. He liked it. He wondered about all the other things he'd never noticed. That perhaps all he'd ever done was run away...and all that was real had passed him by.

Jackson
12.45 pm

His mind had now completely switched off. He had no mediating thoughts. No desire to call out. No urge to reach out.

He stood on the chair.

Like it was meant to be.

He picked up the necktie and made a noose. He then tied the other end around the light chain and slipped the noose around his neck.

He waited.

He wasn't afraid.

He breathed in the silence.

The empty silence.

For a split second Lisa re-entered his thoughts.

He immediately snuffed her out and simultaneously kicked the chair from underneath him.

It fell limply onto the stone floor.

Jackson kicked out.

Then he was still.

Bernie
12.45 pm

He pulled up a chair; stood on it. He took one final look at the mannequin, one final look at how low he'd descended, before tying the rope around the brass chain. He then slipped the noose around his neck. And waited. His heart was pounding. He searched for the *courage* to end his life. And in that moment of acute desperation he heard a voice in his head crying out. He clenched his eyes and let out a silent scream. Then he instinctively reached out one last time – for someone, for anyone to help him…help him find the true Bernie, the real Bernie, the one he'd never been able to set free.

73

Bernie
Saturday, 7 September 2019. 12.45 pm

Sometimes it's impossible to explain things.

Often, bizarre events are attributed to coincidence, or fate, or chance, but in this instance there was only one word for it – luck.

If Bernie's work colleague, James – his only friend, had not noticed a change in Bernie's behaviour. If James had not, yesterday morning, been speaking to Diane from the admin section and mentioned to her that he was worried about Bernie. If Diane had not, at that moment in time, been typing up Bernard Chapman's yearly appraisal. If Diane had not noticed his date of birth and told James that it was Bernie's birthday the next day...Saturday 7th September. If James had not asked so nicely…for Diane to breach confidentiality rules and give him Bernie's address. If James had not decided that he would go round to Bernie's and surprise him the next day, on his birthday. If James had not left at one o'clock, instead of five o'clock as he'd originally intended. If James had not found a parking space straight away.

If.

So pure luck intervened just at the moment Bernie was about to push the chair from underneath his feet.

At first he was startled; he thought he was hearing things. But then it happened again, the sound of the doorbell. He slipped off the rope from around his neck as thoughts cascaded rapidly into his mind.

And then he heard a voice.

'Bernie…Bernie…are you there?'

Bernie stood on the chair – temporarily frozen to the spot. Then it registered…the voice. It was James from work. His friend. His only friend. What was he doing at his flat? Bernie quickly snapped out of his inertia and manically looked around the room.

He needed some breathing space.

'Just a minute.'

He untied the rope from the light chain, ran over to the sofa chair and stuffed it under the seat cushion.

'Is everything alright?'

'One second.'

He then moved the chair he'd been standing on back to the dining table and went straight over to the mirror to check how he looked. A few quick touches and he was ready. He moved over to the door, took a deep steadying breath and opened it.

'James…what a surprise.'

'Happy birthday!' James handed Bernie a present.

Bernie looked at him in astonishment.

'Thhh….thank you. Thank you. I don't know what to say.'

'You can invite me in, that would be a start…or are you entertaining? You look a bit flustered.'

Bernie looked at James, then instinctively shot a glance at the ceiling light as if to check he wasn't having a peculiar post-death out-of-body experience and was actually hanging there.

'Yes, no...sorry...no...I'm...I'm alone...yes, come in, please, come in.'

The first thing James noticed was the mannequin standing in the corner.

'So, you *do* have a guest, you little tease.'

Bernie glanced to where James was looking and immediately chastised himself for forgetting about the mannequin. It had been there for so long that it had almost become a part of the furniture. He needed to think quick. Then he saw a big impish smile on James's face. He decided to play along.

'Alison, meet James.'

James went over and kissed Alison on the cheek.

'Charmed, I'm sure.' He looked back at Bernie. 'She's a bit shy. But delightful...you're a sly old thing; not telling me you had a girlfriend.'

He gave Bernie a mischievous look and they both burst out laughing.

Eventually Bernie regained his composure. And...he'd had enough time to concoct a story.

'I bought her sometime ago, over the Internet, I wanted a virtual audience to listen to me, so to speak, when I was practicing my lines. I dressed her up, for a bit of fun, to make her look more lifelike.'

'You're an actor...you never told me that.'

'No, not really, I just enjoy pretending.' Bernie surprised himself with his reply. He'd never admitted to himself that he wasn't a great actor. It had always been the fault of others – they had never recognised his talent.

'Go on then, pretend in front of me.'

Panic welled up in Bernie.

'I can't...I mean...I...I haven't rehearsed anything.'

'Don't be shy, you must be able to remember something; something you have done before. Macbeth, Hamlet maybe...*to be or not to be?*'

'I don't do Shakespeare.' Bernie said abruptly.

'Then what do you do?'

'Famous scenes from films, stage plays...that sort of thing.'

'Go on then. Give me a scene from your favourite film.'

Before Bernie had chance to engage his reluctant side he found himself acting scenes from *Paddington 2*. Playing Hugh Grant's character...*Phoenix Buchanan.* And he was loving it...hamming it up in the same way Hugh Grant had done. Then, for his final scene Bernie talked to *Alison*...the girl on the bus...the mannequin...just as *Phoenix Buchanan* had done...talked to his mannequins...mannequins he had dressed up as famous fictional characters.

When he'd finished James sat there in silence. Bernie looked at him apprehensively. Then slowly, he began to clap.

'That my friend, was very impressive; mesmerising...really good. You have talent.'

Bernie began to blush.

'You're just saying that.'

'No, really, I never lie to people, you really have a talent. Maybe you should join your local am dram society?'

For a moment Bernie felt the dreaded force of negativity rising up inside of him - he despised amateur dramatic groups with a passion - but this time, he managed to shut the door on it.

'Maybe I will.'

They looked at one another. There was a brief, meaningful silence.

James smiled.

'Come on, I noticed a pub on the corner. Let's go and have a drink. It's your birthday after all.'

Bernie had lived in his flat for 17 years and he'd not once been to the pub at the end of the street. He sensed his demons waiting for him…waiting for him to crack…waiting for the door to re-open.

'I'm not sure…I mean I can't…I'm…'

'Don't be silly, come on.' James grabbed Bernie by the arm and led him to the door. Bernie looked back for his coat. 'You don't need your coat. Have you got your keys?' Bernie nodded. 'Then let's go.'

'Wait, what about the present you bought me?'

'Open it later.'

74

Tawelfan Cottage
Saturday, 7 September 2019. 1.10 pm

Harry was sat on the plain brown sofa.

He was trying to bring some order to his thoughts.

He looked at his watch.

Over an hour and a half had passed since his altercation with Jackson.

He'd had no choice. Jackson had lunged for him…it was his own fault. And in any case, he'd had it coming to him. Best for him that he's in the cellar cooling off. But it didn't matter how many affirmations Harry repeated to himself to justify his actions, he still felt a knot in his stomach. As if everything that should be right, was somehow all wrong.

He got up, put on his coat, but then decided he should give Jackson some water before he left.

He filled up a glass from the kitchen tap and returned to the cellar.

On reaching the bottom of the stairs, he stepped onto the stone floor and looked across.

His grip weakened, the glass dropped, sending it shattering into a thousand tiny pieces.

Harry stood motionless. Then, he moved forward, deliberately, slowly, as if he was drugged. He looked at the old wooden chair that was lying on its side. The dark oak. The worn, slightly concave seat with a crack down the middle. He wondered to himself why the wood had cracked at that point.

He looked vacantly up at Jackson.

Suddenly he felt an impulse to reach out and hug him, but that emotion was immediately replaced by the realisation that a terrible thing had happened.

And *he* had caused it to happen.

He looked to his right and stared blankly at the wall.

Nothing.

He turned his head and forced himself to look back up at Jackson.

The necktie. He must have not tied it properly. He took a deep breath. Why wasn't he surprised. Had he subconsciously done it on purpose...not tied his wrists properly?

Because if he had, he had no explanation for why.

All he knew, was that he had never intended for this to happen.

A terrible coldness permeated through his body. A bitter, biting, numbness rising up from the realisation that he could never go back. And most probably, he could never go forward. He would be trapped in this moment forever.

He returned upstairs and got a sharp knife from the kitchen drawer.

Back in the cellar, he cut his brother down.

He sat with him for a short while, before looking at his watch.

1.25pm.

He knew he needed to think with clarity, to act with decisiveness. Report Jackson's suicide. But it wasn't as simple as that. He would have to admit to his relationship with Lisa. A love triangle. He knew it was classic murder fodder. Suspicions would fall on him. There would be an autopsy. His DNA would be all over Jackson. And the injury to his wrist. And not to mention the cellar. The *Poppy Killer*. If the police did a forensic examination down there, who knows what they would find? It was just too risky. But he knew he was just making excuses...that he should go to the police - like Jackson should have done in 2003, when he first discovered Alison Marchant - but he knew it was already too late. That history was repeating itself. Jackson's words suddenly created a deafening sound in Harry's ears....*you and me are more alike than you can ever imagine*. He tilted his head back as if he was trying to drain the blood away from his brain. He felt weary, like all the spirit had been sucked out of him. Perhaps Jackson had been right...they *were* alike. He'd let Lisa dress him in the Emperor's clothes and he had steadfastly refused to accept what was clearly visible. That the new Harry Black - the Harry Black he thought had been re-born - was in fact just a darker, colder, more heartless version of himself. A version of himself that he justified through his love for Lisa. As if love could justify any behaviour, no matter how despicable.

He looked down at Jackson's body.

He'd killed his brother.

Could love justify that?

He was lost in his own thoughts.

And now he needed Lisa more than ever.

He returned upstairs and phoned her.

75

Lisa. Barbourne, Worcester.
Saturday, 7 September 2019. 1.30pm

Lisa answered her mobile phone.

It was Harry.

He sounded agitated. Upset.

She listened.

Things had taken an unforeseen turn.

Not the outcome she had been expecting.

But then again, she hadn't really thought about what to expect. She never thought about the consequences of her actions...not in any meaningful way. Had life ever thought about the consequences of what it had done to her? She knew the rules. She had learnt the hard way.

It's not that she thought life was a game. Although it may have seemed that way to others. It's just that her field of vision was all mixed up. So to cope, she had learnt to tunnel her vision. To move through life without stopping, without going back, without turning left or right. Without even having any clear destination. Just the righteous notion of a starting point: Monday, 17 February 1997...at the Grange Comprehensive School, Stourbridge...standing in the rain.

She heard Harry's voice...*hello, Lisa, are you there?*

Now Harry had created a problem.

It was nothing more and nothing less than that…a problem.

She thought for a moment before telling Harry exactly what to do.

Then she left his house and headed to Ludlow.

76

Bernie
Saturday, 7 September 2019. 8.05pm

Six hours ago, Bernie had walked out of his flat, laughing and chatting with James.

Then, half way along the street tears had started rolling down his face. He had tried to hide them, but James had noticed. He was concerned for his friend. Bernie had tried to feign a smile but it had just made his tears worse.

In the pub Bernie explained to James that he'd been having a difficult time recently, that's why he'd been so emotional. It had been a release. That's all.

James listened. He did not judge him. He simply listened.

Now, back in his flat, standing alone in the lounge, looking at the mannequin in the corner, he felt more at peace with himself.

The clouds had lifted.

He thought back to the first time he'd read about the *Poppy Killer*. He wondered if things would have turned out the same if he'd not obsessed about him. Not obsessed about his eleventh victim.

He tried to think of how he could rationalise it to himself – his behaviour, but it was something he couldn't explain. Like he'd had some sort of mental breakdown. Functioning, but not functioning. And everything had come to a head.

He sat down.

He felt a bump under the seat cushion. He retrieved the rope he had hidden there. It sent a shiver down his spine.

He looked up at the light shade.

He saw a different Bernie looking back at him. One who had the courage to open his eyes…to be himself.

And now, he could approach life with a totally different attitude.

He looked at the rope.

He shook his head.

Stood up.

He walked over to the chair he'd been standing on six hours earlier.

He picked it up and placed it under the light.

He leaned on the back rest.

It was something he had to do. Something the new Bernie had to do. To take himself back to that moment…when he'd been so close. Wallowing in his self-loathing and self-pity. Unable to face the truth.

He had reached out.

Reached out for the courage to set himself free.

James had answered his call.

As if it was meant to be.

And for the first time in as long as he could remember he felt happy.

He wasn't afraid anymore.

He looked down at the chair.

Impulsively he kicked out at it.

He watched as it fell limply onto the carpet.

He threw out his leg in a moment of joy.

Then he walked back to the sofa, sat down and cried.

77

Harry

Harry had gone to work later that evening - after Jackson's suicide: September 7th 2019. The day the *Poppy Killer* had threatened to strike again. In the end, the evening passed without incident. No murders; just a few extra calls to the police emergency number - jumpy individuals letting their imagination get the better of them.

The author of the letter and the reason for sending it - that had still not been resolved.

Harry had not spoken to DI Bond about what happened that afternoon. If he did want to talk then he knew she would listen. But would she understand? Of course not, not after what he did...what they did...Harry and Lisa. That was something he had to come to terms with. But he was finding it hard.

The next day, Sunday 8th September, just before lunchtime, Lisa reported Jackson as missing. The local force took on the investigation. Harry, Lisa and Lisa's friend, Hannah, whom she had known for over 20 years were interviewed that afternoon - they were all well rehearsed in what to say.

Lisa told the police that they'd expected him to return after an hour or two; and even when he didn't show for the wedding, they still expected him to return in the evening...or the next morning. He was a grown man. He must have needed his own space…had second thoughts about getting married. Yes, he'd been acting a bit strange recently and in hindsight maybe they should have phoned the police earlier, but how could they have known...that he'd been on the edge of a breakdown…that he would disappear?

At first his disappearance caused a few ripples over and above the normal interest for a missing person. A man who goes missing on his wedding day is news fodder, but it only lasted for a day or two. None of the local press bothered digging into the back story of Lisa Hopkins and so Alison Marchant remained hidden from view.

Harry felt so mixed up inside. Jackson was out of the way. His relationship with Lisa could eventually, after an acceptable period of time, come out of its clandestine shadows. The lonely bride, comforted by the best man…*it just happened…it was never planned.* He should have been feeling happy, but he'd never expected it to turn out the way it did. That Jackson would do what he did. Sure, Lisa had predicted it would hit him hard at first…of course it would…she was leaving him; the wedding was off. But Lisa had been very persuasive in assuring Harry that he would eventually snap out of it. That everything would improve. That it would help him get back on his own two feet. Harry felt his heart sink…he hadn't realised just how much Jackson had been in love with Lisa…enough to kill himself.

He still couldn't fully reconcile in his mind why Jackson had sent the *letter* to the police. He'd never asked for proof. Why should he have? He'd taken

Lisa's word on everything. He trusted her implicitly. Or was it more a case that he was afraid to distrust her? He stopped for a second in that thought. He stared at the question...was he afraid to distrust her? His mind transported him back to the cottage...back with Jackson...in the lounge...in the cellar. He could see Jackson's face...his words were rapidly scrolling across Harry's vision. He shut his eyes...he tried to blank out his thoughts. He knew his mind was all over the place – that he wasn't thinking straight. His brother had committed suicide. Perhaps he'd caused it? Perhaps he could have stopped it? He felt terrible. He tried to focus on Lisa...she seemed so together. The fact that Jackson was dead hadn't phased her in the slightest. In fact, if anything, she seemed to be enjoying it. Relishing the challenge of covering their tracks. Like it was a game. But it wasn't a game to Harry. It felt like a situation that could spiral out of control at any moment. And he knew that there would only ever be one loser.

78

Friday, 20 September 2019

Today, Harry's boss, DI Bond was driving over to see him and Lisa. Normally a DI would not get involved with a missing person's case, unless foul play was suspected. Jackson Brown's disappearance was not being treated as suspicious, however, Jackson's parents were angry at the lack of progress, kicking up a fuss with their local MP, so the chief had told DI Bond to go round and show her face; have a word with Harry; speak to Lisa Hopkins, unofficially/officially. Basically go and see if there was anything the local force had overlooked.

DI Bond arrived in an unmarked car. She was wearing plain clothes. Harry, who had driven to Ludlow that morning, answered the door. He'd been expecting her - but he was still caught off guard by her appearance. For some reason she looked different. Not just a detective, not just a woman, but a friend.

He welcomed her to Tawelfan cottage and introduced her to Lisa.

DI Bond had a natural intuition for detective work. She was one of the best. She had skills that you couldn't teach; instincts that you couldn't learn. And right at that moment as she shook Lisa's hand she had a bad feeling about her.

Lisa volunteered to make the tea while Harry and Trish sat down in the lounge.

She looked around admiring the exposed stone and bricked walls. Then her eyes fell on Harry.

'Sorry about the intrusion Harry…you understand…routine stuff...just making sure the covers are straight.'

He nodded.

'The chief…you know what he's like.'

He nodded again.

'I understand you were the best man.'

'Yes, he's my brother.'

'Oh, I'm sorry, I didn't know…..'

'I was adopted. We were reunited last year. I hardly knew him really.'

'You kept that quiet Harry. Do you not think you should have mentioned it to the local plods?'

Harry looked slightly sheepish.

'It was…it was personal. I didn't want it to become the topic for police gossip. Besides, it has nothing to do with his disappearance.'

Trish nodded. She understood the fickleness of the police grapevine, but he should have mentioned something. Disclosures on family members are compulsory. Things like that can get a bit messy if unchecked. If nothing else, he should have mentioned it to her…off the record. That everything was in hand…official channels would be contacted in due course. She felt a slight twinge of sadness that he hadn't. But she didn't have time for that. There would be ramifications, problems that Harry would have to deal with…but not now.

'And this is his house…Jackson Brown's?'

'Yes, he…..'

Lisa entered the room with the tea. She placed the three mugs on the table and smiled nondescriptly.

Warning bells were ringing in Trish's head. It didn't look right. It didn't feel right.

Lisa sat down next to Harry. Trish noted how close they were to one another. The bells were ringing louder.

'Any news?' Lisa asked DI Bond. She shook her head.

'I'm sorry,' said Trish.

Lisa looked visibly upset.

Harry sat there as if he was acting out a well-rehearsed face.

Trish found that odd.

She looked at them both.

'I know you have spoken to the local police, but I'd like you to go over what happened two weeks ago on Saturday, September 7th.'

Silence.

Lisa turned to Harry as if prompting him.

Harry glanced back at Lisa and gave her a faint nod of his head.

Trish found that even odder.

Then Harry began.

'I arrived here just before midday. The day Jackson and Lisa were due to get married.'

79

Lisa
Saturday, 7 September 2019

Lisa came up with an immediate plan.

To make it look like Jackson had disappeared.

She had to, the detective in Harry had gone AWOL.

She called upon her own experience. She knew how easy it was to make it seem convincing. Hundreds of people go missing everyday. All she needed to do was create the deception; implement the deception; and then make sure she and Harry backed-up the deception. Jackson's recent behaviour would do the rest. He'd worked at the butchers in the centre of Ludlow since 2014. He'd never really had any great passion or skills for the job, but for reasons unknown he'd liked it.

She would often go in there. Especially when Jackson wasn't working. Staff had found that strange at first, that she'd come in to buy meat, when Jackson could just as easily have taken it home with him. But after a while they found it more amusing than odd. And they liked her…they liked her a lot.

Lisa would quiz them about Jackson and they were always happy to respond. On more than one occasion, over the last few months, they'd told her he'd been acting strangely. That is, more strangely than normal. What they hadn't been aware of was his impending marriage…Lisa had sworn him to secrecy.

The butchers' statements would further minimise any suspicions that Jackson's disappearance had been anything other than the outcome of a mental breakdown.

He was the type of person that always seemed to be looking over his shoulder.
Greg, Head Butcher

You could never read him. I mean recently…one minute he seemed elated and the next time you saw him it was like the lights had gone out.
Malc, Assistant Butcher

He tended to keep himself to himself. I mean, he hadn't even told us he was getting married.
Pete, Part-time Butcher

Lisa's own deliberations of what would happen after the wedding day showdown between Harry and Jackson had been limited in scope. She'd be spending more time with Harry. And Jackson…she'd thought, hoped even, that the break-up of their relationship would create a tipping point of some sort, but never in her wildest dreams did she ever consider it would turn out the way it did. She'd marked Jackson down as becoming a recluse. Bitter. Lonely. Eventually picking himself up. Maybe finding someone else to follow? But suicide. That had made things easier and trickier at the same time.

As she moved in and out of her machinations, she was unaware of how cold her feelings had become…for Jackson, for Harry, for people. Her conscience had hardened…become non-porous. And the line she once saw between her own genuineness and deceitfulness had all but faded. All she felt was the compulsion to do things. *Normal* felt like an apparition, a scourge. Not that anyone, other than those who got too close to her, would have noticed. She had become adept at hiding her true self. It was all part of her survival plan…not to be yourself, in order to be yourself.

80

Sunday, 8 September 2019
Tawelfan Cottage

The police had arrived.

Harry focused his mind and zoned in on the words that were lined up in his head.

He stormed out...he was totally freaked – he kept saying he couldn't go through with it. I thought he just needed time by himself – time to let off steam. All he took was his wallet and coat – nothing else, not even his mobile – where would he go? I guess it had been building up, but I never thought it would come to this. I thought he would be back in an hour or so. That he'd still go ahead with the wedding. But maybe I should have seen it? I feel really bad that I didn't go after him.

The officers were trained to exhibit the necessary empathetic responses when faced with emotionally difficult situations.

They nodded.

Harry, for his part, performed his role well. He could see how the deception would work...could work. That in itself wasn't a problem. What he was increasingly struggling with was the fact that the deception involved his brother. And in truth it wasn't a deception at all. It was hiding a body. A dead body.

81

Saturday, 7 September 2019

At approximately 2.45pm, following Harry's discovery of Jackson in the cellar - and having subsequently spoken to Lisa on the phone - he drove to Ludlow railway station in Jackson's car. He parked at the far end of the station car park and put on Jackson's coat. He made himself viewable to the people waiting for the next train to London, but he always kept his face just out of sight...including the CCTV cameras.

When the train pulled in, he took off the coat, mingled with the people who had alighted the train and left the station, walking to a nearby street - away from the car park - to where Lisa was waiting in her car.

Lisa would later dispose of the coat.

From Ludlow station, Harry and Lisa headed for the church. At 4.30pm Harry went inside to tell the Rector that the wedding would not be taking place.

****

Subsequent investigations would reveal possible sightings of Jackson at Ludlow railway station: a few of the commuters recognised his distinctive coat, but none of them could remember his face.

It was assumed he had been heading for London, although no CCTV footage was checked at any of the intermediate stations to see if he had got off the train earlier and he was not picked up on the London terminal station cameras. In truth, the police didn't have the resources nor the motivation to follow it up fully. They'd already created a profile of Jackson. They'd interviewed people close to him: Lisa, his work colleagues, and most significantly, Detective Sergeant Harry Black. His disappearance was not being treated as suspicious. Instead, in the eyes of the police, Jackson had become another one of the UK's missing persons...his disappearance most probably caused by mental health issues.

During the days that followed Jackson's disappearance, there were vague, unsubstantiated sightings. That was to be expected – there always were in the early stages of a missing persons case. Harry had spoken to the UK Missing Persons Unit who'd informed him that 180,000 people are reported missing every year in the UK. So he knew that soon the *sightings* would fade and photographs of new missing persons would come to the fore - consigning Jackson to a forgotten face on a shop-window poster.

Lisa's friend, Hannah Wasserstein, faithfully kept to her side of the story: that Lisa had been staying with her in the days leading up to the wedding. And that she too, had waited with Lisa outside the church for Jackson to arrive. She would do anything for Lisa. They had known each other since their time at Children's First Class Catering. In Hannah's mind, they were the best of friends, the closest of friends - it was her duty to look after her soul mate.

The police accepted her statement without investigation.

In truth Hannah was vulnerable. Too trusting. She lived by herself. She needed Lisa's friendship. And she looked up to her. And all the times that Lisa had asked Hannah to cover for her, she had not once questioned why. Not to Lisa, nor to herself.

****

A week after Jackson disappeared, Jackson's mother and father came to see Lisa. It was now clear to everyone that their son *had* gone missing…that he hadn't just panicked and stormed off somewhere to get his head together.

They were very comforting to the distraught bride. They liked Lisa. They'd not met her that many times, considering how long she'd been going out with Jackson, but she had always come across as charming and free spirited - a good person for their son.

At first they were a bit put out at not having been told about or invited to their son's wedding, but that emotion was quickly made redundant by the fear that something terrible had happened to him.

Harry arrived just as they were leaving. They chatted for a while on the doorstep. Jackson's mother asked him how he knew their son. His reply was vague and unspecific: *Through a friend of a friend. We just seemed to hit it off.* She didn't question his answer. She seemed pleased that Jackson had a good friend. Harry didn't tell them that he and

Jackson were brothers. Triplets. That their son had found out he'd been adopted and had met his real father. That...that their son was dead. That was for another day. Or never at all.

82

Friday, 20 September 2019

DI Trish Bond had listened carefully to what Harry and Lisa had said. It had all sounded believable enough. But more than that she was sure that Harry wouldn't lie to her. Then again, she was equally sure that anything was possible. She'd observed them, sitting side-by-side on the sofa. She couldn't be certain, but their friendship looked like it was held together by more than just the fact that Harry was Jackson's brother. And as that notion took root, the detective in her instinctively and clinically computed the facts: that to murder someone for love was second only to greed in the sad and disturbing list of motives that lie behind such a violent crime. Could Harry have had something to do with his brother's disappearance? It seemed totally preposterous. So preposterous that she felt guilty for having allowed herself to think such a thing. She threw it out...Jackson was a missing person...nothing more...nothing less...except...

...she'd not thrown it out far enough.

Love.

She'd seen what it could do to others: impair judgement - make a person believe the insane is sane; the absurd is reasonable; *and*...that something which is clearly wrong is right.

She focused on her gut feeling...that Harry looked spooked. She would have to dig deeper...find out more about Lisa Hopkins. But away from prying eyes. Investigating the potential love interest of a fellow cop, outside of the official channels was fraught with danger. Even if it was done with the best of intentions, it could easily be misinterpreted. She would have to operate covertly, because something was telling her that not only did Harry need help, he needed a friend.

****

Tawelfan Cottage

Back at the cottage Lisa and Harry discussed DI Bond's visit. Harry tried to alleviate any fears Lisa had that his boss would take the matter any further. *It's a missing persons case and that's how it will remain. Everything will be fine.*

Lisa wasn't listening.

She was in her own world.

She had seen that DI Bond was sharp. That she had picked up on things. And that Harry was losing his ability to focus. He was weakening - becoming unsteady, panicky.

She would have to do something about Harry.

83

Friday, 13 September 2019
Tawelfan Cottage

Harry was stood by the inglenook fireplace.

It was 2.10am.

He was dressed to go outside.

Lisa looked at him.

It was time.

Harry gave Lisa an unconvincing nod.

He turned around, put the palms of his hands on the wall above the fireplace and bowed his head. He sighed. He wondered how it had got to this. Everything seemed like an effort. To concentrate, to focus, to feel human...they all had to be summoned.

He returned at 3.35am.

He had buried his brother.

Deep in the woods.

They would not find Jackson Brown.

He was sure of that.

Except...

The guilt.

How could he bury the guilt?

84

DI Trish Bond
October 2019

DI Bond was sat at her desk.

Harry and Lisa entered her thoughts - they reminded her of the call she was waiting for.

She instinctively glanced at the phone.

Three weeks ago when she'd returned to the office, following her meeting with Harry and Lisa, there had been questions eating away in her mind. So, she made a phone call. A discreet phone call. She needed to find out more about Lisa Hopkins. She was just doing her job. That's what she tried telling herself...keep it all strictly professional. But she couldn't stop her thoughts from being contaminated by emotional content. She just kept seeing Harry's face. It was like he wasn't there – that someone else was occupying his body. She needed some answers. That's why she'd called Mickey Maguire. But for now, all she could do was sit and wait. Wait for Mickey to get back to her. Wait for information.

She returned her thoughts to the present. She looked at her computer. She'd been thinking about the *Poppy Killer* case.

There was still no indication of who had sent the letter? There was no evidence of hacking, so clearly it had been a hoax. She corrected that supposition in her head...almost certainly it had been a hoax. But why? Who could it have been? She uploaded the

Poppy Killer case notes onto her computer and scrolled through them aimlessly. Maybe, just maybe something would stand out...something would point to a possible perpetrator. Yes, it seemed pointless. But doing something that seemed pointless was different from doing something that *was* pointless. Trish knew that.

She clicked on page after page. Nothing. Click. Nothing. Click. Then...she paused. There was a sub-folder named 'Alison Marchant.' She clicked on it and read the case notes. The eleventh victim that never was. She knew of her, but the memory was vague. She looked for the accompanying photograph but it had been deleted. It aroused the detective in her. She went to the *back room* and retrieved the hard copy. The photograph had been removed. She pondered for a while. Maybe it had been lost years ago? It wouldn't be the first time case notes or evidence had been lost or *accidently* deleted – especially in a case that had been open for years and had been viewed by numerous detectives. She let that explanation sit in her mind – but it felt uncomfortable.

She looked across at Harry's desk. He was out investigating an armed burglary.

So many times over the past few weeks she had thought he was about to open up to her. He'd start to talk about things. About Lisa. He'd say how hard it had hit her. That she was struggling to cope. Trish couldn't help but think he was referring to himself. And she knew he was trying to protect her, cover for

her. But why? She was back to the notion of love. Love. *That damn thing called love*. She looked at his empty chair. She thought maybe he was in denial; his brother was missing...his state of well-being unknown. It must be affecting him; that he'd not gone after him...stopped him; yet he seemed almost ambivalent as to whether Jackson was alive or not. This worried Trish. This worried her a lot.
She looked back at the computer screen.

She was just about to type the words *Alison...Marchant...Poppy...Killer,* into *Google* when her phone rang. There had been a murder. Domestic. The boyfriend was being held at the scene of the crime. She replaced the receiver and reflected for a moment. She looked at the screen. She thought about the *Google* search. Then she shook her head, pressed *shut down* and left the office.

Just over 3 months later, Harry went missing.

PART 10

85

The Poppy Killer - Tenth Victim
Friday, 14 September 2001

The *Poppy Killer* was back at Tawelfan cottage. It was approaching 1.30 in the morning.

With his tenth victim locked in the cage he returned outside to close the van door.

At that moment, he felt something. He wasn't sure what. Just a feeling. He looked around. The trees, the darkness. Everything, and nothing.

He walked back to the cottage, took one last look out into the night sky, then closed the door...oblivious to the fact that someone had been tracking his movements. Oblivious to the fact that his next victim - his eleventh - would be his last.

86

Alison

Her bedroom door opens. She feels numb. Too numb to be afraid. She can see the man, he's wearing her father's face. She doesn't believe it's really him. It's an imposter. She prepares herself. She lets her mind take her to another place. A place where it's not really happening. He moves towards her. A shadow falls. Then darkness fills the room.

****

"It was all so confusing, the brutal abusing
He'd hurt her, never say why, then apologize
Be daddy's good girl, don't tell mommy a thing
And tell the people who ask you fell off the swing"

****

Alison Marchant grew up in Brierley Hill, south of Dudley, in late 80's, early 90's Britain. There was a vague awareness of her turbulent home life. People would always mouth the words...*her father*, as if subliminally saying the thing that couldn't be said...or couldn't be talked about. Child abuse. It created a pernicious silence. Which meant that whatever was happening to Alison was reduced to the pithiness of hearsay. Because Alison never opened up as to the real cause of her pain...her mental and physical pain.

It was as if she felt she was to blame in some way. That if she talked about it, it would bring shame on her and her mother. Consequently she was passed between the school and Social Services, with neither taking on the responsibility of offering her the proper help and support she needed. As a result, her troubled mind was left to grow unattended to.

87

Monday, 17 February 1997

Alison would often be late for school. She'd feel terrible – physically and mentally.

There was one occasion – a Monday morning – thirty minutes after the bell had sounded, when, as she walked through the school gates, she noticed a van arriving. Her mind was prone to attaching itself to any distraction, especially on the days when *it* happened, so she followed the vehicle round to the kitchen block at the rear of the school. She stood on the pavement adjacent to the nearby sports hall and watched as a man unloaded crates of food from the van and took them into the store room next to the kitchen. She was transfixed.

The clouds opened up.

It was February 17th 1997...she stood alone in the rain...at the back of the school...the Grange Comprehensive School, Stourbridge.

For a brief moment the man looked across at her.

He held his stare for no more than a couple of seconds.

****

Nobody had ever been interested in Alison, that's what she believed. Her father hated her; her mother hated herself, the teachers pitied her; her fellow pupils never understood her.

Her life was dismantling…bit by bit.

Until that day…the day she saw the man with the van…the brief seconds of eye contact that went by in slow motion.

It was such an insignificant moment. Observed and absorbed by no one other than Alison. Yet it would change her for ever. He had acknowledged her for who she was. That's what she believed. And now, suddenly Alison had a purpose in life. A meaning in life. Something that she could channel all her energy into. An outlet for her suppressed mind. A mind that was highly intelligent. A mind that was waiting….waiting to bloom into the wild flowers of obsession.

A few weeks later, Alison was late again. It was a Monday so she decided to make her way to the kitchen block at the rear of the school. This time she hid out of sight behind the large wheelie bins. And she watched, as the man with the van went about unloading the food. Soon she had forgotten her troubles and the only emotion she felt was a sense of being alive.

Shortly after he departed she was just about to make her way to the classroom, when she saw two of the dinner ladies coming out of the kitchen. They stood away from the entrance and lit up. Alison recognised one them, her name was Rita, she had been at the school for years. The other lady, as far as Alison knew, had recently started. She could just about make out what they were saying. Rita was doing all the talking. And it soon became clear to

Alison that they were talking about the man with the van. And that's when Alison first heard his name...William Marshall. And she overheard one other thing...that in the mid 1980's William used to date one of the dinner ladies. A girl called Julie. Apparently, according to Rita, she died giving birth; what's strange said Rita is that the school were given no other details and no one from the Grange was invited to her funeral. And the man with the van, William Marshall, he has never spoken about it to anyone at the school since that day...the day Julie died.

88

September 1997

There was talk that Alison's father had upped sticks and moved to another area, but no one was sure where or why. They were just glad he'd gone away. And on the outside Alison had started to show a different side to her personality. People liked the new Alison. Primarily because they didn't have to worry so much about what to say to her...domestic abuse was a subject most people preferred to avoid.

They started to embrace the new Alison because she had an ethereal warmth to her – a natural gravitational pull. And with it, Alison started to discover how her own behaviour affected the way people reacted to her, the way they viewed her. And she started to use this to her advantage. It was never manipulative, not in Alison's mind. It just felt right.

89

Alison

Alison left school when she was 16. She had no desire to remain in education.

She had a goal...an idée fixe...William Marshall.

In November 1998 she got an admin job for a Catering company in Birmingham. She and another girl - Hannah Wasserstein who had started 6 months earlier - worked for the CEO: Jack Hoffmann.

In addition to the administration team the company also employed another 30 workers: mostly buyers, packers, drivers and salesmen. Alison and Hannah kept all the paper work in order; this involved a variety of administrative tasks from basic HR related duties (responsible for all things staff-related) to ensuring all the ledgers were checked and balanced for the end-of-year accounting and tax returns.

Intellectually, it was way below what Alison was capable of, but she liked the job. It allowed her to feed her growing obsession without distraction.

It was very rare for the company operatives to venture into the admin office. There was no need. The sales team would get the orders; the buyers would order the produce; the packers would load the vans and the drivers would deliver the orders to the schools. All this activity took place on either the shop floor or out on the road. When the drivers returned they would leave the refrigerated vans with the packers who would ensure they were clean and ready for the next day. A few of the workers would occasionally pop up and say hello to Alison and Hannah, flirt a little. But most of them kept themselves to themselves and very rarely, if ever, did they come into the office. That suited Alison. From her vantage point on the first floor, she could subtly watch the daily activities taking place. She could see the drivers arriving and leaving. She was able to observe things. Observe life. Observe people. Especially one person.

90

Alison

Alison had obsessed about him ever since she'd first seen him in the late winter of 1997. Now she saw him from a distance, on Mondays, the day he worked. Just briefly in the morning and then again in the afternoon, but always out of sight.

Now she felt like she needed more. The drug she had administered to herself when she first joined the Birmingham based company - Children's First Class Catering - was starting to wear off. She needed a bigger hit.

She had access to his personal file. And she'd found out a lot about him. She knew his address. She knew he lived alone. She just wanted to be a part of his life.

Stealth mode.

But how?

She hated the term stalker. She knew what it meant. Stalkers were sad, desperate people with no control over their emotions. Alison was in total control. That's how she felt.

It was late 2000 when she first got the idea. It wouldn't be harassment. There would be no crazed, self-obsessed letters, no phone calls, no direct contact. This would be something very different.

She would watch his movements – away from work - from a distance.

Be with him, but never there with him.
Closer to him, but invisible.

91

West Mercia Police Headquarters
Thursday, 30 January 2020

DI Trish Bond looked over at Harrys' empty chair, then she looked up at the clock – 4.00pm. Still no word. It was too early to start phoning around but she could feel it in her bones that something was wrong. Yes, he was a private person, but there was one thing he wasn't – unreliable. So for him not to turn up for work, with no explanation, was unprecedented. She'd requested that a local community support officer call in on him. He'd reported back that his car was parked outside but he'd not answered the door. Add that to the fact his mobile was switched off, meant in Trish's mind that something was definitely wrong.

She weaved different thoughts together. She'd suspected for a while that he was having an affair with Lisa Hopkins – Jackson Brown's *jilted* bride. He'd never said anything and she'd never pressed him on the subject – that was until two weeks ago. Her thoughts coalesced and replayed the video of that evening. It was just after 6.00pm. They were both still at work. It had, up to that point, been like any normal day – if you can class any day as normal in the police force. She heard him shuffle in his chair. She looked up. Then suddenly, as if his whole personality had been hijacked, he asked her if she would like to go out for a drink with him. Trish had been stunned. So stunned that she'd felt an immediate compulsion to say ‘yes.’ And then straight away she had tried to convince herself that it was purely for professional reasons. That he needed help. And maybe, just maybe, he was going to open up to her. Tell her what was really going on. But there was another reason she’d said *yes*...and no matter how hard she tried, she was unable to stop it from entering her head. Harry and herself. She could feel herself blushing. Then her embarrassment turned to sadness as she looked over at his empty chair. She put the thought away and returned to the memories of that evening, two weeks ago....as they walked into the pub. The Plough and Harrow.

92

Thursday, 16 January 2020

Trish and Harry were sat in the Plough and Harrow, which was a couple of miles away from their HQ, on the outskirts of Worcester. There was a pub around the corner – walking distance from work, but they didn't want to go there. They didn't want to be the source of fake news for the gossipmongers.

They were both driving so Harry kept to a half-pint of bitter and Trish had a small glass of red wine. The atmosphere in the pub was convivial. Friendly with just the right level of background chatter to drown out their conversation, but not so loud that they would have to shout at one another in order to be heard.

Trish looked over at Harry. There was a closeness to their situation that went beyond proximity, but it was shielded by the disturbed and troubled look in his eyes.

To start with they chatted about nothing much at all.

Then the conversation faltered.

Trish felt a strange inertia descend over their table.

She noticed Harry glance towards the door as if he was trying to find an entry point to the jumble of emotions in his mind.

They both looked down at their drinks.

Trish felt compelled to break through the ice.

'Are you alright Harry?'

Harry took a sip of his beer. He let it sit in his mouth.

He was fighting with himself. Willing himself to talk, while cautioning himself to hold back...not to say anything he would regret.

The taste of the ale seemed to settle his mind.

He gulped it back.

He was ready.

'Did you ever feel when we were younger...just starting out in the force...the world seemed unsteady, but we always managed to prevent the lens from shaking - we always managed to get a clear picture.'

Trish wasn't sure if it was a question or a statement.

Harry looked down at the table. He picked up his glass as if it was a portal to another time.

'I used to look out of the window and see the truth. You know, the window in your mind. The view may not have always been a picture post card, but it was the truth nevertheless.'

He gazed vacantly around the room.

'Then I started to see faces. Empty, formless shapes. Like I was holding up a mirror to myself. Then one day, just like that, the view was clear. And the world seemed a different place. Brighter. And it didn't seem to matter if I was looking at the truth or lies. It just seemed right.'

He took an empty sip of his beer.

He put his glass down and shook his head.

'It seems as you get older things become blurred - you can't see the sharpness of vision that you used to take for granted. And then...' He stopped mid sentence and looked straight ahead – as if Trish wasn't there. Like the memories required his own space. Then he picked up his glass and moved it onto a different beer mat, as if prompting his mind to change tack. There was a long silence. Trish hovered over her wine. She knew what her role was in the context of that moment: to listen, to nod and not to interrupt. Long silences were all part of the process. 'And then one day you realise you are living a lie and the truth has got buried, lost even, within the deep layers of the lies. ' He paused. His eyes glazed over. Trish felt an incredible sense of desolation in his silence. 'I believed in myself...once; that my way was the right way. It didn't matter if I didn't get the promotion I deserved; it's what I believed in that mattered. And as long as I was authentic; true to myself...I could live with that.'

His posture seemed to sink a few inches.

'But now I'm not so sure who I am...what I want. I feel like one of my father's magic tricks; like I've gone into a box and disappeared; I'm still out there.' He shook his head. 'But all people can see is the empty box.'

He looked at Trish as if he was waiting for her to respond, but then he quickly finished his drink and asked her if she would like another one. She declined. She still had most of her wine left. He returned with a glass of sparkling water. Trish was about to speak but she could see he was ready to continue.

He took a deep breath.

'You know don't you...you know about me and Lisa, I can tell.'

Trish nodded.

'How long have you known?'

Trish didn't answer. She looked around. People were deep in conversation. She watched them talk - inaudible chatter. She thought to herself that you never really know what's going on in people's lives. She looked back towards Harry.

'I never...' Harry shook his head and sighed. '...it just happened. It's a cliché but it's true. Two people...lost...finding a common ground in their emptiness.' He sipped on his water. 'I love her, and...and I try to convince myself I'm happy, but deep down, deep down I know I'm not. That I've never been happy with Lisa. I mean, is that possible, to love someone without ever feeling happy?'

Trish stared into her red wine.

She knew there was no definitive answer. That in matters of love there was no absolute right or wrong, only perceptions of right or wrong.

She let the question drift off into the background chatter.

Harry picked up his glass and swished the sparking water around anticlockwise as if rewinding a thought.

'Do you know what I see now.' Trish gave a faint shake of her head. 'A world that has been turned inside out...but...but it doesn't matter anymore...it doesn't matter what I see...because it's too late.'

Trish straightened up.

'Too late for what Harry?'

Two men were sat nearby. The man facing Trish had a Paddington cap on. It looked slightly odd on him, as if he was wearing it out of a sense of duty – like he'd been given it as a present. He was laughing and Trish noticed how happy he looked. At that moment his gaze wandered slightly and fixed in on Trish. He smiled at her. She was taken by how piercing his pale blue eyes were. She quickly turned back to Harry. The corners of his mouth had curled upwards. An ironic smile. The smile of a man who felt no joy. The smile of a man who found no comfort in what he was saying or what he was about to say.

'Too late to close the blinds…too late to look away…too late to comprehend the truth,' he said.

'Harry?'

Harry's expression paused for a moment.

'Are you in trouble?'

Harry knew the answer. But he was still struggling to accept it. He recalled what his father had said to him shortly before he died: *love is a wonderful friend, but an evil master.* He'd never really been sure what he'd meant – as if his words were to be stored and understood at a later date. But now he knew. He'd followed a road, unaware of where it would lead. He'd been driven by desires; desires that had been consumed by the journey; so much so that he'd never taken the time to think about what might happen. He had been overpowered. And at that moment, sitting in the pub with his boss, the reality of his situation suddenly hit him. He couldn't involve Trish. Lisa was too strong. He was on his own.

He raised his defences.

‘I’m sorry...’ Trish went to interrupt him but he held up his hand. ‘No please.’ He lowered his hand. ‘I’ve been talking like…like…’ He looked around as if searching for the right words. ‘I guess…I guess I just can’t work it out…maybe it’s me, I don’t know.’ He paused. Trish widened her eyes and nodded for him to continue. He looked straight through her and in that moment she saw a crushing sadness in his face.

He finished his glass of sparkling water, then looked at Trish’s glass. She let it sit there with one sip left.

‘I should go.’ He glanced at the door. ‘Thank you.’

‘What for?’

He let his eyes answer the question.

‘Harry…’

He shook his head. Then stood up.

Trish sighed.

She looked down at her glass. It felt unfinished, but she knew it was no use. She picked it up.

As they walked back to their respective cars Trish thought about Lisa Hopkins. From the moment she’d first met her she’d had an uneasy feeling about her. That she was a manipulator. But it wasn’t just that, there was something else about her, something she couldn’t put her finger on.

When they reached Trish’s car, Harry paused. There was a fleeting moment of ambiguity. Then Harry turned around and started to walk away.

Trish felt compelled. She had to try one more time to reach him.

'Maybe you *don't* love her.' Harry stopped in his tracks. 'There is a difference between needing someone and loving someone Harry – a big difference. Needing someone comes from a different place – maybe that's why you've not found happiness? Needs can be destructive. You've seen that in our line of work just as much as I have.'

Harry smiled wryly to himself, then turned back around. He looked into Trish's eyes. It stirred something inside of him; a feeling. It was faint; it was transient; but it was there and for a split second he was almost tempted to kiss her, but he knew she could not save him. And it would only make matters worse.

'Do you know something Trish.' Her face straightened. 'All this…all this is the result of my search…for my birth father. At the time…God it seems so long ago…but at the time it seemed like such a good idea. My adoptive father had died. It was curiosity. A distraction from work. How could I have ever known what it would uncover?'

Alarm bells sounded in Trish's head.

'What did it uncover Harry?'

Harry flinched.

'Jackson, Lisa, me, we're all scarred.'

Trish's mind was racing.

'I don't understand what you're saying Harry.'

'There is no way to understand it.'

'You need to stop talking in riddles Harry. You need to tell me the truth.'

'The truth can never be told.'

'*Harry.*'

'He died. My birth father. He went off to Europe, no one knows where. No one knows what really happened to him. All he left was everything you would want to forget. But it can't be forgotten. It will never be forgotten.

'We're all damaged goods, but Lisa, she's sanded down everything…to the point where you can't see any of the imperfections. Everything is hidden. All the damage is tucked away out of sight. And I love her for the person she is…and that's why I can never be happy with her. Because the person she is, is the person she isn't.'

'Harry, what are you saying? It doesn't make any sense. You've got to come clean with me.'

Harry shook his head and gave Trish an uneasy smile.

'I'll see you tomorrow,' he said.

He walked away, leaving Trish with a disturbing knot in her stomach. She got into her car. As she drove home she tried to read between the lines, to find the meaning behind his words. There was so much hidden. What had he uncovered? What can't be forgotten? Why can the truth never be told? Why are they all damaged goods…Harry, Jackson, Lisa? Was he talking on an emotional level or something else? She went over all the things she should have asked him. But she knew it was a futile exercise, because if she had pried, if she had pushed him, he would have backed away. *Be patient,* she kept telling herself. *Be patient. He'll open up when he's ready. He's a good cop…a good man. He'll find his way back.* She hoped. But she wasn't confident.

93

West Mercia Police Headquarters
Friday, 31 January 2020

DI Trish Bond was sat in her office.

Harry had been missing for 36 hours.

She was feeling restless.

She stood up and paced around.

She was thinking back to a few months ago when she'd been looking through the *Poppy Killer* files. She'd noticed the photograph of Alison Marchant was missing. Sometime after, she can't remember exactly when, she'd asked Harry about it. At the time his answer had seemed perfectly reasonable - that he had wondered the same thing - what had happened to the photograph? Trish had let it rest at that...there had been more pressing things to be getting on with. But now, as she replayed that moment in her mind, she remembered something else - it was a split second thing, but now she could see it in slow motion. His eyes had shot a glance at the top hat on his desk.

She stopped.

She looked curiously at the top hat.

He'd explained to her the history behind it. That his father had been a magician; it had been his most favourite prop. Made of silk. He'd told her it had originally been used by a famous magician who'd performed in the early part of the 20th century. But she couldn't remember his name. She picked it up. She wondered where the magic part was - the hidden compartment. All magic hats had one - she was sure of that - that's why they were called magic hats. She prodded and poked around for a while until, purely by accident she activated the collapsing mechanism. And there inside the secret compartment was a photograph.

It was a picture of a girl. Her heart skipped a beat...it was Lisa Hopkins. More youthful looking, longer hair...but it was definitely her. She was puzzled. She understood his need for secrecy, but why had Harry chosen to keep a much younger-looking photograph of Lisa Hopkins?

Before she'd had chance to consider a possible explanation, the answer leapt out at her. On the back of the photograph was a name: Alison Marchant.

It was glaringly obvious now. And for a moment DI Trish Bond was annoyed with herself for not having made the connection earlier. Especially after what Harry had told her two weeks ago, about Lisa...that she hid everything. But she knew she was being hard on herself. Without the photograph – why should she have made the connection? She remembered the moment when she discovered it was missing – she'd been about to look up Alison Marchant on the Internet, but she'd been interrupted. A murder as far as she could recall. Some hapless boyfriend. She held back a silent curse...if she hadn't been interrupted maybe she could have helped Harry. Prevented whatever has happened to him from happening.

Lisa Hopkins had certainly covered her tracks well...Harry was right about that. Trish wondered what else she was hiding – the eleventh victim that wasn't - maybe she was the eleventh victim that was? She was letting her thoughts run away from her. She needed to take a step back.

It was approaching lunchtime. She decided to get some air.

An hour later having distracted her mind with a nondescript sandwich and an insipid cup of tea she was back in her office with a clearer head.

For the rest of the afternoon she delved back into the life of Alison Marchant. Looking at information in the files and on the internet; research that revealed that in 2005 Alison Marchant left her home village to start afresh. Then references to her life after that all but dropped off the radar.

She tried to think logically. Alison Marchant went missing for over 50 days. It eventually transpired that she'd had some form of nervous breakdown. A time-bomb that had been ticking inside of her; suppressed memories of her abusive father that had suddenly exploded in her mind.

Then Alison, in starting afresh, must have, at some point, moved somewhere near to Ludlow, under the name of Lisa Hopkins. And that's how she'd met Jackson Brown. It seemed plausible. Then Harry - from his own investigations into his birth parents - finds Jackson, his brother. And the two are reunited. Then on his wedding day Jackson has a break down and decides he can't go through with it and leaves…disappears. Another missing person. Harry comforts the grieving bride and they end up in a relationship. And now Harry has gone AWOL.

Trish looked inquiringly at Harry's top hat as if willing it to reveal one more secret. Yes, she thought to herself, all of that could have happened. People go missing all the time and coincidences are common place. But what if there was something much more sinister going on? She knew she was in danger of putting two and two together and getting five. That she might try and force out an explanation that was neither true nor provable. She turned and looked at the door. If only Harry would walk through it. She would be a lot more vigorous in her questioning of him this time. Tough love. Not that she was in love with him. She'd never loved a man before, but she did like him. Just a little. The door remained closed. An eerie silence filled her mind. And just at that moment the phone rang, making her jump.

'DI Bond?'

'Yes.'

'It's Mickey Maguire.'

She'd been waiting to hear from him.

She'd contacted him last September, following her first meeting with Lisa Hopkins.

She knew Harry used his services. That their arrangement was a mutually beneficial one. All detectives had their 'unofficial' channels; it was part of the official unwritten culture.

She'd told Mickey Maguire to look into Lisa Hopkins. She'd had the feeling that whatever was wrong with Harry, Lisa Hopkins had something to do with it.

Just routine stuff she'd told him, knowing that he wouldn't believe her. He'd reminded Trish that he and

Harry were *friends*; that they went back a long way. She knew there was some truth to his exaggeration, but when she remained silent, she knew he understood – not to ask questions. And more importantly, she knew she could trust him. She hadn't wanted the rest of the police station to know - and she especially hadn't wanted Harry to know - that she was investigating Lisa Hopkins. That's why she'd contacted Mickey Maguire – she knew it would remain strictly between the two of them.

'Mr Maguire…I hope you've got something for me?'

'Sorry it's taken so long. I've been extremely busy. It seems like there is a virus of distrust spreading around the nation. Not that I'm complaining; business is business. But hey, Lisa Hopkins. Now, *there's* a story. Are you sitting comfortably?'

'One moment.' Trish popped her head out of the door and shouted for a coffee. Then she settled down to listen to Mickey Maguire.

'Go on.'

'She's a bunny boiler.'

94

West Mercia Police Headquarters
Friday, 31 January 2020

There was a knock on the door.

'Hold on a second.' DI Bond said down the phone.

A young boy dressed as a police constable handed her a cup of coffee. She thanked him, shut the door, sat down and shook her head.

She took a sip of her coffee, shook her head again and picked up the receiver.

'Take me through what you've found out.'

Trish heard Mickey Maguire take a deep breath.

'At first I was getting nowhere. Lisa Hopkins was not a social media enthusiast. So I focused on the lead you gave me, Hannah Wasserstein. The girl Lisa had been staying with before the wedding. That lead proved invaluable, even though the contact details you'd given me for her were wrong. Don't you check up on these things?'

Silence.

'I figured it wouldn't be hard to find someone with the name Hannah Wasserstein. At first there was nothing. Then I found a Hannah Wasserstein working for a company called Children's First Class Catering in Birmingham. They deliver food to schools. So I phoned up the company and bingo...she answered the phone. As soon as I mentioned the name Lisa Hopkins I knew she was our girl. At first she denied knowing her but when I mentioned the wedding and spun her a line about how she'd broken the law by giving false information, her defences cracked and she got herself into a right pickle. Said she suffered from panic attacks. She ended up transferring me to the CEO: Jack Hoffmann. Turns out Lisa Hopkins was not Lisa Hopkins back then. Get this…she was Alison Marchant. And I checked it out. She was the same Alison Marchant that had been headline news in 2003, when, for a while it was thought she had been abducted by the *Poppy Killer*, that she was his eleventh victim.'

Mickey Maguire waited for the sound of astonishment from DI Trish Bond. There was nothing. He rustled his notes in frustration before continuing.

'She left First Class Catering in 2004, just before she changed her name. Jack Hoffmann was very complimentary about her. Good worker; she got on well with everyone. *Deceptively intelligent* was the phrase he used. Anyway, he didn't hear from her for a couple of years. Then in 2006 she phoned to tell him she'd changed her name and that he may receive a reference request in the name of Lisa Hopkins.'

'And did he?'

'Yes, and I persuaded him to dig it out.'

Mickey tilted his head towards the receiver.

Still no praise.

He continued.

'Which was fortunate because without it the trail may have gone cold. He was very helpful, Mr Hoffmann, very helpful. If only everyone was as…'

'What happened then Mickey?'

Trish's abrupt interruption caused Mickey's posture to straighten and his arm tensed up ever so slightly. Then he looked back down at his notes and just as quickly he relaxed.

'This is when it gets interesting. She gets a job at a company called Fab Textiles in Shrewsbury which is about 30 miles north of Ludlow. Well, in 2009 she leaves this job under a cloud. To begin with the owner was reluctant to reveal any more than that, but I soon charmed my way into his confidence.'

Mickey paused.

He listened.

He heard the sound of coffee being slurped.

He looked at the receiver and shook his head.

'At first he thought she was a breath of fresh air – slightly weird but in an ethereal way...fascinating, exciting, mysterious. But then she became dark, obsessive, humourless and unhinged. They were all *his* words, not mine.'

'But why did she leave?'

'He didn't say, but things will become clearer. That was just the beginning.'

'Next, she turns up at Minster Carpets in Kidderminster. Excuse me a sec.' Trish could hear the slightly muffled voice of Mickey Maguire telling his PA, Aurora to hang up on *him*. 'Sorry about that. Some people won't take *no* for an answer. Anyway, where was I?...oh, yes...it was a similar MO. She started well and then things gradually started to change.'

'What's the time frame Mickey?'

'November 2009 to 2012. It was roughly the same time period with each job. I pressed the proprietor. A man named, believe it or not, John Pile.' He shook the phone as if willing it to laugh. Silence. He continued. 'And he admitted to having had an affair with Lisa Hopkins. He was very open about it. I think he thought I was a therapist, not a private detective.'

Mickey didn't wait for a response to that quip.

'He said she became and I quote a *crazy lady*. He wouldn't go into details but mentioned harassment. He said, in the end, she just left. He was glad to see the back of her. Six months later he received a reference request.'

'Did he give her a reference?'

'Yes, he said he was afraid not to. In case she caused a fuss. Made things difficult for him at home.'

'And let me guess, much the same thing happened at the next job.'

'You've got it.'

There was an unplanned but coordinated break in proceedings as Trish Bond dealt with an enquiry on her mobile while Mickey Maguire told Aurora to hang up on *him* again.

With distractions dealt with, their conversation continued.

'So what happened next?'

'This time she turns up in Worcester. She never played at home...never got a job in Ludlow. Probably didn't want her dirty laundry displayed all over town; especially, as I'm guessing her extracurricular activities were not a topic of conversation at home. Anyway, she's now with Champions Trophy Makers.

All her roles were admin based. Book work, low level accounting, that sort of thing. This time I spoke to Dan Ottewell. The company was a partnership. He said exactly the same thing as the others: to start with you couldn't have asked for a better employee; everyone warmed to her odd eccentricity. But then and excuse my French, things went tits-up. She had an affair with his business partner, Mark Cook. All was fine until he tried to cool things between them. Then he started seeing a different side to her personality. She went mental...as he put it. Started phoning him at all hours. Then, just when he thought he might have to call the police, she left...3 years after she'd started, in 2015.'

His voice goes quasi-muffled again. *Aurora, what are you doing?...he said what!...look, I'm sure he didn't mean it...I'll sort it out when I'm done here.* There was a long pause, as if Mickey was waiting to see if Aurora had calmed down...making sure she was okay. Trish wondered to herself what the real Mickey Maguire was like; the one that hid behind his private eye alter ego.

'Sorry about that. There are some *real* weirdos out there.' Trish smiled. 'Now we have déjà vu. Reference request. Owner too scared not to reply. Lisa Hopkins moves on unabated. It makes you wonder how much you can trust a reference these days.

'Anyway, exactly the same thing. Nice, vulnerable, slightly dotty Lisa turns into psychotic unhinged Lisa.'

'So she had another affair...with the business owner?'

'Bullseye. Mr Albert Bayliss of Bayliss Shoemakers in Hereford. Apparently they are a trusted name in bespoke footwear. Sounds like a load of cobblers to me.'

Mickey held his breath.

There was a deathly stillness on the line.

He wondered to himself if Trish had had a sheltered upbringing.

'I mean, you couldn't write it. Four jobs, each lasting approximately 3 years and four affairs – all with the owners. She was consistent if nothing else.'

'What happened with Mr Bayliss?'

'She was gaining in psychotic confidence. The guy broke down on the phone. Said that when he ended the affair she totally changed. She started blackmailing him. He thought he was going to lose everything. His business, his wife, his kids. She started stalking him at his home. And...' he paused. '...these were his words...*she was like Glen Close, from that film, Fatal Attraction. A right bunny boiler.*'

Trish Bond shuddered. She hated that term...the way it was used to bully women into passivity. To suppress their empowerment. To stifle their independence. It allowed for the creation of a stereotype that was both judge and jury before the evidence had been heard. Mickey Maguire may or may not have been right about Lisa Hopkins. And Trish knew herself, that she had already made judgements about her. But by Mickey using that term...*Bunny Boiler*, it made Trish feel uncomfortable and it made her realise that she had to temper her assumptions about Lisa Hopkins, not become the judge and jury. Not until she knew the truth. The absolute truth.

'So what happened?'

Mickey looked over to Aurora. She was no longer on the phone. She was busy flicking through a file. She looked calm. Contented. Mickey felt a warmth in his stomach.

'Just like all the other jobs...she suddenly left...in October 2018. He's not heard from her since. The poor guy's voice was shaking. He was clearly traumatised by the whole thing.'

There was silence.

'Hello?'

Trish was mulling over what she'd just heard. All those affairs. Had Jackson known about them? Maybe he'd found out - before the wedding? That's why he'd not gone through with it? But then again, he could have been totally oblivious to everything. Trish knew of men, police officers included, who'd had affairs - *were* having affairs - and their partners were totally unaware. They seemed to be able to turn their home life and their 'affair life' on and off at will. Switching from one persona to the other in a seamless set of coordinated deceptions. She shook her head as if to clear that thought from her mind. But it came rebounding back. Had Harry been just another one of Lisa's affairs? Had she turned on him? Had she caused him to run away from everything?

'DI Bond?'

'Yes, I'm here. Thank you...thank you Mickey. That has been invaluable.'

'Is Harry there? I've not heard from him for a while. There's something I need to ask him. You know…a favour.'

'Yes, I know how it works Mickey, but he's not here.'

'Oh…err…can you tell him…'

'Mickey, you must keep this to yourself. Do you understand?'

'DI Bond, if I didn't understand, I'd be out of business.'

'Of course.'

She paused. There was something about Mickey that she didn't particularly like, but she trusted him.

'DI Bond?'

She was thinking of Harry. Snippets of what he'd said in the pub entered her mind. Stuff about his birth father. It had all started when he began his search for him. That's what Harry had said. She wondered what he'd meant by the phrase *it had all started*.

And the other stuff…*we're all damaged goods*. As if it was his birth father, not Lisa that was…that had been the problem. What was it about his birth father? She wanted to ask Mickey about what he'd uncovered but she knew he wouldn't break his client confidentiality relationship, no matter what the circumstances. But she was going to ask him all the same.

'But first there is something I need to ask you. I know you can't tell me everything. But just answer this one question. When you found out about Harry's birth father. Was there anything that seemed odd? Alarming maybe?'

'Is there something wrong?'

'I'm not sure yet.'

'Is he in danger?'

'I'm not sure....do you have *anything* for me Mickey?'

'I found out his last known address, that's all. I'm trying to find out what happened to him, where he's buried, but everywhere I look is a dead end.'

'And the address?'

'A cottage near Ludlow, I can't remember the exact address. Do you want me to look it up?'

Every hair on Trish's body stood up. She forced herself to remain calm.

'No. You've been most helpful.'

'So, what about Harry?'

'He may have gone missing. It's not been made public yet, make sure it stays that way.'

Trish Bond replaced the receiver and sat back in her chair. She looked around the room. At Harry's desk, at the window, at the half-empty cup of cold coffee. She sighed. It was time for her to pay Lisa Hopkins another visit. This time she was determined to get to the bottom of what was going on. She logged out, picked up her keys and left.

An hour and a half later she was driving up the lane that led to Tawelfan cottage. The cottage she now knew was Harry's birth father's last known address. Had he owned it? Did he leave it to Jackson? What must Harry have thought? Jackson had the cottage; Jackson had Lisa. Then Jackson goes missing...the last person to speak to him was Harry. And now...Harry has Lisa; maybe he'll inherit the cottage? A horrible feeling welled up inside of Trish. A feeling that she desperately hoped was misplaced.

She parked up and looked around.

Then she closed her eyes.

Focus, focus, focus.

When she opened them she saw Lisa Hopkins standing at the front door. And a very strange sensation surged through her body.

95

Alison
2000

Alison's obsession - William Marshall - had become a part of her - the norm. As normal as the beat of her heart. Constantly there, in the background, keeping her alive. It meant she could slip in and out of her life with effortless ease. And so no one knew the real Alison Marchant. It gave her a sense that anything was possible. No matter how irrational it was.

So it was that in late 2000 a light went on in her head. She read an article in the Sunday Times Magazine about the emergence of the global positioning system (GPS). It consisted of a network of satellites orbiting the planet, beaming down signals to anyone on earth with a GPS tracking device. The article made reference to how the system had grown rapidly since 1994 when it had first gone fully functional. And over the past few years the application of the GPS had been applied to vehicle tracking. Mainly fleet tracking, but devices were being developed that allowed individuals to track the location of their own vehicles...for security, as well as mapping.

Over the next few months she researched tracking devices. The technology was becoming more sophisticated every year. Expensive, but possible to obtain for the early adopters who had the money to spare and the nouse to operate them.

She had the money.
She had the intelligence.
She had the desire.

96

Alison
Children's First Class Catering
Monday, 18 June 2001

It was a Monday like any other Monday.

Other than the packers, who had moved across to the storeroom, most of the workforce were out on business. The delivery drivers, as normal, had arrived early, parked their own vehicles in the company car park and had started on their daily rounds using the Children's First Class Catering refrigerated vans. The sales team and the buyers had been in at 8.00am for a meeting with the boss, Jack Hoffmann and were now out on the road, meeting prospective clients or suppliers.

The mid-morning calm had descended. Alison and Hannah Wasserstein were sat working their way through the usual start-of-the-week admin tasks.

Alison mentioned in passing to Hannah that she was popping out for 5 minutes.

She made her way to the private car park at the back of the building. A secure location. No need for CCTV. The car park was half full. She walked over to the white transit van. She knew it was William Marshall's, the registration of all employee vehicles was kept on file. She looked around. There was no one in sight. She looked up at the beautiful blue sky. Then she crouched down. She took the tracking device out of her pocket. She felt the sun on her face. She traced around the edge of the undercarriage with her hand. She felt for the right spot…the right place to attach the device.

At that moment in her heightened state of arousal her senses felt animated. She could smell the lush grass…grass cuttings left over from his gardening business that had nestled in the back of his van. She could hear the leaves dancing in the trees that lined the street outside: blurred, abstract sounds, but so beautiful; she imagined the orchestra of nature – pitch perfect and heavenly. She touched his car and a warm feeling ran through her body as though she was somehow touching him…William Marshall…her unconditional obsession. It made her feel alive. So alive.

She felt the flat plate magnetic base of the tracking device snap into place underneath the van. Out of sight. She peered through the front window of the vehicle next to William Marshall's. There was still no one around.

She returned to the office.

Hannah looked up, smiled and then continued with her work.

Later that evening, Alison switched on her computer to test the tracking device.

To save battery life she had programmed the device to send a signal every hour.

At first, the application she was using on her computer to monitor the signal kept flashing the message…*error in signal detection.*

She felt deflated.

Hours passed.

She was about to turn off the computer in frustration when it suddenly lit up a map of Ludlow. It was pointing to a location about a mile to the west of the town centre.

Her heart jumped.

She had been told that the signal may not be 100% accurate. Especially if the antenna was having difficulty in picking up or maintaining a satellite signal. There were bigger devices on the market. Bigger antennae's. Allowing for more accuracy. But she'd had to compromise on size in order for the device to fit under William Marshall's van.

But it *was* working. There he was, William... flashing on her screen.

She felt a surge of adrenaline rush through her body.

Up until then the whole scheme had been more an exercise in just doing something. And in truth, she hadn't expected the device to work at all. But that thought hadn't seemed to matter. She just liked doing things in which William was at the forefront of her mind. It felt exciting.

It fed her obsession.

97

Alison
Summer/Autumn 2001

Weeks, months went by.

Nothing much happened.

She discovered William was a creature of habit. On Monday he would drive to Birmingham to do his delivery job. And even though specific parking spaces were not allocated at Children's First Class Catering, he always parked in the same place – furthest away from the back of the building. Then, Tuesday to Friday he was dotted around various locations in Ludlow, working on his gardening business. And other than a short trip into town, 10.00am, every Saturday, which, if the map marker was accurate, was to Tesco, he never went out at weekends or in the evenings. He seemed to have little in the way of a social life. Alison knew he was unmarried. It was on his file. And even though she had no evidence to back up her beliefs, she just knew he was single, unattached...a loner. It's what she wanted to believe. And that's all it took in Alison's mind for it to be the truth.

The tracking device had limited power, therefore every so often she changed the battery. She was always very careful, making sure she was never spotted.

But still nothing much happened.

She was beginning to tire of the exercise. It had lost its sense of excitement. She was starting to think of other things...something different that she could do. Other ways to satisfy her obsession with William Marshall. That was until August 2001. Suddenly, he broke from his normal routine. He started making trips to Coventry. Three visits over the space of one month. Always on a Saturday. Mostly in the evenings, often returning in the early hours of the morning. She couldn't be sure of the accuracy of the map marker, but it was consistently pointing to an area approximately one mile due north of the city centre.

Initially she'd feared he was travelling to see a woman, that he'd found a girlfriend. She was gripped by a terrible sadness. But then, on Saturday, 15 September, following his forth trip to Coventry, she heard on the news that Kevin Kenny, a doorman, had vanished in the early hours of Friday morning. Believed abducted near to an industrial estate on the route he regularly walked home on - just over a mile outside of Coventry city centre. His mobile phone had been found on a quiet country lane two miles from the suspected abduction sight. The press were already calling him the *Poppy Killer's* tenth victim.

Some weeks later she read that the body of Kevin Kenny had been discovered in a remote spot 30 miles from where he'd been abducted. The news came as no surprise to Alison.

98

Tawelfan Cottage
Friday, 31 January 2020

DI Trish Bond and Lisa Hopkins were sat opposite one another. Steam was rising from the two mugs of coffee that were resting on the table between them.

DI Bond looked down at her coffee. *Too hot* she thought to herself. She looked up at Lisa.

'You said when I arrived you'd been expecting me. Why was that?'

'He's gone missing hasn't he?'

Trish didn't answer.

Lisa thought for a moment. She knew Trish would ask her, so she wanted to pre-empt the question.

'I know you know about us,' said Lisa. 'He told me on Wednesday. I was angry with him... but...but it doesn't seem so important now...I was just being silly.'

Lisa looked despairingly at Trish.

'Why don't you tell me what happened Lisa.'

Lisa sighed.

'I'd picked him up...in the afternoon; we'd driven out to the countryside. We'd had a nice time. Romantic.' Lisa's smile got lost in translation. 'Then we drove back here. I was cooking. Nothing special, but it was my treat. In fact the whole day was on me...that's why I was driving. To give him a break from everything. Then later that evening I was going to drop him back home. He couldn't stay, he needed to get up early the next day. Work related stuff. That was fine. I was happy to do the driving for once. So when we got back here he opened a bottle of wine, and that's when the atmosphere started to change. He was doing most of the drinking as I still needed to drive. Then he seemed to drift into a deep melancholy. That's when he told me about the conversation you'd had in the pub. Like I said, I was angry with him, not just because he'd told you about us, but it had taken him two weeks to tell me about your meeting. Then one thing led to another and we had an argument. I ran up the stairs and he quickly followed me. But when he got to the top he seemed to go dizzy, maybe it was the alcohol? Maybe he'd moved too quickly? I don't know. It was like slow motion. He just seemed to fall backwards down the stairs. It was an accident. He was momentarily concussed. When he came round, he seemed disorientated. I tried to calm him down, I tried to stop him, but he just walked out. I expected him to come back...but…'

Lisa started to sob.

'I didn't run after him. Maybe I should have. But I was still angry with him. When he didn't come back I tried phoning, but it went straight onto his voice mail. I thought he must have got a taxi home or something…I could have…should have kept trying, but I was tired and I thought it would be better to let him sleep it off…give him some space.' She reached forward and took a sip of her coffee. '…but just then, when I heard a car approaching, when I saw it was you…I knew. When you've had bad things happen to you all your life you expect the worst. He's not turned up has he...he's gone missing.'

Lisa wiped back her tears. 'First Jackson, now Harry. I can't believe this is happening.'

Trish was fighting with herself not to jump in too soon. She wanted Lisa to fill in the silences.

'Maybe it's a malfunction in their genes or something? Maybe it was pre-programmed to happen?' said Lisa.

'You don't really believe that do you.'

Lisa shook her head.

'Did you know their birth father?'

Lisa's head shot back defensively.

Her tears were gone.

'No, I never met him.'

Trish thought she was lying but she could think of no reason why she would.

'I believe this is where their birth father used to live. Did he own the property?'

'I think so.'

'And Jackson got the cottage, not Harry?'

Lisa nodded.

'Don't you think that's a bit strange?'

'I guess it's difficult to understand what went through their father's mind. And I can only go on what Jackson told me. And he only met him once. I suppose that's why it was never really brought up in conversation. It was a question that could never be answered. So Jackson just seemed to accept it and I never heard Harry mention it. Maybe their father thought Jackson needed it more? He would certainly have been right on that count.'

'What do you mean?'

'Nothing really, I'm just being flippant.'

Trish looked at Lisa disbelievingly.

'Do you know what happened to him – their father?'

'Only that he left for Europe. Suddenly. That he went there to die.'

'Harry said something...about his birth father...that all he left was everything you would want to forget. What do you think he meant by that?'

'As far as I'm aware Harry never met him, so he never discussed him. Not with me at least. Maybe he and Jackson talked about him? I'm not really sure. I guess he was someone who could never be explained...a mystery. Harry certainly never said anything like that to me. Maybe it doesn't mean anything?'

Trish could feel her body tense up.

'But you still think he's alive don't you Lisa.'

Lisa turned her head away.

'Lisa.'

'What difference does it make what I think?'

Lisa felt a sense of unease that Trish was starting to dig a little bit too close to the truth. She needed to get her off the subject of William.

'All I know is what you now know,' said Lisa. 'That they have never found him...they've never found where he's buried. But does that mean he is still alive after all these years?' Lisa shook her head.

Trish thought Lisa's answer, her body language, lacked conviction and she wanted to continue her line of questioning, but she had nothing else to go on. So she let it go.

There was a tense silence.

Lisa made to pick up her coffee, but hesitated, letting her hand rest on the handle of the mug.

'Have you found him yet…Jackson?'

Trish shook her head. She knew Lisa's tactics…she wanted to give herself breathing space. So Trish made an immediate counter-move.

'Why don't you tell me what *really* happened to Harry?'

Lisa rubbed her hands. She looked unnerved. Trish fixated on her. Lisa stood up and moved to the window behind where Trish was sitting.

'You probably didn't…don't approve of our relationship.' Lisa looked at the trees blowing gently in the wind. 'Sometimes life brings people together, not because of love, but because of need…and yes, we needed each other…we didn't need to love one another.'

'Is that how Harry feels?'

'Harry wasn't…' Lisa checked her words. 'I'm sorry, I don't know why, but it feels like he's gone. Like he's already in the past. I think I'm just a bit freaked out by everything.' Lisa composed herself. 'To answer your question, Harry's not very good at talking about his feelings. Most of the time you have to interpret them.'

Trish silently acknowledged Lisa's words.

She stood up and looked around. Her eyes came to rest on the cupboards under the stairs. They looked incongruous, out of keeping with the rest of the décor. Her mind drifted. Then her thoughts were interrupted by the sight of Lisa walking in front of her line of vision.

'I know about your past Lisa. I know about Alison Marchant.'

Lisa had had the feeling, ever since their first meeting, that DI Bond would find out…eventually.

She let Trish's words hang in the air before answering.

'It was a long time ago. And yet…and yet, sometimes it feels like it was only yesterday.'

Trish got drawn into Lisa's eyes; she couldn't help herself. There was something incredibly seductive about her. She now understood why so many people had fallen for her. She tried to resist. She tried to dismiss the thoughts that were entering her head.

'It must have been very traumatic…to have lost your memory like that.'

Lisa looked across to the window.

'They tried to label it as an extreme form of post-traumatic stress.' She laughed ironically to herself. 'It sounds like *it* is in the past…that what happened to me...has somehow been healed.' She straightened her head. 'But it never heals. You can't look back, you daren't look forward and you haven't the confidence to stay in the present. Do you understand what I mean?'

Trish knew it wasn't a question. She went back to her seat. She felt oddly alone, as if her police persona had deserted her and she was left with just the woman inside of her. A woman she'd been hiding from for as long as she could remember. She was having to fight to stay focused. She dug deep.

'I'm sorry about...about your childhood. About what happened to you. But...'

'*But what?*'

'I've been doing some investigative work. That's my job. After Jackson went missing I had someone look into you.'

Lisa moved from the staircase and sat back down. She took a deliberate sip of her coffee. It had gone cold, but she didn't care.

'I know about the men...the affairs. How you reacted...the...'

'How *I* reacted. Is that what they are saying...that it was *my* fault?'

'And was it?'

'If I was to blame for anything it was having needs. Yearnings. And yes, it happened more than once. I didn't fight those needs I rolled with them. They were a distraction.'

'*A distraction*...is that what you call them.'

'And what do you think I was to them? It was a two-way street. But when I closed off my side of the road, the same thing happened every time. They became obsessive, crazy. I guess you didn't hear that bit did you.'

'You're manipulating what happened Lisa. Trying to deflect the blame, but your behaviour got progressively more psychotic. Didn't it Lisa. Wouldn't you agree?

DI Bond was turning up the heat, but Lisa remained cool.

'Not more psychotic DI Bond. More frustrated. They were all the same. They'd always got what they'd wanted in life and when they couldn't have me, when I ended the relationships, they didn't like it.'

'That's not what I heard. Your behaviour became unhinged, obsessive. That's what you're like…isn't it Lisa.'

'Have you spoken to them?'

Lisa could see by the look on Trish's face that she hadn't.

'I bet the person who…your investigator…I bet he's a man, isn't he. Am I right?'

Trish thought back to what Mickey had told her. She trusted him. Trusted his discretion. Trusted him with the truth. But did she trust him with the absolute truth? Yes, she was certain the affairs happened, but did they end the way Mickey had said they did? Clearly there was sufficient doubt. And that made her think that maybe she *had* passed judgement on Lisa too quickly? That maybe - and this was a thought Trish didn't want to have to consider - maybe she was feeling emotions towards Lisa that she shouldn't have felt.

Lisa had moved back to the window…she was shaking her head.

'You don't get it do you. *I* finished the relationships. If I was guilty of anything it was believing that the next one would be different. But they never were. I got bored. Moved on.' Lisa shrugged. 'What can I say. They didn't like it. That's not my problem.'

'What about Jackson – did he like it?'

Lisa looked into and beyond Trish's eyes.

Trish could see Lisa was drifting. She was anxious to maintain some form of momentum.

'He said you were damaged. Harry. That you were hiding it all.'

Lisa's eyes re-focused on Trish.

'I'm not denying what happened to me. But *I* was the victim DI Bond.'

'Do you really think that you're the only one who has suffered. That you're the only one who is feeling pain. And that you can justify anything in your battle with yourself. Because that's what it is Lisa. You are fighting with yourself. There is no unseen entity, no heartless God conspiring against you. Life is hard. The only thing that is unfair is that it's so much harder for some people than others. But that doesn't give you the right to do what you did.'

Lisa's face congealed.

'What *I* did. You're not listening to me are you DI Bond.'

Trish felt a resurgence of her police mentality. A hardening of her resolve. Harry was missing, Jackson was missing. She had to remain professional.

'In October 2018 you left Bayliss Shoemakers in Hereford and you've not worked since. Why is that?'

'I'm tired of being used.'

'Was it because Harry had entered your life, and now you had someone else to focus your damaged mind on...now Harry could become another one of your affairs?'

Lisa's eyes widened.

'That's what *you* want to think. You want that to be the truth don't you DI Bond, but you're wrong. Harry was different. The others…they were nothing, weak, just pale imitations of…' Lisa paused violently in mid sentence.

'Of who Lisa…of who?'

Lisa and Trish sat mirroring each other's posture, staring intently at one another.

Lisa allowed a faint smile to appear on her lips.

'Harry, he wanted me for who I was, or at least who he thought I was. But the others, they wanted me to be normal…passive…their plaything. That was never going to happen.'

'And you expect me to believe *you*, over the statements of four men.'

'I expect you to believe the truth. Four men, twenty men, it makes no difference. When will you understand that *I* was the victim.'

Lisa leaned back in her chair. The sound of a woodpecker echoed off the trees and into the room. She tilted her head back. 'He didn't know.'

Trish tried to ease the tension in her head.

'Jackson…he didn't know about any of them. We were never really that close. Well, maybe Jackson loved me. And I guess I loved him…but in a way that never really felt like love .'

'Is that why you agreed to marry him, out of pity?'

'I thought it might save us, but I was wrong.'

'Do you think he's dead?' Asked Trish.

Lisa looked at the table; the half-drunk mugs of cold coffee. She sighed to herself.

'You're the expert, but from what I've read on the Internet, people disappear for two reasons: to escape the world or to escape themselves. Those who disappear to escape themselves very rarely come back.'

'You think he's committed suicide?'

'Yes.'

'And that doesn't bother you?'

Lisa adjusted herself as if trying to find a more comfortable position for her thoughts.

'Any emotions I once had were swept up and discarded years ago…as if they never really mattered. Like they were just minor irritations that needed disposing of.'

Trish's eyes fell on the inglenook fireplace. It looked unused. Unloved.

'And Harry. What about Harry? Was he like all the others?'

Lisa moved forward in her seat.

'No DI Bond, I've already told you. Harry was different.'

Trish continued to stare at the fireplace. Hypnotised by it's cold, dark secrets.

'You like him…Harry…you like him don't you.' Lisa said conspiratorially.

Trish's eyes darted back into focus. She saw Lisa smiling.

'Harry is a good cop.' Trish sharpened her voice. 'If you know where he is, you must tell me.'

'You like him, but you don't fancy him.'

'Do you know where he is?'

'You don't fancy him because…'

'Tell me where he is!'

Trish stood up with a start. She glanced over at the stairs. Lisa noticed. She answered back quickly.

'I don't *know* where he is.' She immediately softened her tone 'Harry has been good to me. And yes, I'm worried about him, but I honestly don't know where he is.'

'Do you *really* expect me to believe that?'

'As I've already said, I expect you to believe the truth.' Lisa said curtly.

Trish sat back down. She took a deep breath.

'So, Harry's disappeared. That's what I'm meant to believe. People seem to disappear all around you Miss Hopkins.'

'I've just been unlucky in my choice of men.'

Trish let Lisa's frivolous remark fall flat.

An indistinct calm descended. Silence filled the room. Lisa looked up to the heavens – her eyes glazed over.

'Do you believe in God?'

Trish gave an infinitesimal, almost resigned shake of her head.

'I've looked for a god, but every time…all I see…is just a black hole where *he* is meant to be.'

Trish only partially heard what Lisa had said. When people talked about God her mind automatically wandered off elsewhere. She tried to sum up what she had learnt from talking to Lisa Hopkins. But things still weren't any clearer. Either she was one of the most psychotic, manipulative, femme fatales she had ever encountered or she was the hopeless victim of a life that had dealt her one bad hand after another.

'I must go,' said Trish.

They both stood up and walked to the door.

'Can't you trace his mobile? Lisa said.

Trish shook her head.

'No, it's switched off.'

Trish thought she saw relief on Lisa's face, but her mind was elsewhere.

'I hope you find him,' said Lisa. 'He's been good to me. He...' she stopped mid-sentence. Her face went absent.

Trish looked at Lisa. She knew that whatever it was Lisa was going to say; whatever it was she may have revealed, it would be locked away...forever.

'So do I. And Jackson,' said Trish.

Lisa nodded.

'Goodbye Miss Hopkins.'

'Goodbye DI Bond.'

DI Trish Bond took two steps away before turning back around. Lisa was still standing in the doorway.

'If he doesn't turn up by tomorrow, I will get a search warrant.'

Lisa shrugged.

'Go ahead. I have nothing to hide...you can have a look around now if you want?'

Trish shook her head. *Now* wasn't the right time...she would need to bring a team with her...do a proper search of the premises and the grounds.

She gave Lisa a faint smile and walked back to her car.

As Trish Bond drove home she couldn't shake that feeling. That strange sensation she'd had when Lisa Hopkins had first opened the door. And even though she'd fought vigorously to stop it...she couldn't. And now, as she cut through the darkness she hoped - irrationally and in defiance of all that the policewoman inside of her was telling her - that Lisa Hopkins was innocent.

99

Alison
Autumn 2001

It was fait accompli.

William Marshall *was* the *Poppy Killer.*

Of course, Alison Marchant had no way of being certain it was true. Just circumstantial evidence. The tracking device. But was it accurate? Did it really mean he'd actually done it...abducted and killed Kevin Kenny? She'd not actually seen him do it – William was just a dot on a map on her computer. But his van *had* been there – the night of the abduction and the night Kevin Kenny's body was disposed of. It had to be true.

It was fait accompli.

Not once did she ever question the sanity of her thoughts. Not once did shock ever register in her mind. Not once did she ever think that maybe she should have gone to the police. That maybe she could have saved Kevin Kenny's life.

The life of William Marshall was more important.

She just wished...she just wished they could be together. She hid that thought. From herself. But she knew where to find it...that it wasn't really hidden at all.

100

Alison
Autumn 2002

In the Autumn of 2002, Alison's world was thrown into disarray. Disaster struck. The CEO, Jack Hoffmann, informed her that William Marshall was retiring; on October 15th...his 65th birthday. Alison was to sort out the paper work. She'd always known it would happen, but she still felt devastated when she heard the news – not that anyone would have noticed. She concealed her emotions...her pain.

He told her that William had been with the company since 1954. She didn't tell him that she already knew that fact; that she knew his file inside out. *48 years service* Jack Hoffmann said; he wanted the company to give William Marshall a special retirement present.

Alison organised it all.

But on his last day, she phoned in sick. She didn't want to deal with it...she didn't want to deal with it on a number of levels. But most importantly she didn't want William to see her. They had been anonymous work colleagues for nearly four years. She didn't want that to change...not now. Because this wasn't the end...this wasn't the end by a long way. For Alison, this was a new beginning.

****

Alison didn't think about death – it was something that just happened. Something you had no control over. And she had developed a morbid fear of anything or anyone that she couldn't control. So she dealt with the thought of death by giving it no emotional weight whatsoever. Giving it no fear.

She didn't view herself as a control freak, she needed to control things in order to survive. She'd experienced the horrors of not being able to control what was happening to her. And she never wanted to feel that way again.

****

Alison was becoming increasingly self-absorbed in her fantasy of being with William. So much so that she no longer tried to hide it from herself.

But could she somehow find a way of actually being with him?

Then one day it clicked. It seemed so obvious that she wondered why she hadn't thought of it sooner. She would become his next victim. In Alison's mind it was that simple. She had the tracking device. She had the means. And she had the desire...to become his eleventh victim...the eleventh victim of the *Poppy Killer*. Even if it meant dying. Because as soon as the thought had entered her head – to go to him, to be his next victim - she'd immediately rationalised that it was the only thing that would keep her alive.

Alison was too blinkered by her obsession to comprehend the magnitude or the reality of the thoughts that were going through her mind.

But could it happen? Yes, the tracking device was on his van. All she had to do was wait...wait for a change in his routine. But the battery would soon be running out. If only she could find a way of getting to his vehicle; now that he didn't work for Children's First Class Catering anymore. She knew his home address, but that was too risky, too exposed. Her mind floundered. Nothing of substance entered her head. She went into the kitchen to make herself a cup of tea. There on the floor leaning against the back wall was a bag with some shopping in it. Household stuff from her last visit to Tesco that was waiting to be unpacked. She looked at the bag.

Tesco.

TESCO.

TESCO!

It hit her.

William was a creature of habit. She'd found that out already. He always went to Tesco at 10.00am every Saturday. If he followed his old work convention he would almost certainly park at the far end of the car park. She could wait for him to arrive and then, when he was in the store she could park next to his van, retrieve the tracking device, quickly change the battery and snap it back in place. If she parked close enough, her open door would provide a natural shield.

She made her plans.

Three weeks later she pulled into Tesco in Ludlow. It was Saturday morning - 9.45am. She waited. At 10.00am she felt her heart slam into her chest. A white transit van. Then her heart sank...wrong number plate. But when she got a closer look she whooped to herself...it *was* him. She smiled as she remembered that every couple of years he bought a new van. Same model – a small ford transit – brand new number plates. Now she understood why.

She watched him park in a secluded spot at the back of the car park. Her heart was pounding. It was raining. Light rain. He got out of his car. She so wanted him to see her, for him to give her that look, but she forced herself to stay out of sight. He entered Tesco. She drove over and parked next to his van. She got out of her car and felt the rain on her face. It felt good.

On her way back home she replayed the whole scene a hundred times. It had gone like clockwork. She was beside herself with self-satisfaction. She was starting to believe it could work...the plan: to be abducted by William...to be with William. And that's all it took. That's all it took in Alison's mind for it to become real. It gave her hope. And that to Alison was the most important thing...having hope. It didn't matter if the plan was fanciful. That was the nature of her obsession: the irrational became rational; the outlandish became grounded; the impossible became possible. And it was in that moment of euphoria that any doubts she'd had disappeared totally from view. She was going to be with him. She was going to be with him, come what may.

That afternoon she visited her local library. She wasn't sure if Internet searches on a home computer could be traced, so when she wanted to look up information on the *Poppy Killer* she always did it at the library. A part of her thought she was being ridiculous, but her mind was hyper and everything was brighter, louder and more animated...making her more suspicious, more cautious than ever.

He'd struck 10 times over a 15 year period: 1986; 1988; 1989; 1990; 1992; 1993; 1994; 1996; 1999; 2001. She knew this already, but she wanted to be sure. Be certain of the dates.

He'd been slowing down.

She needed to be patient...to wait.

Wait to see a change in his routine.

Wait for him to put on the mask of the Poppy Killer.

101

Alison
Spring/Summer 2003

Alison never felt like it was pointless.

Everything else was pointless.

But gradually her sense of purpose began to wane. Nothing for fourteen months. She was willing him to do it. To strike again. To start planning for his next victim...his eleventh victim.

Then in May 2003 his routine suddenly changed.

He made a trip to Nottingham.

Then another.

And then another.

Alison's belief was reinstalled...the fourteen month wait instantly forgotten. And her mind slipped effortlessly into her plan of action.

By 2003, technology had improved and she'd updated the tracking device. She was now able to programme the device to receive a signal every few minutes without draining the battery too quickly. She still had to change it every month or so...do the Tesco run. But she was now able to pin-point with more confidence where he was at any given time.

She searched on Google Map for a possible abduction site near to where the signal had indicated he'd parked in Nottingham...three visits...three different locations. So she drew a line through each of them. She'd researched his MO...she was looking for an industrial area. And there it was, right in the middle of where the three lines intersected. A street lined with factories and businesses, located approximately three quarters of a mile out of the city centre.

It had to be the place.

She had made her decision. She had her plan: calculated, controlled...compulsive.

She was ready.

She'd written down three key steps in order to maximise the chances of her plan being successful:

Step 1: In 2001 he'd struck on his fourth trip to Coventry. Therefore she would go on his fourth trip to Nottingham. He typically operated on a Friday or Saturday evening, but she would maintain a level of readiness on all the nights, just in case. She was confident that she knew where in Nottingham he would be heading. When she picked up the signal that he was on his way she would leave immediately. She had calculated that she could get there an hour before him.

Step 2: She would park approximately half a mile from the industrial area.

Step 3: When she felt the time was right she would walk to the street where she believed William Marshall would be waiting.

The fact that she couldn't be 100% sure he *was* the *Poppy Killer* no longer mattered. The fact that her plan, like the evolution of life itself, was relying on nothing more than luck, no longer mattered. The only thing that mattered to Alison was that her plan *felt* real. And that reality was founded on the unwavering and blinkered belief that the successful execution of her plan was the only way she could ever be with William Marshall.

The date was Friday, 6th June 2003.

It was 10.10pm.

Alison was sat in front of her computer.

She had the application for the tracking device open.

As with each of the previous seven nights she was waiting...waiting for him to make his move...to make his fourth trip to Nottingham.

She was ready to go. Ready to leave. Ready to disappear.

Then at 10.35pm the map marker started flashing.

He was leaving.

Alison felt a surge in her heart rate.

She opened the settings on her computer. She clicked on the tracker app, selected the uninstall option and then removed the programme. If things didn't work out tonight, then...? ...her mind's eye had not looked beyond that point.

She picked up her keys.

She deliberately left her mobile phone on the table, next to a half drunk cup of tea. She then left her flat and headed for Nottingham.

As she made her way north, she could see the moon high in the sky, bright, illuminating. Her mind was detached, but in the moment. She didn't want to think about what might happen. She just knew she had to try. To be with him. To be with William Marshall. Life had taken whatever it had wanted from her, and life had felt no debt, no remorse. Now it was her turn to take what she wanted. *She owed the world nothing. She believed that without reservation.*

102

DI Trish Bond
Saturday, 1 February 2020

Trish received a phone call. It was just before 10.00am. A body had been discovered in Mortimer Forest on the edge of Ludlow...approximately a quarter of a mile from Tawelfan cottage. She felt a wave of nausea overwhelm her. She slammed down the phone.

Ninety minutes later she was at the cottage.

Lisa did not answer the door.

Trish made her way to the grave.

The area was taped off.

Forensics were already on the scene; scouring the area like they were on an archaeological dig. Trish surveyed the scene. Lucy Wayside looked up and smiled at her. Lucy was a red head. Slight of build, but large in personality...full of life. It always struck Trish as a slightly incongruous trait for a forensic scientist. Lucy informed Trish that the body had been in the grave for some time. She guessed at between 5 and 6 months. Significant decomposition. Trish took a look at what was left of the face. It could have been Jackson, but she'd only seen photographs of him. It didn't look like Harry and besides the timeline was all wrong for it to be him. She felt a sense of relief, which was immediately followed by guilt...yes, it wasn't Harry, but it was still a dead body.

The local police constable approached her. She recognised him: Paul Blackhurst; he'd served for three...or was it four decades with the Ludlow station? Trish wasn't sure. He'd never sought a promotion, he loved what he did and had never had any ambition to change things. She admired him for that. He was loved by the community that he'd served faithfully all his life.

He told her that the body had been discovered by a man walking his dog. Trish wondered to herself how many homicides would have been left unsolved if it wasn't for man's best friend? Constable Blackhurst then got out his note-book and relayed verbatim what the dog walker had told him...*my dog suddenly got a sniff of something and darted off into the woods. When I eventually caught up with him, he was sitting patiently, waiting for me. That's when I noticed the half-finished grave. Like you see in cemeteries, when they're preparing for a new burial. Soil all around the edges waiting for the coffin. Only in this instance, the body...I mean it looked like there was a body in there...partially covered by soil. My dog didn't do it...dig up the soil I mean, I can assure you of that. After that, I called the police. I wasn't certain if there was anyone in there...a body I mean, but I couldn't just let it go. That wouldn't have been right...it wouldn't have felt right.* Trish thanked PC Blackhurst for his above-and-beyond-the-call-of-duty thoroughness and went back to talk to Lucy Wayside.

'He's one in a million isn't he.'

Lucy saw Trish nod in the direction of Constable Blackhurst.

'He's not just a textbook cop, he *is* the textbook,' said Lucy.

Trish smiled to herself and then returned her thoughts to the job in hand.

'What have we got?'

'Interesting,' said Lucy. 'There's physical signs of recent ground disturbance; the soil around the edges has been dug up, but the soil covering the body has solidified.'

'Meaning?' DI Bond asked.

'Meaning that the body was placed here some months ago, but someone has recently returned to the grave. As if they were attempting to move the body but got disturbed.'

'Or someone wanted the body to be found,' countered Trish Bond.

Lucy acknowledged Trish Bond's hypothesis, but in a way that made it sound less plausible than hers.

'Any guesses...cause of death?' Trish asked Lucy.

'Most probably hanging. There's evidence of blackening of the skin around the neck. Possible ligature mark.'

Trish hid her sadness behind a thank you smile.

She returned to Paul Blackhurst to tell him to do what he was already doing: to keep the public and the press away from the area.

Constable Blackhurst had seen it all before...the prima donnas, the hot-shots, but DI Bond...she was one of the good ones. Not just a great detective, but someone who understood people. She knew how to make them feel valued. And he knew the obstacles she'd had to overcome to get to where she was today. He'd heard the whispers on the grapevine...he seemed to be a magnet for the gossip mongers. As if they trusted him to do what they were clearly unable to do...keep a secret. And yet, whenever he met her, she never came across as cynical. No, he liked DI Bond, but he could see that the discovery of the body was troubling her...troubling her a lot. He wanted to help, but he knew it was beyond his station. Instead he smiled politely and respectfully.

DI Bond acknowledged his smile, turned around and looked out to the forest.

Her gut was telling her that the body was definitely Jackson Brown's, and that once the coroner had examined it and confirmed her suspicions, she would be opening a murder investigation. No question about it...people who hang themselves, do not bury themselves.

She went back to the cottage...rang the bell...knocked on the door. It was 1.05pm. There was still no answer. She went over to the garage. It was locked. She took out her mobile. She needed to act quickly. Her heart was racing.

103

Saturday, 7 June 2003
2.00am

Alison Marchant was in Nottingham.

She was on an industrial road – just under a mile out of the city centre.

She was walking in the moonlight.

She loved walking.

She admired the beauty of the sycamore trees.

She breathed in her own thoughts.

She knew what she wanted.

She started skipping.

Around the cracks in the pavement.

Thinking of her dream man.

And then.

And then…

…she collapsed into his arms.

104

Wednesday, 29 January 2020
Tawelfan Cottage

Harry was hovering over the kitchen sink trying to get the dirt off his hands and out of his fingernails.

Lisa walked in - stood opposite him - in front of the dark green Aga.

'It smells good.' Harry turned his head and nodded at the oven.

'Are you okay Harry?'

Harry quickly turned back to face the window that was above the sink.

'Yes, of course, why do you ask?'

'I told you this afternoon…I'm worried about you. You've not been yourself lately…but you didn't want to talk about it then.'

Harry gave himself an ironic smile.

'I'm not sure what being myself is anymore.'

'So everything isn't okay…why don't you talk to me Harry?'

'It's just one of those days.'

'We all have bad days Harry, Christ, my life is a continual roller-coaster.'

Harry forced a smile.

'I'm sorry; I'm being selfish.'

Lisa walked over to him.

'Harry.'

Harry turned around

She took hold of his hands and glanced across to the glass of red wine stood on the worktop to the left of the sink.

'You've had some wine. It can make a person feel melancholic.' She kissed him on the cheek and playfully rocked his hands back and forth.

'Your hands are still wet,' she said and looked down at them. She suddenly unclasped her grip and stepped back.

'Your hands…your nails, they're dirty. Did you fall over?'

Harry dropped his hands as if he was trying to hide them – he looked uncomfortable.

'Why did you go out Harry? We've been out all afternoon. Why the sudden need to go out again?'

Lisa could see Harry tensing up.

She moved back towards him and took a firm hold of his hands.

'You did what you had to do Harry; you'll have to learn to live with it or it will destroy you…it will destroy us.'

Harry snatched his hands away, turned back towards the sink and continued scrubbing his nails. Lisa put her hand on his shoulder. He stopped and took a deep breath. He looked out to the empty view in his head.

'Suppose you've been driven…' said Harry, '…driven by a desire that is so strong that everything else you do is blocked out. And then one day…' He took his hands out of the water, picked up the towel next to the sink and started drying them. 'And then one day you suddenly realise that you're on your own and there's nothing but darkness all around. And the journey...the road you have taken to get to this point...it seems like a dream. Only it isn't a dream. And, as you stand all alone you have two choices. To go back and face the consequences of your actions, or, continue to shut things out and move on forward into the darkness.'

Lisa let Harry's words reconfigure in her head.

'There's always another choice Harry.'

He spun around.

'*What*...what other choice Lisa...what is the other choice?'

Her eyes drilled into Harry's weak spot.

'You learn to live with it. Only then will you see beyond the darkness in your head.'

Tears welled up in Harry's eyes but he held them back. He could feel her words burning into his mind...*you learn to live with it*. Like she had learnt to live with her abduction by the *Poppy Killer*...William Marshall...his birth father. Like she had learnt to live with the fact that the man she still obsessed over was not only a mass murderer, he was also a ghost. Maybe she was in an acute form of denial. Perhaps she always has been? He turned back around and stared out of the window. The view no longer seemed to matter.

'I'm not like you Lisa. You've never grown up; you're still Alison...Alice in Wonderland...the little girl who wants to escape. Only now, you've learnt to manipulate; not just other people, but yourself. You have no concept of normal life; no concept of normal feelings.'

Lisa's face turned cold.

'I thought you were stronger Harry.' She took the towel from him. 'You can't bring him back. You did what you did because *you* wanted to survive. You wanted *us* to survive. He'd become unstable...remember...the *letter*...all the other stuff...he could have hurt me. You did it for me Harry...at least that's what I thought?'

Harry reached for the doubts in his head. He thought of what the Rector had said...that Lisa had made the booking in 2018...the month after he'd first met her. He thought of what Jackson had said...that Lisa thought he was a troubled soul.

He flinched, as if he was struggling to keep a grip on things.

'Why did you do it Lisa? Why did you lie about booking the church? The Rector told me you made the booking in November 2018. Why Lisa? Was all this a game? Had you planned it right from the start?'

Lisa's face changed from surprise, to shock, to anger, in a seemingly seamless animation.

'I booked it because I thought I might need it someday. As a way of calming Jackson down. I've told you this...my concerns about him. I lied about the booking because I knew you wouldn't understand. The only way you *could* understand, is if you were in my position. But you're not...*are you Harry*.'

'I'm sorry Lisa. It's just all this, everything, it's just getting too much. I mean, the date written in the letter...September 7th...the date the *Poppy Killer* was going to strike again. For it to have been the same date as the date you'd chosen the year before, when you booked the wedding...I mean, it's one hell of a coincidence.' Harry looked despairingly at Lisa. 'Did you send it Lisa? Did you send the letter?'

Lisa gave Harry a playful smile.

'Harry, you're meant to be the detective, yet you've missed the obvious thing. Jackson must have found the booking confirmation. He was always prying into my stuff. It was a symptom of his insecurity. Maybe he thought I was having an affair and that I was going to marry someone else? I don't know, he never talked to me face-to-face about things. When he found the booking form, he must have panicked, decided to act, do something and I guess sending the *letter* was his way of bringing things out into the open. And, I suppose, for a while he must have thought it had worked. That's why I played along with it. Pretended I needed him, that I wanted him to protect me. I had to...you know that...who knows what he might have done if I hadn't. Which is exactly the reason I booked the church in the first place. But to be honest I never thought it would come to anything, I just needed to be doing something. That's important to me...that sense of being in control. And...okay, yes, it was a spur of the moment thing and now...and now, maybe I could have chosen a different route, but how could I have known, how could I have known that events would unfold the way they did.'

Harry's head was throbbing. It was all getting too much. He felt like he was caught in a maze full of lunatics...shouting, screaming, pointing. Each one certain they know the way out…but unaware that in reality, there *is* no way out.

'I'm not sure of anything anymore. I mean, it's one hell of a thing to do. Can't you see how it looks?' Harry moved to the kitchen door and turned to face Lisa. 'It doesn't look good Lisa. It doesn't sound like the actions of a sane person…no matter how much you try to rationalise it.' He walked into the lounge and sat down. Lisa moved to where Harry had been standing. He could see the hurt on her face, but he tried to see through it. 'I'd do anything for you Lisa, you know that, but I'm starting to doubt things...doubt who I am. Who *we* are. It's so difficult, you're always manipulating things; you always seem to have an answer for everything. It's...' Harry shook his head. 'But you can't see it. You can't see that you're driving me into the abyss…just like you did with Jackson. He killed himself because of *you*. How can you live with that?'

'No Harry…you can't do this.' Lisa walked into the lounge.

'He deserves a proper burial. His parents deserve…'

'No Harry.'

'It's time to face the truth Lisa. It's time to stop running. It's time for you to get the help you need.'

'No Harry.'

Lisa looked at Harry and gave him a faint nod of her head. It was a gesture he knew well. She was reeling him in. A voice in Harry's head was telling him it wasn't real…she was putting it on…like she had with Jackson. But the raw passion, the raw love he felt inside was tearing down his defences.

Lisa calmly walked up the stairs.

Harry thought for a moment before following her.

When he got to the top of the stairs, she was waiting for him.

The look on her face had completely changed. It was a look he had never seen before. As if she was possessed.

'Lisa?'

'Why are you trying to hurt me Harry?'

'I'm trying to help you. Don't you understand?'

'I saw you, I saw you go out to the forest and then I saw you walk into the garage before you came back inside. I went and had a look, just now, before I joined you in the kitchen. I saw the trowel Harry. You'd just left it there. Like you wanted it to be found. There was fresh soil on it. What have you done Harry?'

Harry's mind started to rush.

'I told you, he needs a proper burial.'

Lisa towered down on him.

'They will accuse *us* Harry, they will say *we* did it...*we* killed him and then what will happen to us.'

'We *did* kill him. Maybe not directly, but we killed him...you killed him. You don't realise...and yet...' Harry bowed his head.

Lisa thought of William...*You must be ruthless. It will help you survive.* 'I thought you were different Harry, that you possessed your father's character. But you don't. You say you love me, but now you're trying to make out that *I'm* the bad person. That's not love Harry, that's...'

Lisa's voice started to crack. Harry looked up. He looked into the eyes of the woman he loved...his heart ached...he had to try...try one last time to reach her.

'You must come with me,' he said. 'I will protect you.'

Lisa shook her head.

'You know you can't do that Harry.'

'They will find the body. I had to do it Lisa. I couldn't live with it on my conscience.'

'You're a fool Harry.'

She turned her back on him and started walking towards the bedroom.

Harry began to panic

'I've told her.'

Lisa stopped in her tracks.

'Who Harry? Who have you told?'

'DI Bond. About us.'

Lisa's eyes solidified. She turned around.

'Two weeks ago. I...I needed someone to talk to. We went to the pub...after work. But...I wanted to...but I just couldn't...I couldn't tell her...tell her the *real* truth.'

'What *real* truth Harry?'

'About Jackson; about what my birth father did.'

Lisa shook her head.

'Why didn't you tell me sooner? That you'd talked to her. That you'd told her about us.'

Harry's face took on a childlike quality as the policeman in him started to fade.

'I just blabbered. It was a mistake.'

'Do you love her?'

'What!'

'You heard me Harry, do you love her?'

'Do you know how ridiculous that sounds? We went out for a drink. Nothing more.'

'There is no such thing as *nothing more* Harry.'

Lisa moved towards him.

'Lisa, please.'

'You shouldn't have told her about us Harry. She won't let it go. She'll tear us apart.'

Harry started to feel uneasy.

'Come back downstairs Lisa, please. Let's talk about this down there.'

Lisa shook her head.

Harry steadied himself.

'We can't go on like this. They will find out soon enough. And then...and then I will have to tell them the truth. *You* will have to tell them the truth. There is no other way.'

'I can't let you do that Harry.'

Lisa took two steps forward; Harry saw her eyes dilate before her whole body engulfed him.

105

Lisa
Friday, 31 January 2020

Lisa Hopkins watched as DI Trish Bond drove off. As she closed the front door she immediately looked at the time. Soon they would either find Jackson, or DI Bond would return with a search warrant and they would find Harry.

For a brief moment she thought about trying to cover her tracks, but she knew it was no use.

That before long, she would be arrested.

And then what chance would she have?

She'd never get a fair trial. She'd never *had* a fair trial...why would life suddenly favour her now? She'd be vilified by the press. Powerless to stop it. Her guilt pre-ordained; her sentence inescapable.

And yet, there was a small part of her that felt DI Trish Bond believed her...that she was on her side. But the feeling wasn't strong enough for her to trust it.

Instead, it had become patently clear in her mind that she couldn't risk staying around any longer.

She stood for a while.

Calm.

Focused.

She'd feared this day may come - when her past would catch up with her. So she'd first come up with the idea of an escape route in 2009 whilst she was on holiday in Madagascar. She'd wanted to survive...after William left. But more than anything, she had wanted to believe that William was still alive. That she had to keep on going for him. So Madagascar was a perfect destination to escape to. A perfect location to keep her dream alive. A place where she could easily melt into the tourist-centric laissez-faire. Self-isolate if need be. And it was a country that the UK had no extradition treaty with. So over the years, with each subsequent holiday to Madagascar, the concept of using the destination as a place to escape to had grown and grown, until it had become a well researched plan.

She went up to her bedroom and started packing.

Her life squeezed into one holdall and one medium-sized suitcase.

She retrieved her passport. She looked at the name: Alison Marchant. She glanced around the room. She could feel his presence…William Marshall. She smiled to herself.

She knew what she had to do.

106

Saturday, 1 February 2020

When, at 1.05pm, DI Bond had been unable to locate or communicate with Lisa Hopkins - following the discovery of the body in the forest - she'd immediately phoned the chief. They were facing a situation where obtaining a warrant would have caused a delay that would have most likely defeated the ends of justice. So the chief agreed to allow her to exercise her power to enter the premises without a search warrant. Very soon after, she'd had no other recourse but to conclude that Lisa Hopkins had absconded. She made another call instructing her acting detective sergeant, Steve McCann, to issue a BOLO ('Be On the Look Out for') for Lisa Hopkins née Alison Marchant, to be circulated on the Police National Computer as *wanted*. She told him that the BOLO must include the airports and seaports, and that Lisa Hopkins must be prevented from leaving the country. With her mind racing, she forgot to reiterate that the BOLO *must include* her current and previous names.

****

Just four hours earlier Alison Marchant had left the cottage and driven to Birmingham Airport where she'd boarded the early afternoon flight out to Gibraltar. From there she'd caught a ferry, crossing the Straits of Gibraltar to Tangier, Morocco. At Tangier she'd boarded the train to Casablanca and then she'd flown on to Cairo, Egypt. At Cairo she'd caught a flight to Antananarivo, Madagascar, in the Indian Ocean. At Antananarivo she'd hailed a taxi, north. Finally, three days after leaving England, she arrived at her destination: Hôtel Ambatoloaka; the hotel that she'd stayed at on at least half a dozen occasions in the past; it was situated in Nosy Be, eight kilometres off the north coast of Madagascar, in the Mozambique Channel.

She was exhausted, but she felt an incredible sense of elation. Elation because she knew that her escape plan had worked. She had successfully disappeared. She felt safe.

****

Shortly after Alison Marchant had caught her flight from Birmingham Airport, the image of Lisa Hopkins appeared on the airport security screens. Her original name was carelessly missing from the accompanying details; when Alison Marchant was finally added to the BOLO, Birmingham airport police quickly identified her as a passenger on a flight to Gibraltar. Initial elation was soon dampened when it was discovered that the plane had landed at Gibraltar International Airport 3 hours earlier. After that, the police were always playing catch up. There were reports of a person fitting her description on a ferry, crossing the Straits of Gibraltar. But soon after that the trail went cold. As if she had vanished off the face of the earth.

Two days later, her car was found abandoned at Birmingham Airport.

107

Tuesday, 4 February 2020

Alison was in her hotel bathroom. An hour had passed since she'd checked into the Hôtel Ambatoloaka.

She was standing in front of the mirror. She thought back to when she'd changed from Alison to Lisa. How she'd learnt new ways to apply makeup to change her features. Tied her hair up. Wore clear lens glasses. It seemed like a lifetime ago. She wondered if she'd ever actually needed to do it....to disguise herself? She'd felt self-conscious at first, that everyone was looking at her. But then she realised that people were looking through her, not *at* her...that they weren't really registering anything at all, just filling the empty spaces in their minds with fleeting images of the things that passed before them. And so gradually, as the years passed by, she stripped away her disguise. Firstly the make-up, then the hair and finally the glasses, until she looked like an older version of a person she used to know.

And now...

...her life had gone full circle.

Lisa Hopkins was dead.

She felt at peace with herself.

She looked in the mirror.

She watched Alison smile.

She liked having her back.

108

Wednesday, 5 February 2020

'DI Bond.'

It took a split second for DI Bond's mind to shift into gear.

'Lisa Hopkins. Where are you?'

'Don't bother with a trace, you won't find me.'

'You can't hide forever Lisa.'

'You are right Trish, you can't.'

There was a pause.

'We found the cellar.'

'I figured you would.'

'Harry.'

Lisa could hear Trish's voice faltering.

'Why Lisa, why did you kill him…them…why did you kill Harry and Jackson?'

Lisa watched as people came and went, easy in their own lives, oblivious to what had happened to the girl on the phone.

'I didn't kill them. Jackson…Jackson committed suicide. And Harry…it was a terrible accident. It wasn't me…I'm sorry…I'm really sorry about Harry…and Jackson…but it wasn't my fault.'

Trish was trying to un-pick the tone in Lisa's voice.

'You're lying Lisa. You are doing what you do best…trying to cover your own tracks…trying to manipulate things…trying to deflect the blame away from yourself.'

'You're wrong. Harry and Jackson. They'd had an argument. On our wedding day. They had a fight. Harry overpowered Jackson and took him into the cellar to cool down. When he went back, a bit later, to talk to him, that's when he found him. He...he'd hung himself...'

Trish could hear Lisa sobbing. Crocodile tears she thought to herself, but without seeing Lisa's face, without seeing her body language, she couldn't be sure.

'Harry told me over the phone. I knew how it would look. I knew the police, the press, they would start prying around and...and then everyone would blame me. I was going hysterical. Then Harry...he suggested...to bury him in the woods. To make out he'd gone missing. He said people go missing all the time. That nobody would suspect a thing. He sounded so sure...I...I trusted him.'

'Stop lying Lisa. I think Harry was trying to tell me something. But he couldn't quite bring himself...' Trish paused to compose her voice. 'I think *you* killed Jackson and persuaded Harry to bury him. He loved you, he needed you. You knew that...that he'd do anything for you. But it was eating away at him, wasn't it Lisa and so *you* killed Harry because he was weakening – he was feeling guilty. I think it was Harry who dug up the grave. He wanted it to be found. His mind must have been in turmoil. But you found out. You killed him, didn't you Lisa, you killed him.'

'No!'

Lisa looked out across the hotel lobby. For a moment the whole scene seemed frozen in time. She lowered her voice.

'You've got it all wrong DI Bond. Yes, I did lie to you about what happened, what *really* happened, because I knew you wouldn't believe me. But the truth remains the same. I did not kill Jackson and I did not kill Harry. I have never sought to hurt anyone.'

Trish fixated on the top hat on Harry's desk. She imagined the secret compartment. The hiding place. She wondered if that's what Lisa was doing…finding a hiding place in her mind for all that she had done.

'You cannot go on thinking that whatever happens…whatever you do…it's not your fault. That you can forever hide behind your misguided belief that you have done no wrong.'

'So, you know what happened do you DI Bond. Are you certain of that?'

Trish could hear Mickey Maguire's voice in her head: *She's a bunny boiler*. She shuddered. Questioned herself. Had she become no better than Mickey Maguire? Judge and Jury. Had she found Lisa guilty, without *really* listening to what she was saying? She forced herself to slow down.

'Then tell me Lisa. Tell me what *really* happened.'

Lisa took a slow deliberate breath.

'I've told you what happened to Jackson.' She exhaled. 'With Harry, it was a terrible accident. We were at the top of the stairs. We'd had an argument. I went to hug him, but he stepped back. I don't know why, but he did. And he just seem to fall, he lost his footing, the wine? I don't know, something happened.

He fell down the stairs. When I got to him his neck was all twisted and horrible. I panicked. Dragged him into the cellar. I didn't know what else to do. I couldn't think straight.'

'You've lied to me before Lisa, why should I believe you now?'

'Because it's the truth.'

'If that *is* the case then why didn't you come and see me…talk to me?'

'Well, that's the problem isn't it DI Bond. You *don't* believe me. It's always *my* fault. When anything goes wrong. I'm the one to blame.'

'Murdering someone is a bit more than *something going wrong*.'

Trish heard Lisa sigh.

'I phoned you…I phoned you to tell you that I'm sorry. I'm sorry about Harry, but I swear on my life, it was an accident.'

It was Trish's turn to sigh. She knew she had to push.

'You know…when I last saw you, shortly after Harry…shortly after he'd gone missing, I…I genuinely hoped you were innocent. I felt for you…as a woman. And I prayed that Harry would turn up, alive and well. Then after our meeting, when I was driving back, it felt like I was in a trance – I hardly remember the journey. Suddenly I was sat in my office. And that's when I realised something; something that I'd suspected right from the beginning, from the first time I met you - you are dangerous…you are a dangerous woman Lisa Hopkins. A very dangerous woman. Year after year, you've become more and more detached. More detached from reality. Haven't you Lisa. '

There was a moment of silence on the line.

A man and woman sat down on one of the plush hotel lounge sofas that was positioned across the way from where Lisa was making her call. She watched them without registering their faces.

'It's not me who's dangerous DI Bond...I told you, *I'm* the one who's been victimised. The only way I've survived is by telling people what they want to hear. My teachers; social services; my friends; my bosses; Jackson. But it was never enough. And the more I gave of myself, the more intrusive they became. They always wanted more. It was always about them. And no one understood *me*...what I'd been through. What I'd *really* been through. Not then...not now.' A bell sounded in the background. Lisa looked across at the reception desk. An elderly couple were waiting. She watched them as they stood and looked around. She followed their eyeline...then her thoughts returned to a random place in her mind. 'Do you know what separates us from all the other species on this planet...our ability to perceive. We can see into the distance and for some the horizon is unlimited. But for others, it's shortened and narrow. They can't see beyond what's in front of them...they don't *want* to see beyond what's in front of them. They have no ambition other than what's in their reach. Jackson was like that and Harry to a degree. But I'm not like that...I've never been like that...that's why...that's why I've gone away DI Bond, because you're just like the rest of them...aren't you. You think you know best; you think you know what really happened...but you haven't a clue...you need to see into the distance DI Bond, only then will you find the truth.

Trish reflexively looked across to the window behind Harry's desk before deadening the impulse.

'Lisa, can't you see. It's all in your head. The fight you are having is with yourself. Only it's spilled over and other people have been drawn into your battle, other people have died. Isn't that right Lisa...isn't that the truth.'

Lisa felt her grip tighten on the phone.

'Do you know what it's like to be frightened. I mean really frightened Trish. So frightened that you hear every noise, every vibration. And you jump at the sight of your own shadow. And all you want to do is run away; it doesn't matter where; it doesn't matter in which direction, you just want to get away. But you can't...you can't run away. Because no matter where you run to, it's always there behind you...following you. Haunting you. People tell you to talk about it. They think words will make it disappear. And if you don't seek help it's your fault. Your fault that you haven't dealt with it. But you can't Trish, you can't deal with it...you can't talk about it...you can't even think about it. You just have to learn to live with it. And yes, you were right...you have to fight with yourself. But what you don't understand is how other people make that fight so much harder.'

Trish's mind seemed to empty itself.

The line went eerily silent.

Lisa held out the receiver in her hand. She looked at it intently then rested it against her chest. She could sense Trish Bond. Like she was there next to her. She felt a jolt in her spirits.

'You should come and join me...escape,' said Lisa. 'You and me are more alike than you think.'

Trish felt a gentle shot of adrenaline pump into her blood.

'We just want people to understand us. Appreciate us for who we are. But they don't, do they Trish.'

She let that remark resonate.

'The innocence has gone hasn't it Trish...for the likes of you and me. We'll never rediscover the child within us like other adults do. They hang on to their youthful spirit no matter what their age. We'll never feel like that...young at heart...will we. Life has taken that away from us. That's why we're alike. That's why you should come and join me.'

A knot tightened in Trish's stomach. She felt Lisa's words suffocating her. She had suppressed her feelings for so long that she no longer knew what it was she was suppressing. She took a deep breath.

She looked over at Harry's empty chair.

His *empty* chair.

She regrouped.

She knew that she couldn't hold back the question any longer. No matter how painful the memories were for Lisa. Trish had to be ruthless. Lisa was a double murder suspect. She owed it to Harry...and to Jackson.

'Tell me about your father.'

Lisa rested her head against the backboard above the phone. Trish could hear the muffled sound of background chatter.

'The information in the file stated that he left you and your mother in 1997.'

Black and white images flashed into Lisa's mind.

'So, I dug a bit deeper. Reports relating to his disappearance, newspaper clippings, that sort of thing. They all said the same thing, that he'd upped sticks and left. He seemed to be a man that nobody was particularly interested in finding. Better off without him, was that the case Lisa? Is that what you made people believe?'

Lisa could feel a sharp pulse-like sensation in her head.

'That your father had left, disappeared. Like Jackson, like Harry. Only they didn't disappear did they Lisa...they are dead. Is that what happened to your father? Did you kill him? Did you kill your father?'

A tune started to repeat in Lisa's head...

> *The Shoop Shoop Song (It's in His Kiss)* by *Cher.*

She hated that song.

The terrible memories.

'You got away with it didn't you Lisa. And having got away with it once, you thought you could get away with it again, and then again. That's how killers work...don't they Lisa...they get more confident with each kill.'

> *Does he love me I want to know*
> *How can I tell if he loves me so*
> *Is it in his eyes?*
> *Oh no! You'll be deceived.*

'And the date your father supposedly left home. As soon as I saw that date I knew. The *letter*. The letter claiming to have been written by the *Poppy Killer*. You sent that letter didn't you Lisa.'

Is it in his face?
Oh no! That's just his charms
In his warm embrace?
Oh no! That's just his arms.

'September 7th 1997, that's the date your father left home. The date he disappeared. But he didn't disappear did he Lisa? You killed him, didn't you Lisa. And then you got your mother to bury him. I'm right, aren't I?'

If you want to know if he loves you so
It's in his kiss
That's where it is
It's in his kiss
That's where it is.

'And maybe you *were* abducted by the *Poppy Killer*? Or maybe Harry told you things from the file that he shouldn't have? One way or the other that's how you knew so much about the *Poppy Killer*. That's how you knew what to put in the *letter*.'

Silence.

'I'm right aren't I…this has all been a game to you. Your way of ensuring that life repays the debt it owes you. You killed them…killed them all…didn't you.'

Oh no! That's not the way
And you're not list'nin' to all I say

Lisa looked up at the glass roof. Up to the wispy, early morning clouds. Up to and beyond the sky. And then…

The music in Lisa's head stopped abruptly.

'Is that what you think, that I'm some crazy woman, going around killing people? Is that what you think or is that what you want to think? Because you are wrong DI Bond. You are wrong but that doesn't seem to matter does it, because the truth...the real truth...is that you don't *want* to see the truth. Because it's easier for you to hide behind your false beliefs. It means you don't have to face up to your real feelings. Isn't that the truth Trish. Isn't that the real truth.'

Trish tried to free her mind.

'It is you who is hiding behind your words Lisa. But they cannot protect you...not this time.'

Trish thought she heard the sound of a muffled laugh.

'You are wrong detective. They are the only thing that *can* protect me. Because within them, lies the truth.'

'We will find you Lisa, you know that don't you. The world is a small place. Justice will prevail.'

The woman on the plush lounge sofa looked up at Lisa. Her insincere smile flashed briefly in Lisa's mind – like an insipid two-dimensional face on a billboard. Then she returned her thoughts to DI Trish Bond.

'Jail is not an option for me. I cannot let myself be in a situation that I cannot control. I hope you understand DI Bond.' Lisa smiled back at the woman on the sofa who was no longer looking at her.

'Lisa you...'

'Goodbye DI Bond. I'm sorry about Harry, I really am. And I hope…I hope you find someone…one day…someone to love.'

Trish tried not to let Lisa's words stick in her mind.

'Oh…and DI Bond…it's Alison. My name is Alison…Lisa is dead.'

Alison adjusted her sunglasses.

The line went dead.

'Lisa, Alison, Miss Hopkins…Alison…Alison.'

Trish replaced the receiver and sat back in her chair. She felt as if she should be doing something…trying to get a trace on the call, but she knew it was a forlorn hope. She tried to sit up straight, but her whole body felt uncomfortable. And she knew deep down that her discomfort was just a symptom of her mind. She tilted her head back and looked up at the ceiling. She needed time to think. She needed time to rid herself of the way she felt. She needed time to see the real truth. She lowered her head to look at Harry. She desperately wanted to see his face. But all she could see was the face of Lisa Hopkins. And no matter how hard she tried she couldn't get the thought out of her head…that when you stripped away everything and looked at the person…who really was the victim?

She took one last look over towards Harry's desk, turned off the light and then left the room.

109

Thursday, 6 February 2020

Alison was sat on her sun lounger. She idly looked around. People looked like casually drawn impressions against the clear blue, motionless sea. She continued to pan around. And then a sight made her stop and rapidly rewind her vision. There sitting by himself, at the beach bar, looking directly at her, was an old man. Her heart missed a beat – could it be him?

She straightened up, her eyes were transfixed. The sun was shining brightly yet she felt a dampness against her skin. A couple ambled across her view. When they had passed, he was gone. She sat and stared at the empty stool in the distance. Her mind felt confused, then aroused, then nostalgic. Snippets of her life filtered into her consciousness. She wondered how she'd survived. She shook her head. She tried to think of who it was that said *to survive is to find meaning in suffering*. She couldn't remember his name but she knew it to be true. She tried not to think of what had happened. Her father. But it was still there – her past. The horribleness of it all. Nothing could change that. But now, for the first time, she realised she had no more bitterness, no more resentment. She could finally move on. Be free of her own shadow. Wake up in the morning and be herself.

She looked back over to the beach bar. She smiled to herself. William Marshall had been her obsession, her glorious obsession. Her escape. The drug on which she had become dependant. And then, the tables turned and men obsessed about her. She couldn't find any reason for it. As if everything that had happened to her, had just...just happened. Even her own abduction – so meticulously planned – had just happened. She'd never been in control of the outcome. But, through it all, she had somehow survived and even though she'd never felt like a part of society, she'd always found a way of living within it. And now...now it felt like she'd come full circle and she was back...closer to William Marshall...closer than she had been for years. For 17 years.

She lay back down and looked up to the heavens.

A lone rain cloud appeared. Incongruous in the blue sky.

Alison tilted her head and looked across.

A young man was now sitting on the stool where *William* had been sitting. Had it *really* been him?

She sat up.

She thought back to the times when she'd listened to William reading his father's poetry.

She reached into her bag and took out a pen and paper.

She had no idea how to compose a poem or what made a good poem. She just felt overcome with an incredible urge to express her feelings.

She came up with the title immediately: *Three Missing Words*.

She began to write.

Alison's pen hovered over the final line. She put dashes in the place of where the words should have been _ _ _ _ _ _ _ _ the *three missing words*. For a moment she thought about filling them in. The pen felt alive in her grip...as if it had its own energy. She rested her head back down on the lounger. The sun felt comforting on her face. She closed her eyes and gently fell asleep.

110

The muted sound of children playing in the sand drifted into Alison's dreams.

She felt William next to her…she twitched.

She tried to reach out to him but her arms felt heavy.

She could see his lips moving…hear his words.

I knew it was you. As soon as I got back. When I laid you down on the bed. In the cage. In the cellar.

You used to surreptitiously shoot me a glance. From up in your office. Then you would look away, duck out of sight. But I knew...knew your face. And whenever I went up to the office, you'd always popped out. Even on my last day, the day I retired, you were off sick. Like you were trying to avoid me. I couldn't think why...why you were being like that. Then, after I left, I forgot about it. Until that night. And then I knew. It was you. The girl who'd been avoiding me for all those years.

I couldn't comprehend it at first. It was a coincidence. It had to be. There could be no other explanation. And yet, it was too much of a coincidence to be a coincidence.

Alison didn't know if she was dreaming. It seemed so real. His face, his voice, it was so vivid.

I still don't know why you did it. Or maybe I do? Obsession. I see it in you. We all have it. But you have it more than others.

It took me a while to figure it out. How you did it. How you knew. The time, the place. It was very ingenious of you...the tracker. It made me see you in a different light.

A child's voice lifted above the others.

I'm glad you survived.

Alison felt the sun go behind the lone cloud.

I'm sorry I had to leave you. Leave you with Jackson. I hope you understood why. I could see no other way out for me. For you. But I would never have let you die...if he'd not come...Jackson...I would have come back for you. But it was for the best. You know that...don't you.

Suddenly the children were silent. Lost in the breeze.

I know about them...what's happened to them, Jackson and Harry.

Alison felt a chill run down her spine.

I was never close to my sons. I only kept a watch on them out of loyalty to Julie...to the memory of her. And yet...a part of me has always blamed them for her death. But I never blamed you.

You did the right thing – leaving the cottage, coming to Madagascar. I thought you would. I've been expecting you. But soon they will know the truth. The police, the public. About the Poppy Killer. So I must remain dead. And you must remain here. But I'll always be there with you Alison. Never forget that.

111

Alison woke up.

She felt the sun come from behind the lone cloud and caress her face.

She looked at the time...an hour had passed.

Had it been a dream?

It had seemed so real.

It had felt so real.

William, next to her, talking to her...the sound of children playing in the background.

Or had her subconscious mind brought William to life?

And had she just heard the words in her head that she'd wanted to hear?

Everything suddenly seemed so quiet.

She looked down at the poem she'd written.

The *Three Missing Words.*

They were filled in.

She stared at the paper.

She tried to think about what she'd done before she fell asleep.

Had she filled in the words?

She was going to, but had she?

She desperately tried to remember, but she wasn't sure.

She looked at the handwriting.

It didn't look like her writing...but it could have been.

Maybe she'd written it, in that half grey moment, in the seconds between being awake and dropping off?

Or had he been there?

Had he really been there?

Had William filled in the three missing words?

Just at that moment a woman with a dog strode over to her. She spoke in a language that Alison didn't understand. Alison looked down to her right to where the woman was pointing. There, on the sand, next to her sun-lounger, was a red shoe. A ladies shoe. The woman picked it up and shrugged her shoulders as if she was unable to explain how it had got there. Then she pointed at the dog as if that was the only plausible explanation. Alison smiled at her in polite confusion. Then as she watched the woman walk away, she was suddenly struck cold with a thought. The poem...*The Red Shoe*...the one William had recited to her in the cellar. The one his father had written. Had William placed the shoe there....for his Cinderella? Or had the dog actually brought it over?

She looked out to sea.

It looked so still.

She felt trance-like.

She looked back down at the poem.

She smiled to herself, then picked it up and started reading it.

Three Missing Words

Below,
Sad rain falls pinpoint upon me. Me
An empty figure too damaged to see
Above,
Between the dark wailing clouds
The blue sky has surrendered...
...my terrible nightmare, lest remembered

Was I dreaming?
Alone,
When I saw you
Against the beautiful rain
You
When my life stood still
When your eyes, so bewitching, answered my will

And into the gentle arms of impassive fate
I placed my soul to end my wait
For in the moonlight hour did I fully give
Myself to you, in order to live

From darkness to light, and on to the stars
I stretched out my arms – walked through the bars
And though my spirit felt such pains
You set me free from my darkest chains

And you, you alone, you understood
The real person, hiding, so misunderstood
Allowing me to live. Live again
To know my heartbeat was no longer in vain

And now as I look, such wonder I see
For my vacant heart to absorb, to be free
Riding on the wings of the uncaged bird
Let me hear it again, that four letter word
Let me hear it again, a whisper will do
Those three special words, to me from you
Those three special words, I've waited to hear
one more time, year after year.
Those three missing words, that once were true
Those three missing words *I LOVE YOU*

As she read the last line, she looked up to the beach bar, to the empty seat where William had been sitting. Her heart felt on fire. She got up. Stood for a while...staring. Then, with her mind floating high in her spirits she said the three missing words out loud...*I love you*...and she imagined William - his eyes glistening - whispering back to her...*I love you.*

112

West Mercia Police Headquarters
Thursday, 6 February 2020

Detective Inspector Trish Bond is sat in her office. She looks at DI Harry Black's desk – at the top hat; at the empty chair. Soon his desk will be cleared. A new detective sergeant will be taking his place.

The office feels melancholic.

Her mind feels drained.

She looks around. She notices a mark on the wall that she's never seen before. It looks like it's been there for years. Her eyes fixate on it. It seems so pointless, so meaningless; yet it seems so alive, so animated. She tilts her head back and closes her eyes. The self-remonstrations float back into her head. Is there any way she could have found out what was going on behind the scenes? Picked up on any of the seemingly implausible and improbable chain of events that led to Harry's death? Could she have prevented it? She takes a deep breath. She lets her self-doubts roam freely in her mind.

She opens her eyes and stares at the ceiling.

She wonders where Lisa Hopkins is now. Lisa Hopkins née Alison Marchant. Her face lights up in her mind. She hears her voice. And then she hears the question, the question that is still pounding away in her head...and her heart. Killer or victim? Killer or victim?

Trish gets up out of her seat and walks behind Harry's desk and looks out of the window. Snow is falling but all she can see are the thoughts in her head. And the only clarity she can find is the sure notion that after what has happened she will never be the same person again. A shiver runs down her spine. Her gaze returns to Harry's empty chair. Time evaporates. She drifts further away. Macbeth floats into her thoughts. *Round about the cauldron go; In the poisoned entrails throw.*

A familiar sound filters into her consciousness. She comes out of her daydream, walks back to her desk and picks up the phone. It's Forensics. The other hair samples found in the cellar; they've had a match on the national DNA database. She hears two names: *Marie Hurst and Kevin Kenny.* Then the voice on the phone suddenly becomes distorted. Her heart thumps into her chest. She asks him to repeat what he's just said. *Marie Hurst and Kevin Kenny*. Her eyes contort and all the oxygen gets sucked out of the room. She whispers him a question that she already knows the answer to and she hardly hears his reply...*Yes, they were both victims of the Poppy Killer...can you...* His voice tails off. She can hardly breath. The room is spinning. She collapses back into her chair and ends the call. Time condenses. The phone rings again. She ignores it. She staggers back to her feet and returns to the window. She stands motionless. The answer was there...right there in plain sight...and she never saw it. She watches the snow fall as tears roll down her face.

EPILOGUE

July 2021

Trish Bond walks out of the local supermarket. Small but convenient. She nods politely at familiar but unknown masked faces and utters a few courteous pleasantries in her broken French. She's not sure if they understand, but they nod politely back.

As she heads down the street towards her home, she spots a police car approaching. Her heart skips a beat as it always does when she sees the police. But as usual they drive on by with nothing more than the hint of a passing smile behind their veiled faces.

She follows the car in her vision as it disappears down the road. She turns back around and continues walking; the image of the police car still in her mind. She knows what will come next: a cognitive replay of last year. When her life changed forever. It's a process she has to go through. She understands that. Such a major life change, such a major decision, such...such an irrational move requires time to be processed. Of course, it was the right move, she believes that without a shadow of doubt, but it will still take time to adjust. For her rational, sensible self to catch up with her more enlightened, free-spirited self.

She smiles, as she recalls the Chief's face - last August - when she handed in her resignation. His star detective. Although in truth he always interjected that phrase with the word female…his star female detective.

She'd not been right for a long time. The constant battle to justify her position had in reality taken far more out of her than she'd ever realised. Because in truth, she'd not challenged it…the casual sexism, the subtle innuendoes, the non-verbal put-downs. Instead she had tried to rise above it all, but all she'd done was become a part of it. Yet, somehow, that had seemed the easier option. A trade off. A way of distracting her mind from the truth. The truth that was eating away inside of her.

And then that day, the day she went round to see Lisa Hopkins. It was shortly after Harry had gone missing. She remembers it like it was yesterday. It sends a shiver down her spine. That moment when Lisa answered the door and a sensation surged through her body the like of which she'd never felt before. Was that the moment? She'd asked herself that question many times before. It was certainly a pivotal point. But she was still in denial then. She was still DI Trish Bond.

Then at the beginning of February last year, Lisa disappeared, and the re-born Alison had phoned her. She had pressed Alison hard, really hard. She had to. But all the time, deep down, it had felt wrong.

> *So, you know what happened do you DI Bond. Are you certain of that?*

And then…

> *You should come and join me…escape. You and me are more alike than you think.*

And then…

I hope you find someone…one day. Someone to love.

After then…

She had tried to carry on. But her investigation into whether Lisa was innocent or guilty had gradually started to consume her until she could no longer function. And that's when it hit her…the realisation. The realisation that she was in love.

****

William Marshall, the *Poppy Killer*, had been headline news throughout most of February and early March 2020. The eyes of the world had been on the West Mercia Police Force. And the deaths of Jackson Brown and Harry Black had been squeezed into the background.

Then *it* happened.

Covid-19.

Mid to late March.

A pandemic was spreading around the world.

It meant the investigation into what had happened to William Marshall was suddenly overshadowed, firstly in the chaos that surrounded the coronavirus outbreak, and then the lockdowns.

And the search for Lisa Hopkins, née Alison Marchant got swept away in the global maelstrom.

Then, July last year - July 5th - Trish will always remember that day. She was in her office. The phone rang. There was a brief silence and in that silence she knew instinctively who it was. But more than that, she knew how she was going to react. She'd already gone over things a thousand times in her head. And every time she'd come to the same conclusion. Alison wasn't a killer. It wasn't her fault. Everything was circumstantial: Harry; Jackson; her father. And what Mickey Maguire had told her...well, there was always two sides to every story. Lisa's only crime had been to go along with Harry's suggestion to bury Jackson's body in the woods. Not to report his suicide. But Trish understood why. She understood a lot of things now. She understood that she loved Alison. And that Alison had been the victim all along.

So when her phone rang on July 5th, she'd already made up her mind. And she knew immediately that Alison understood. That Alison trusted her. That she felt the same way. After that, it was just a matter of making plans and putting them into place. Trish's parents were surprised but not shocked at the news that she was taking an unpaid sabbatical from work - seeing the world. At least that's how she'd worded it to them. And they knew that only someone with their daughter's mentality would make such a decision during a worldwide pandemic. She had always been headstrong – their baby girl.

Yes, it was definitely the right decision. And every time she went over things in her head the closer she got to really believing that fact. Now she wasn't running away from the truth. Now she wasn't hiding. Now she was happy.

As she approached the front door to her apartment she looked across the promenade. The people walking on the sand were silhouetted against the bright sun. She felt a warmth in her stomach. A car went by breaking her reverie. She turned around and entered the apartment.

'Breakfast is ready,' said Alison Marchant as she watched Trish remove her face mask and hang it by the door.

Trish turned and smiled. 'It smells wonderful,' she said, and went over and kissed Alison on the cheek. 'I'll butter the bread. It's freshly baked.'

Alison's face lit up. 'Perfect,' she said, 'just perfect.'

'Love you,' Trish said, as she walked into the kitchen.

Alison moved over to the window. She looked out to the distant sea. There he was. Totally still. Looking at her. His dark shape, his outline. She knew it was him. She looked towards the kitchen before turning back to the window.

She waved to the silhouette.

Then she mouthed to *William Marshall, I love you.*

July 2021

Nosy Be, Madagascar

A man stands on the sand with his back to the sea.

A lady who is walking nearby looks over at him. She has never seen such captivating eyes before. She suddenly feels a lightness in her stride.

The man remains motionless.

His mind is clear.

Then…

The lady sees him wave at someone in the distance. She follows his eyeline but there is no one there.

She thinks about approaching him but decides to move on.

The man watches her pass, then he looks back into the distance.

And he gets that feeling inside.

The Poppy Killer

References

p.53: Mr Jaggers & Abel Magwitch. Reference from Great Expectations by Charles Dickens.

p.185: Stockholm syndrome. Reference from Wikipedia.

p. 209: What a piece of work is man! Quote from Hamlet by William Shakespeare.

Lyrics on Page 314 from the song "Hell Is for Children" by Pat Benatar. Written by Neil Giraldo, Roger Capps and Pat Benatar. Pat Benatar started writing the song after being shocked by a series of articles on child abuse in the New York Times.

P 407: The Shoop Shoop Song (It's in His Kiss) by Cher. Written and composed by Rudy Clark.

p. 411: Survive is to find meaning in suffering. Quote from Friedrich Nietzsche.

p.422: Round about the cauldron go, In the poisoned entrails throw. Quote from Macbeth by William Shakespeare.

Printed in Great Britain
by Amazon

43968141R00243